Martin Pippin in the Daisy Field

ELEANOR FARJEON

MARTIN PIPPIN

IN THE

DAISY-FIELD

Illustrated by
ISOBEL AND JOHN
MORTON-SALE

J. B. LIPPINCOTT COMPANY

Philadelphia and New York

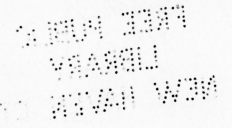
Copyright 1937 by Eleanor Farjeon

Lithographed in the United States of America

LIBRARY OF CONGRESS CATALOG CARD NUMBER: 63-9857

To the children of Sussex

who skipped in my lane

Contents

Important Persons
Who Aren't in this Book

JOAN:	SALLY'S MOTHER
JOYCE:	SOPHIE'S MOTHER
JENNIFER:	SELINA'S MOTHER
JANE:	SUE'S MOTHER
JESSICA:	SYLVIA'S MOTHER
JOSCELYN:	STELLA'S MOTHER

Unimportant Persons
Who Aren't in this Book

CHARLES:	SALLY'S FATHER
MICHAEL:	SOPHIE'S FATHER
TOM:	SELINA'S FATHER
JOHN:	SUE'S FATHER
OLIVER:	SYLVIA'S FATHER
HENRY:	STELLA'S FATHER

You who read this book,
Are you Sussex-born?
Do you know the look
Of our sun at morn
And our moon at night?
They come up Amberley crown
Like bowls of yellow light,
Big bowls turned upside down
With all their light to spill
On table-land and hill.

You who read this rhyme,
If you're Sussex-bred,
You've seen many a time
Those bowls above your head
To golden bubbles grow
And up the blue air swim,
Blown by some child below
Amberley's green rim,
Some child that once you knew
Who wants to play with you.

Prelude in the Daisy-Field

I

'Now which of those children,' said Martin Pippin, 'is mine?'

He was standing on the plank that bridged the Murray River at the bottom of his garden. All about and around the garden were the trees of the forest. Over the Murray River, which, as everyone who hasn't been to school knows, is the biggest river in

Sussex and the world, lay the daisy-field. It spread to the far foot of the Downs, like a green table-cloth full of crumbs. All the birds of the air, picking all day, could not have cleared them away in a week. All the mice in the grass, nibbling all night, could not have cleared them away in a month. But there were no birds to be seen, for the nests were asleep; and no mice, for the children were not. The only pickers in the daisy-field were six little girls, filling their pinafores.

Two were standing, two were stooping, two were sitting at their chain-making; and as they strung the daisy heads, they sang scraps and snatches of songs, no longer than a daisy-stalk. In the very middle of the field stood a wicker clothes-basket without any lid, and every now and then one of the children got up to drop a daisy inside it, and then went back to what she had been doing before; standing, or stooping, or stringing daisies as she sat.

Overhead the sky was going green, and the stars were making pin-pricks where the green was deepest, and the moon a yellow hole where it was palest, along the shoulder of Rackham Hill, and the dome of Amberley Mount. It was high time that the six little girls were in bed.

Martin thought so. And though he was afraid of nothing so much in the world as girls big and little, he made two strides across the boundless river, and stood in the daisy-field.

★

Sally. It's him!
Sylvia. What's he come for?
Sue. To send us to bed, you know.

Stella. I shan't go.

Sally. Let's shut our eyes tight, so he'll think we can't hear him.

Sophie. I shall put my fingers in my ears.

Stella. *I* shan't. I just won't go.

Selina. I wonder why it's so horrid going to bed, when it's so nice being there.

Sophie. Oh it isn't, S'lina. There's nothing to *do* in bed, except go to sleep.

Selina. There's such a lot to do I never go to sleep.

Sally. Did you hear that? Selina never goes to sleep.

Sue. She's fibbing, you know. Are you fibbing, Selina?

Selina. I don't fib. I only make things up.

Stella. That's fibbing.

Sophie. Don't quarrel, or he'll say we're quarrelling, and time to go to bed.

Stella. If Selina says she never goes to sleep, she's fibbing.

Selina. Well I do go to sleep sometimes then, but when I do, I *do* things just the same.

Sylvia. What sort of things?

Selina. Dreaming-things.

Sue. ⎤ Me too!
Sophie. ⎢ And me!
Sylvia. ⎢ And me!
Sally. ⎦ And me!

Stella. That's nothing. Anybody can do dreams when they're asleep. I don't.

Selina. Can't you?

Stella. I could if I liked.

Sylvia. Why don't you like?

Stella. Dreams interrupt.

Sylvia. What?

Stella. I shan't tell.

Sally. Being asleep she means. I wish I didn't do them. Dreams can be so nasty.

'And so nice,' said Martin Pippin.

They had forgotten about the enemy while they talked, and here he was in their midst. 'I have come,' he said, 'to send my child to its dreams.'

The six little girls shut their eyes tight, and put their fingers in their ears.

II

There is no better chance to consider a little girl than when she's not looking or listening. Martin sat down among the daisies, and considered them one by one.

Sylvia had a mischievous inquisitive little face, with a tilted nose. Her hair was light-brown, and her eyes, when you could see them, were hazel.

Selina was very slim. She had a dreamy look, and her mouth was always a little open. Her hair was so fair that it was all but silver. Her eyes, when you could see them, were chicory-blue.

Sue was small and solid and brown all over, like the best eggs. Her round elbows had dimples in them, and her hair was almost black and very smooth, with a fringe cut straight across. Her serious eyes, when you could see them, were almost black too.

Sophie was quick and gay and carefree. She smiled to herself as well as to other people. Her hair had a lot of gold in it, and curled at the ends. Her eyes, when you could see them, were bright and brown.

Sally had a small queer face, with a pale skin and several freckles, and surprised eyebrows, and a pointed chin. Her hair was short and very fine, and flew out in a spindly way like the hair on the cat's spine when it meets the dog. It had no colour in particular, but her eyes—when you could see them—were green on the whole.

Stella had a crooked nose and a straight mouth, and a very cream skin, and a wild-rose patch on each cheek. Her hair was *not*-red-whatever-you-say. Her eyes were violet as the night—when you could see them.

★

'It might be any one of you,' said Martin; and getting no answer he went and looked in the clothes-basket. There lay a baby, without any hair, no nose to speak of, and bigger eyes than it had any right to. They were as grey as the sea, and it was quite clear that they knew all. So Martin leaned over the basket and whispered: 'Tell me, Sibyl, which of them is my daughter?'

'Not fair! that isn't fair!' shouted six voices at once, and, tugged backwards by six pairs of hands, Martin measured his length in the daisies. Before he could get up again, Sylvia and Selina had him by the shoulders, Stella and Sue by the ankles, Sally was perched on the peak of his two knees, while Sophie straddled his chest, thumping it like a metronome as she repeated: 'Asking—isn't—fair! Asking—isn't—*fair.*'

'You've got to guess,' said Sylvia in his right ear.

'And if you don't guess right——' said Selina in his left.

'None of us—
   will go to bed—
      at all—at *all*—at ALL!'
chanted Sally, bumping up and down on his knees.

'Not,' said Sue, squeezing his right ankle gravely, 'that you can send the rest of us to bed, you know. You're not *all* our fathers, you know.'

'Fancy not knowing your own child!' scoffed Stella, pinching his left ankle scornfully.

'Fancy,' Martin admitted meekly. 'Might I sit up now?'

'I think he might,' said Stella to the others, 'if he agrees to our rules.—Do you?' she asked quickly.

Martin asked cautiously: 'What rules?'

'That's for us to say,' said Sylvia.

'We haven't made them up yet,' said Selina.

'We always make things up on the spur of the moment,' explained Sally.

'It is the best part of the moment,' said Martin, 'to make anything up on, and I will abide by any rules you make up without thinking.'

The children got off most of Martin, and Martin got most of himself off the grass. He sat up with a good deal of it in his hair; and the six little girls sat in a semicircle in front of him.

Martin (*pointing his finger quickly at Sylvia*): Sylvia?

Sylvia. The Rule *is*, a story at bedtime.

Martin. Sophie?

Sophie. The Rule *is*, a story *each*.

Martin. Selina?

Selina. The Rule *is*, a song to go to sleep on.

Martin. Sue?

Sue. The Rule *is*, a song apiece.

Martin. Stella?

Stella. The Rule *is*, if you guess wrong, she needn't go to bed at all.

Martin. Sally?

Sally. The Rule *is*, not ever to ask Sib.

Martin. Sib?

Sally. Sibyl. The Baby. You know she is, you said her name yourself.

Martin. Why, so I did. When you had your fingers in your ears, and couldn't hear a thing. Now how, I wonder, did I come to know the Baby's name? Well, that's no matter. I agree to your six Rules, and you must agree to my one. The Rule *is*, that you shall tell me the names of the Fathers and Mothers you share among you, and if I guess the right parents after the story is told and the song is sung, you will go to bed at once and no more talking.

The children put their heads together, and whispered. 'I think that's fair!' whispered Stella. 'Yes,' whispered

Sylvia, 'and he's sure to guess some of us wrong.'
'And then, you know,' whispered Sue, 'those ones
needn't go to bed at all.' 'Not ever?' whispered Sally
eagerly. 'Not ever!' whispered Sophie; 'and he might
guess us *all* wrong!' 'Well then,' whispered Selina,
'let's tell him the names all mixed up.'

The six heads separated, and the six pairs of eyes
fixed Martin where he sat, chewing the juice of a
grass-stem.

'Well, little owls?'

Sylvia said: 'One of the Mothers is called Joscelyn,
and one of the Fathers is called Michael.'

'Another of the Mothers is called Jennifer,' said
Stella, 'and another of the Fathers is called Tom.'

'Another of the Mothers,' said Selina dreamily, 'is
Henry, and another of the Fathers Joyce. Oh no, I
mean——'

'We know what you mean,' giggled Sophie, 'and
my Mother is Jessica and *my* Father Oliver, only not
really, of course.'

'It might be really,' said Martin, 'if you were very
very artful.'

Sally looked at Martin very very artfully, and said:
'*My* Mother's Joan, and *my* Father's Charles.' After
this her surprised eyebrows were more surprised
than ever.

'Oh dear!' said Sue. 'Then my Mother's Jane and
my Father's John after all. Oh dear! how funny.'

Martin. What is funny, Sue?

Sue. Well, I had to have the two what were left,
you know, didn't I?

Martin. There was no help for it.

Sue. So p'r'aps Jane and John aren't my ones at all,
you know.

Martin. The chances were all against it.

'Yes, they were, weren't they,' said Sue happily, 'so you won't say Jane and John for me, will you?'

'I'm not such a goose,' said Martin, 'as to take your word for it.' And the little girls stifled their giggles, while he leaned slowly back till the tall grass made an emerald net between his eyes and the sun. 'But the funny thing *is*, that in all this talk of fathers and mothers there has been no mention of my name or Gillian's. Yet my only object in bothering about you at all was to discover which of you is my daughter. It looks as though you are going to be too cunning for me.'

His head came to rest against Sib's basket, and it began to rock very gently, while Martin hummed under his breath:

> *'Moon for your cradle,*
> *Dark for your cover,*
> *Star for your night-light,*
> *Me for your lover,*
> *Hush-a-by, hush-a-by,*
> *Baby, lie over.'*

'What baby?' inquired Sylvia.

'My baby,' said Martin, 'whoever she is.'

The basket stopped rocking, and the six little girls crammed their fists over their mouths.

Because if he had noticed them laughing, you see——

But Martin Pippin hadn't noticed anything. He was the sort that any child can hoodwink.

III

'Where,' asked Martin Pippin, 'shall we begin?'

The children didn't help. Each of them started a new daisy-chain, as though it were no concern of hers.

Martin tried again. 'Shall we begin with the youngest?'

'We're all the same age,' said Stella, 'though it may not appear so.'

'It doesn't and it isn't. For let me tell you,' said Martin, 'there's no such thing as the same age, even if you were born on the same day in the same hour to the minute.'

'Well we were, you know!' cried Sue.

'I suspected as much,' said Martin.

'Guess when,' said Sylvia.

'The day was the first day of April, and the time was one minute to noon.'

'You *are* a good guesser,' said Sally.

'It is my only gift. But though I have hit the fact, the truth, which is another thing altogether, is that some of you are younger than others of you, and others of you are older than some.'

'Of course,' said Selina.

'Of course not,' said Sue.

'It might,' said Sally.

'But how?' asked Sylvia.

'Does it matter?' said Sophie.

'No,' said Stella, 'it does *not* matter, because even if it's true, and I never said it was, if you don't go by facts where *are* you?'

'Just where we were,' agreed Martin, 'before facts tried to lead us astray. So it all comes back to, which first?'

Being first has sometimes its advantages, but not when it is going first to bed. None of the six was eager to get her story over while the light lay on the land. They went on threading their chains, and Stella looked haughty, and Selina looked dreamy, and

Sylvia looked mischievous, and Sue looked obstinate, and Sally looked somewhere else entirely; so Sophie looked round, laughed, shrugged, and said obligingly: 'Me if you like.'

'I do like,' said Martin.

'What do you like?' asked Sylvia, for now it was safe to come in again.

'I like Sophie.'

'Why do you like her?'

'She laughs. That is one reason.'

'She cries, you know, sometimes,' said Sue very solemnly.

'I like her for that too.'

'How peculiar of you,' said Sally. 'Laughing and crying are *other sides*.'

'There are two sides to everything. If you took one away the thing wouldn't be there. And if you like one, you'd better like both.'

'*I* see,' said Sally.

'I don't,' said Sue.

'Do there *have* to be two sides to everything, Martin?' asked Sylvia.

Martin said: 'Think of a penny.'

They all thought of a penny.

'Now take one side of it away.'

There was a short silence in the daisy-field.

'I keep on taking and *taking* it away,' said Sally, 'but it's still there.'

'Mine's getting awfully thin,' said Sue, 'but I *can't* make it go.'

'Which side are you taking away, Stella?' asked Sylvia.

'I'm keeping Britannia. I like her best.'

'I'm for the Queen!' sang Sophie.

Sophie

'My penny is gold,' drawled Selina softly, 'and it spins like a ball. It hasn't any sides at all.'

'S'lina's made up some more poitry,' said Sue, 'and anyhow I like Sophie when she laughs but not when she cries.'

Martin. Isn't that unkind of you?

Sue. I don't like *me* when I cry.

Martin. You are the soul of squareness. Still, I am glad to hear that you too sometimes cry.

Stella. Isn't *that* unkind?

Martin. No. For who'd escape rainbows? And the Old Saying goes:

> 'The child who laughs as well as cries
> Will find a rainbow in his eyes.'

Sue. Sophie's a girl, you know.

Martin. I wouldn't have her otherwise. 'His' was merely a manner of speaking.

Stella. It's a bad manner then.

Martin. The English tongue is full of them. Men sometimes try to mend them, and seldom for the better.

Sophie (wriggling). Is it going to be lessons?

Martin. At seven o'clock in the evening? Heaven forbid.

Stella. I don't trust that Old Saying, anyhow. I never heard it before in my life.

Martin. You are a sceptic.

Sylvia. What's that?

Martin. An unbeliever.

Stella. How *can* I believe what I've never heard before?

Martin. Some people can believe nothing else.

Stella. We aren't talking about people. We're talking about Old Sayings. You made it up.

Sue. Making up's cheating, you know.

Martin. Of the very best kind. Let us all make up Old Sayings.

Sylvia. What about?

Selina. Trees of course. The Birch is a fountain.

Sophie. The Willow's a bower.

Sally. The Elm is a mountain.

Sue. The Poplar's a tower.

Stella. The Chestnut's a chapel.

Sylvia. The Aspen's a song.

Martin. The house of the Apple holds right things and wrong.

Sue. The Cedar's a table.

Sophie. The Maple's a flame.

Selina. The Fir-tree's a fable.

Sally. The Mulberry's a game.

Sylvia. The Beech is a ceiling.

Stella. The Pine is a mast.

Martin. The Oak has the feeling of first things and last.

'Your line was all wrong, Sally,' said Stella.

'What for?' asked Sally.

'There was one-and-a-quarter too much of it. And how can a Mulberry be a *game*, you silly?'

'Because here we go round on a fine and frosty morning.'

'That's a bush,' said Sue, and Selina reminded Sally gently, 'It's trees we were old-saying.'

'I like mine, and I won't change it for anything,' said Sally fiercely, and then looked rather frightened of herself.

But Martin took her side and said: 'You need not.

For the Mulberry is really a tree all the time, though he turns himself into a little bush for play, as a grown man, to please you, turns into a bear under the table. I never saw a Mulberry yet that wasn't elderly; but it was once the tree of the best singer in Warwickshire, and can be what it likes, young and old, green and grey, withered and still fruitful. No berry is sweeter, or so leaves its mark on its enjoyers. And he who planted it to outlive him, wrote many a line with one-and-a-quarter too much that will outlive the tree he planted. So let us pass Sally's old-saying among the rest, and stick this sleepy daisy behind Sophie's right ear, with a toffee all round to keep your tongues busy in one way, while mine keeps wagging in another.' Saying which, Martin Pippin took a paper bag from his pocket, and in it there were exactly six toffees. Six mouths opened as round as young birds, and Martin popped a toffee-piece in each; but when he came to Sophie's he stopped to ask: 'What would you like your tale to be about?'

'Pharisees,' said Sophie promptly.

'So it shall be,' said Martin. 'No more talking.' He plucked a daisy, and twiddled it for a moment or so, looking it full in the eye as he said, more to himself than to the toffee-suckers:

> 'They are fairies in Norfolk
> And fairies in Suffolk,
> And fairies in Cumberland
> And in Northumberland;
> They are fairies in Dorset,
> And fairies in Devon,
> And fairies in Worcestershire,
> Durham and Gloucestershire;
> They are fairies in England

Where else you may please—
But in Sussex the fairies
Are Pharisees.'

This seemed to settle his thoughts; and lying back
against the clothes-basket, he slipped the daisy behind
his left ear, and began the tale of

TOM COBBLE AND OONEY

WHEN Tom Cobble of Southways was seven
years old, he got stolen by the fairies. Perhaps
it would be better to say that he got himself stolen,
for he certainly did it on purpose.

At about that time of life he was feeling rather
offended. He was then living with his Grandfather,
who kept one of the Lodges of the Duke's Park. The
Park ran up hill and down dale, and the wall that
went round it was twenty miles long, so that it had
a great many Lodges, some of which were on high-
roads and by-roads, and others in woods and meadows.
Tom Cobble's Grandfather's Lodge was lucky enough
to lie in a dale, with the river flowing just outside,
where fishermen would come and sit in the reeds in
the middle of the night, with lanterns and creels
beside them. The lanterns had lights in them, but
the creels had nothing at all, except a little green
grass at the bottom. Sometimes Tom would get out
of the window when his Grandfather was snoring, and
go and talk to the fishermen, but they were all deaf
and dumb. This was a pity, because Tom had a lot

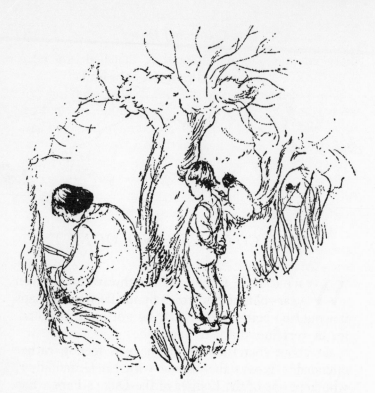

of interesting things to ask them, and even more to
tell them.

'Why doos you fish in the dark?' said Tom Cobble.
'There ain't never no fish in the river at night; they
all goos and swims in the sky. Why doos you bait
with worms and gentles? I don't like gentles I don't.
You'd ought to fish with parsley sauce you did. Why
doos you sit with your feet in the reeds? There was
a fishingman once and his feet took root and growed
there, and he couldn't goo away never no more, and
so when my Grandad killed the pig I bringed him
toasted chitterlings I did, but one time they mowed
the reeds for thatching and so the fishingman ain't

there no more he ain't, but they thatched him into Betsy Ware's lean-to and that's where he is.'

The fishermen never answered his questions, or even said 'Oh!' to his information, but some wind or other would always blow up, and the reeds would say 'Shish! shish!' This offended Tom Cobble.

Just inside the Lodge gate was a knobbly grass hollow, with fruit-trees and chickens and patches of flower-beds, and a sheet of vegetables, and a green bucket lying on its side half in and half out of a weedy pond. All this was Tom's playground, but a bit farther back the beeches and wild cherry-trees began, at the foot of a slope; the wild cherries got tired before they reached the top, but the beeches went all the way up. Tom Cobble was not supposed to go farther than the first two cherry-trees, but he often tried to get as high as the top beech. This was difficult, because the ground was in ridges that were hard to climb and hollows that were easy to tumble in. They were covered and filled with beech-mast, as brown as a fishing-sail on top, and as black as pickled walnuts underneath. The mast lay so thick in the hollows that Tom Cobble sometimes tumbled into a drift of beech-leaf as deep as snow, and he came out with the old leaves in his hair and down his neck, and sticking to every part of his little person before and behind; and his palms and knees were as black as walnut-juice. Then his Grandfather knew where he had been. So he needn't have asked:

'Where you been, Tom?'

But he did.

Tom said: 'I seed a little rabbit with horns on its head I did, and I runned to catch it by its little tail, but the tail comed off in my hand, and the Duke comed by with gold boots on and said if I would plant the little tail in the beech-mast another little rabbit would grow on it come Michaelmas, and so I did, Grandad, you come and see.'

But his Grandad didn't come and see; he went instead to the chimney-piece where his carpet slippers were warming, and he laid his grandson across his knee, and the slipper said 'Slap! slap!' This also offended Tom Cobble. For Tom Cobble saw the world in his own way, and if other people saw it different, he couldn't help that.

It was these things which made him get himself stolen by the fairies.

He knew how, quite well. He went one evening to the mushroom field before the moon was up, and lay down in the middle of the biggest green ring there without saying his prayers. When the moon came up, the fairies came out and got him.

'It's no manner of use, Tom Cobble,' they said, when he woke up under the Hill. 'We've got you fast for seven years, and it's no manner of use to cry.'

'I aren't crying I aren't,' said Tom. 'Ol' Betsy Ware she cried when the fox got her chickens, she cried so hard she did 'at the Duke's Steward comed in a pink satin coach and laid a gold gutter down her garden to catch her crying, with a little pool for gold-fishes at the bottom. But her tears was that hot 'at the goldfishes frizzled, an' she eat 'em for supper, 'an she gived me one and it tasted like treacle pudden.'

The fairies listened attentively, and then they looked worried and said, 'What shall we do with him?'

'Let's let him go,' said one.

'We can't do that,' said a second, 'we've bound him

fast for seven years, and who knows what he'll pick up in that time? Why, once he gets the hang of it, he'll outdo Puck himself.'

'Hang o' what?' asked Tom Cobble.

'Magic,' said a thoughtless elf—and clapped his hand over his mouth as he said it.

'We's got the hang o' magic at home we has,' said Tom Cobble. 'We hanged its flitch in the chimbley-piece the day afore I comed away; an' I left my Grandad a-plaiting of Puck's chitterlings I did, and the rest of him's in the pickle-tub.'

At this an old Enchanter limped forward and said: 'Give the brat to me. I'll keep him out of harm's way. He shall serve his time as my kitchen-boy, and learn no more than I choose.'

So the fairies handed Tom Cobble over to the Enchanter and went back to their dancing.

*

The Enchanter took Tom to his own part of the Hill, where he lived in three caves, one leading into the other. The first cave was the kitchen, full of pots and pipkins with fires under them. The fires were of different colours, rose and scarlet, gold, blue, and green, and in the pipkins the Enchanter brewed his spells. It was to be Tom's job to look after the fires and clean the pots when necessary.

'Doos we cook the charms for supper?' asked Tom.

'No,' said the Enchanter, 'we don't trouble to cook supper.'

'Doos we goo without supper?' asked Tom.

'No,' said the Enchanter, 'I just wave my wand.'

Tom was to sleep in the kitchen.

The second cave, which had a table in it, was where they lived, and it was also the place where Ooney slept. Ooney was the Enchanter's daughter; she was about as old as sixteen, Tom thought, and she was very beautiful. Like the other fairies, she had a sort of moonshine frock on, but over it she wore a big check apron with pockets, and in her hand she had a feather duster, with which she was dusting the table. The only difficulty was that as her duster touched the dust, the dust turned into silver pennies, which, pretty as they were, littered the table dreadfully. The Enchanter looked rather crossly at her and said:

'What a lot of work you make!'

'One must make something,' said Ooney.

The Enchanter waved his wand and the dust all vanished, and Ooney's apron untied itself and hung itself up on the wall; but Ooney fetched it down and put it on again, and taking a leather from the pocket, fell to polishing the table vigorously, saying: 'Who's that, father?'

As she polished it, the table began to sing as sweet as a nightingale. This pleased Tom, but it seemed to vex Ooney; she said: 'Stop it, can't you? Stop it at

once!' However, the table went on singing, so Ooney
gave it up and asked again: 'Who's that, father?'

'It's Tom Cobble from Southways,' said the Enchanter. 'We fetched him away tonight, and have
got him for seven years.'

'Betsy Ware had a table with a leg in the middle
like a lion's foot,' said Tom, 'an' she polished an'
polished the top till she polished it right off and only
the leg was there. So it runned away to the spinney,
an' it met a lion without any legs because of William
Jenks's rabbit-trapses, an' the lion he sat down on the
top of the leg and it runned back to Betsy, so she has
her dinner off the lion's back now, and when she has
done he turns his head and licks off the crumbs.
What's in the next room, mister?'

'That is *my* room,' said the Enchanter, 'and what is
in it is no concern of yours. Nobody goes in that
room but me.'

And nobody did, during all the time Tom served as
the Enchanter's kitchen-boy. The Enchanter kept all
his magic in that room, and sometimes when his
charms were brewing he came out with a big brown
book under his arm, and read in it as he stirred the
pot; then he might say: 'Give me a pinch of that fern-
seed, Tom Cobble,' or 'I want half a cupful of morning
dew from the big round bottle,' or 'Weigh me out an
ounce of last year's thistledown,' or 'Measure me out
a yard and three-quarters of spider-silk, quick now!'
And Tom did as he was told, and tried hard to find
out what the Enchanter was doing, and sometimes he
almost succeeded. But there was always one little bit
he could never quite discover.

Nevertheless, he learned how to make the fires
under the pots, and what gave them their beautiful

colours, but I shall not tell *you*, for this very good reason: you might go doing it too. And who knows what would happen then? For if you boil your breakfast egg over a fire-coloured fire of coal or coke or wood or peat, it is still an egg for breakfast; but if you boiled it over a blue or green or purple fire built of the old Enchanter's secret fuels, it might come out of the pot made of pure gold, or of grey rubber, or it might have wings on it and fly away—but whatever happened to it, it would no longer do for your breakfast.

At the end of his seven years, Tom was a nice tall lad of fourteen years old, and Ooney was still a very pretty fairy of sixteen. She had taken as good care of Tom as his own elder sister could have done. She had washed his face and hands, and brushed his hair, and darned his jacket, and she always got him clean and smooth and neat. Tom did not really mind that after she had washed him his face underwent some change—it might be that his skin gleamed as though it had been gilded, or his nose was like a blackbird's bill; and when she had brushed his hair it would start growing up instead of down, or perhaps it would change into long green grass with buttercups growing in it. As for his jacket, the holes were mended right enough, but afterwards the jacket itself was never quite the same—it might be a blue velvet coat with brass buttons, or a bronze breastplate inlaid with copper, or a linen smock like Davy's, the Duke's head shepherd. Whatever it was, Tom Cobble put it on, for it was the only one he had. But as soon as the Enchanter saw him, he would wave his wand, and in a moment Tom had his right face and hair and coat again. Then the Enchanter would frown at Ooney and say:

'You see what a lot of work you make.'

'Well, father,' said Ooney, 'who's to look after the boy if not me?'

When his time was up, and Tom came to take leave of Ooney and her father, the Enchanter said to him: 'You've been a good boy, Tom Cobble, and to reward you I'll give you whatever you can carry away in your pocket.'

'I'll have your brown book,' said Tom, without thinking twice about it.

The Enchanter looked vexed and said: 'Come now, let me give you the Purse of Fortune.'

'No, thank you,' said Tom.

'The Invisible Cap, then.'

'Nor that neither,' said Tom.

'Take the Flying Slippers,' said the Enchanter.

'I'll take the brown book,' said Tom.

The Enchanter saw there was no help for it, and gave him the book; but at the same time he blew on Tom's left eyelid.

Then Tom went back to Southways.

★

Southways was exactly as Tom had left it, for it was the sort of village that only changes once in a hundred years, when the Missus at the Garland Inn hangs up red curtains in place of chintz ones, and behind the flat little shop-window you see brandy-balls in the bottles instead of lollipops. It did, however, occur to Tom, as he walked down the street, that a good many new people had come into the place while he was away, for he didn't see a single face he remembered. He stopped at the shop to buy two ounces of brandy-

balls, and the woman behind the counter wasn't Goody
Green any more, but somebody quite different. She
weighed out the brandy-balls and handed them to
Tom, and he felt in his pocket and found he hadn't
any money. So he said: 'Wait a bit,' and looked in the
Enchanter's book, and fiddled with one of the brandy-
balls from the packet, and said something the woman
couldn't catch; and the brandy-ball turned into a
sixpenny bit, and Tom gave it to the woman, who
gave him fourpence change, as her sweets were a
penny an ounce, with four to the ounce. But as Tom
had used one of the brandy-balls to turn into sixpence,
there were only seven left in the packet, so she gave
him another one out of the bottle as a make-weight,
and he put it into his cheek and went down the lane
that led to his Grandfather's Lodge by the river. This,
too, was just as Tom had left it; the barndoor fowls
were still picking about the grass, and the green
bucket was lying on its side in the pond, but a tall,
gaunt old woman he didn't know at all, about as old as
sixty-five, Tom thought, was hanging out the washing
on the line.

Tom walked through the gate up to the Lodge, for
he wanted to find his Grandfather and his elder sister,
but the old woman called 'Hi!' in such a sharp voice
that he stopped.

'If ye've brought them groceries at last,' said the old
woman, 'ye can just fetch 'em here for me to count,
and *I'll* take 'em in.'

'I haven't brought any groceries,' said Tom. 'What
sort were you wanting?'

'What sort, indeed!' said the old woman irritably.
'Where's my coffee-beans, I'd like to know, and
where's my oatmeal, and my salt? And what have

ye done with the lump sugar, and the castor sugar, and the yaller soap, and the candles? Lost 'em on the road, I suppose!'

'Wait a bit,' said Tom Cobble, and he sat down and opened his book; and after a short read he began to fiddle with the twigs and the stones and the leaves and anything else that happened to be handy, and soon he had seven nice fat parcels done up in blue silk paper with silver stars on it, which he gave to the gaunt old woman. She handled them suspiciously.

'What's this here?' she asked.

'Lump sugar, I think,' said Tom.

She opened the parcel, and it *was* lump sugar, but it was all in one lump, and shaped like a duck, which quacked three times at the old woman and then laid a little lump of sugar in the palm of her hand. The old woman tossed her head, and undid another packet, and this was coffee-beans. They looked all right, but as she opened the packet a little more they rose up like a cloud of bees and swarmed on the low branch of a plum-tree close at hand. The old woman sniffed and fetched a skep, and shook the coffee into it, and set it on the bench with the other hives, where, instead of humming, it made a comfortable grinding sound, and smelt very good. The other parcels all had some peculiarity; the oatmeal was like gold-dust, but Tom said it would cook all right, and the yellow soap was striped with all the seven colours of the rainbow, and had a lovely poem in seven verses engraved one on each stripe, and the salt tasted like castor sugar, and the castor sugar like salt, and the candles were just one candle that grew longer and longer as the old woman pulled it out of the parcel, so that she never got to the end of it. When she had pulled out twenty yards or so she put it down, and set her hands on her hips, and looked at Tom and said:

'A nice grocer's boy *you* are.'

'I'm not a grocer's boy at all,' said Tom Cobble.

'Then what have ye come for?' said the exasperated old woman.

'To see my Grandad and my big sister,' said he.

'Nobody lives here but me and my son,' said she. 'What was your Grandad's name?'

'Barnaby Cobble,' said Tom.

The old woman looked at him very hard. 'And what's your big sister's name?'

'Molly Cobble,' said Tom, 'but she's going to marry William Jenks when he gives up poaching.'

The old woman looked at him harder still and said: 'Oh, indeed! and what's *your* name?'

'Tom Cobble,' said Tom Cobble.

Then the old woman looked at him hardest of all, and said: 'Tom Cobble who was stole by the Pharisees?'

'Seven years ago,' said Tom.

'Seventy,' said the old woman.

Then she took her hands from her hips, and pegged an apron on the line, and said: 'Well, you've come back now, and there's no help for it. Your Grandad died fifty year back, and your sister Molly forty year back, and I'm your niece, her daughter, and I keep the Duke's Lodge. My father, William Jenks, turned keeper, and died thirty year back, and twenty year back my husband, Bob Drake, died. Sally Drake's my name. My son's name's Jack, and he's the Duke's Head Keeper. Now, uncle, just take them things into the kitchen and put 'em away in the cupboard, and cut that candle up into sensible sizes, and don't start pulling on it any more for mercy's sake.'

Tom did as his niece told him, and later on his great-nephew Jack, a sturdy man of five-and-thirty, came in, and was told by old Sally that her young uncle had just come back from the Pharisees and would live with them now, and the sooner they settled down together the better.

★

Tom's return created a good deal of interest in the village for a day or two. People whose grandfathers had been babies when Tom was stolen would stop him on the road and ask him how he was after all this time, what he had been doing all these years, and what he proposed to do now. To these questions he answered: 'Very well, thank you,' and 'All sorts of things,' and 'I haven't made up my mind.' Then one night Prince Carlo's Circus came along and pitched its tent in Half-Moon Meadow, and everybody's thoughts were full of lovely spangled ladies, and black-and-white ponies, and red-and-white clowns, and strong men who could carry worlds on their shoulders, and slim youths who could leap through the air like birds from one bar to another; and their ears were full of the sound of brass music, and their eyes of the sight of flaring torches, and their noses of the smell of grass and sawdust. Tom went with the rest of the village to the twopenny seats, and liked it immensely, and after the Circus had departed the people talked of its wonders for a week and thought about Tom no more. And nobody but Sally Drake, his grim old niece, bothered to ask him what he proposed to do for a living.

'For it's high time, uncle,' said she, 'that a handy

young lad of seventy-seven like you should be put to some trade.'

'There's no hurry,' said Tom. 'I think when I'm older I'd like to be one of the Duke's keepers, and perhaps Jack would take me round with him so as I can get the hang of things.'

Jack was agreeable, and they spent long days together in the wild Park; and Tom was taught how to handle a gun, and all the other ways of a keeper, with which I am not very well acquainted, so I cannot tell *you*. All I know is that one morning, as Jack and Tom were going through the Park, the Duke himself came up to them and said to Jack: 'Good morning, Drake. Something very funny's going on in this Park.'

'Is it, your Grace?' said Jack Drake. 'I hadn't noticed particular.'

'Come along with me, then,' said the Duke, 'and I'll show you.'

So they went along, all three, to one of the rabbit warrens, and there were hundreds of rabbits racing along the runs they had scratched on the hill-side; and big and little, brown and white, old and young, they all had horns on their heads.

'That's queer now,' said Jack Drake, rubbing his eyes.

'And that's not all,' said the Duke, and went a bit further on to a glade much favoured by his deer. And one and all, dun and dappled, doe, buck, and fawn, they had wings on their backs.

'That's queerer still,' said Jack Drake, scratching his head.

'Then what do you think of *this*?' said the Duke, and led the way to the biggest tumulus on his estate;

and there, on the very top, stood a handsome mahogany table-leg with a claw foot, and planted a-top of it was the body of a splendid lion, roaring in a friendly way and wagging its tail with pleasure.

Jack Drake rubbed his chin and said: 'That's the queerest yet.'

'It is,' said the Duke, 'and I don't like it at all; and as my Head Keeper I'll thank you to keep it from occurring again.'

'I'll do my best, your Grace,' said Jack Drake; and then he stared so hard at the Duke's feet that the Duke looked down too, and saw, to his great annoyance, that he had golden boots on. They looked very grand, to be sure, but they were hard and heavy, and most uncomfortable to walk in. He hurried home and changed them for his bedroom slippers, and sent to the bootmaker for another pair of leather boots; but after this, so sure as he walked in the Park he walked in gold. Before long he had a whole cupboardful of golden boots and shoes.

And this wasn't the end of the queer doings in Southways that summer. When the fish began to leap, the fishermen came as usual with their reels and creels and lanterns to fish in the river outside the Lodge gates. No doubt they were the grandsons of the men Tom Cobble used to see there, but they looked just exactly the same. There they sat in the dark among the reeds, as deaf and as dumb as of old. Tom Cobble came and watched them, but he did not ask them questions any more. While *they* fished in silence, *he* lay on the bank and read in his brown book. And one night a fisherman, atten ̣ ̣g to his bait which had just been carried away by a saucy perch, discovered to his vexation that his bait-box, instead of worms

and gentles, was full of parsley sauce, and the other
fishermen were in just the same case. So there was no
more fishing that night.

The next night the fishermen came again, and cast
their lines in the river, and Tom Cobble came too
with his book, and sprawled in the reeds beside them.
It was a lovely rainy night, and the fish were jumping
a treat. But all of a sudden the rain stopped and the
moon appeared as big as a silver plate, and no sooner
did they see it than the jumping fish jumped clean out
of the water and went leaping through the air till they
were safe in the dark blue sky; and there, as though
they had been in their own sweet river, they swam
round the moon all night, some swift, some slow,
perch and bass and dace and little minnows, making
the prettiest patterns with their supple slippery bodies
and wavy fins. Several of the villagers turned out to
see the sight when they heard what was happening;
but those who preferred to keep their beds asked what
it was like in the morning; and the fishermen went
home, for there was no more fishing *that* night.

However, it is the hardest thing in the world to
discourage a fisherman, and on the following night
they were there again, and there, too, was Tom Cobble
with his book. And this night the fishermen did not
go away, but fished in peace with their usual sort of
luck. But when the morning came and they thought
they would make a move, they found they couldn't,
for every man had taken root in the reeds where he
sat, and there he was whether he liked it or not.

The village children were very nice to the fishermen in the reeds, and bought them licorice shoe-
strings from the shop to cheer them up, and whenever
the fish jumped they cast their lines contentedly and

hadn't such a bad time of it after all. Except one, who
had the misfortune to be mowed down with a bundle
of reeds, where he was overlooked by Jem Turner
the thatcher, who thatched him into the gable-end of
an old cowshed that wanted patching up. However,
his arms were left free, so the children put a bucket
of rainwater on the ground below, and gave him his
fishing-line to drop into it, and then he was as happy
as the day was long.

I relate these events just so that you can know the
sort of thing that now began to happen in Southways,
and went on for the next seven years, but these were
mere nothings. If I told you even a fiftieth part of
Tom Cobble's lop-sided magic, you wouldn't be in
bed before breakfast-time. Sally Drake suspected him
and his book from the first, and pretty soon told her
son Jack to be quit of the boy as a keeper, and
apprentice him to the village Cobbler.

The Cobbler took Tom on for a year, during which
time Tom made boots and shoes very deftly, but
something was always wrong. The right-hand shoe
was perfect, but the left-hand shoe was queer. The
first pair he ever made was for Harry Blossom, the
Potman of the Garland Inn. He pulled them on
behind the bar, and made one step forward with his
right to serve Jem Turner with a draught of porter—
and the next step he took he was over the counter and
standing on Doctor Daly's onion-bed, a quarter of
a mile down the road. He started back with his right,
and then his left plunged forward and landed him
breathless in the school-house, where the children
were chanting:

'Twice one is two!'

'That depends,' said Harry Blossom, sitting down

quick on the floor before he was betrayed into another
step; and he pulled off his boots and walked the half-
mile back to the Garland Inn in his socks.

The next pair Tom Cobble made was for the
Parson, who wore them one Sunday to church. The
right boot was a sober boot enough, but the left boot
was given to dancing. So sure as it touched the
ground, up it flew like a Columbine. The Parson
was late as it was and couldn't turn back; he managed

to get to the church unseen, but he created some surprise when he pirouetted into the pulpit, where for safety he stood the whole morning on one leg to deliver his sermon. Or perhaps Tom's left shoe had the power of flying, or the knack of pinching you whenever you told the least little fib—Tom Cobble himself was a strictly truthful boy—or perhaps his left slipper might be made of pure glass.

Well, the Cobbler passed him on to the Blacksmith, where he made horseshoes that galloped off the anvil and up the hill without waiting so much as to make the acquaintance of the horse standing to be shod; it was an alarming thing to meet one of Tom's red-hot horseshoes racing through the fields, taking the gates and ditches, and fetching up at last in the stable, where it stood waiting for the horse to come while it cooled off. So the Blacksmith passed him on to the Farmer, where the clover and the corn, and the poppies in among them, came up that year made of silk and calico, like the flowers in the Squire's Lady's Sunday bonnet, and in little Daisy Martin's market-hat. And when one day the speckled hen, who was such a fine layer, stopped her proud cackling in the yard, and marching into the kitchen said to the Farmer's Wife, 'I'm come to inform you, ma'am, that I've just laid a beautiful egg,' the Farmer paid Tom Cobble his wages, and told him to go.

So back he went to Sally Drake, and spent the time in reading his book, and doing whatever he fancied; such as making the river run backward; and the snow turn to white sugar icing when it fell; and the school-house settle itself in the top of an oak tree, where the children had to climb through the leaves to their lessons; and Farmer Jolly's sheep on the Downs transform

themselves into a flock of white clouds, when the
Butcher came to fetch them away, that rose bleating
softly into the blue summer sky, and after a short
while disappeared. But after that, every now and
again, when the white clouds came sailing over Southways, one of them might be heard to bleat as it passed,
and the villagers would tell each other: 'There's one
of Jolly's sheep going by.'

In due course Tom completed the seventh year of
his return from Fairyland, and to all intents and pur-
poses was twenty-one years old.

★

On his birthday, as he was walking by the river, he
saw kneeling in the grass a pretty girl who did not
belong to the village. She wore a silver frock that
glistened in the sun, but over it a check apron was
tied; her hair hung loose from a wreath of stars, and
on top of this was a sprigged sun-bonnet. She had a
little trowel in her hand, and was busy weeding the
buttercups that grew thick on the river-bank. Where-
ever she pulled up a weed a gold ring was left in the
ground, so that the wild meadow was sprinkled with
enough to marry all the maidens of Southways three
times over. Tom looked at her for a bit and then
said: 'Good morning.'

'Good morning,' said the pretty girl, driving in her
trowel.

'What are you doing?' asked Tom.

'I'm weeding the world,' said the pretty girl.

'It'll take some time,' said Tom; 'wait a bit!' He
looked in his brown book, plucked a spire of purple
loose-strife, waved it three times, and every weed in

the meadow immediately disappeared; but at the same time the buttercups turned blue.

The pretty girl looked vexed. 'There's my job gone,' said she, 'and just see what a mess you've made of things. Blue buttercups indeed! It's not nature.'

'No,' said Tom, 'it's magic.'

'I hate magic,' said the pretty girl. 'It spoils a body's jobs.'

'It saves a lot of time,' said Tom.

'What for?' said the pretty girl. 'Time's got to be spent somehow.' She rose from her knees, looked at Tom, and said: 'Why, to be sure, you're Tom Cobble!'

'And you are Ooney,' said Tom. 'You're still sixteen years old, I see, though seven years have passed.'

'Minutes,' said Ooney. 'Why, 'twasn't ten minutes back since you walked off with my Father's book, but haven't you grown in the time!'

'What have you come for, Ooney?' said Tom. 'You can't have the book.'

'*Bother* the book!' said Ooney. 'It always spoiled my fun. If you want to know, Tom Cobble, I'm out of sorts with my own folk and I've come to get stolen by the humans. Believe me, Tom, you people aren't one whit more curious about Fairyland than we are about Southways; so I'll just step up to the village and let somebody catch me.'

She nodded to him and tripped away, and Tom saw no more of her that day. But next morning, happening to pass the Garland Inn, he saw Ooney wiping mugs behind the bar, with Harry Blossom showing her how. 'Ye'll soon get the hang of it,' said Harry Blossom, 'but 'twould be better, my dear, if ye could keep 'em from filling with rose leaves and pearls after ye've wiped 'em dry—it only makes work twice over.'

'I'll try,' said Ooney, 'but one can't get rid of one's upbringing all in a moment. There's Tom Cobble at the door. Come in, Tom, and have a drink. I'm maid-of-all work at the Inn here, now, for the Missus caught me nicely with her clothes-line yesterday evening, and so I'm stolen safe and sound and can't go back to Fairyland for seven years. What will you have?'

'I'll have a ginger-pop,' said Tom.

Ooney ran for a bottle, and undid the wires with great care, and the cork popped up to the ceiling, and a skyrocket popped after it and dropped coloured rain all over the sanded floor.

'Try again,' said Tom.

So she fetched another bottle and tried again, and the cork popped as before, but when Ooney went to pour out the drink there was another cork in the bottle; and however often she drew it, there was always a cork to take its place.

'Third time's lucky,' said Tom, and Ooney hoped it would be. The third cork came out quietly, and the ginger-pop foamed into the mug; and as soon as the froth was settled Tom saw the whole of his past and future life reflected in the clear drink. However, that didn't trouble him, and he drank it down and enjoyed it.

Ooney said: 'That will be threepence, please'; and Tom, who never had any money, picked up a pinch of sawdust from the floor, and changed it into threepence and gave it her. Ooney shook her head and said: 'Oh, this magic! will you *never* learn to do things in the ordinary way?'—and put the pennies in the till, where they immediately began to spin themselves, one fall down t'other come up, till closing time.

Ooney served her seven years at the Garland Inn,

but the whole story of it would take too long to tell you. During this time Sally Drake, who was nearly eighty years old, and as spry as forty, continually plagued Tom to stop messing about with things and get some sensible work to do, and Tom always answered: 'Wait a bit, there's no hurry.' When, however, Jack Drake took it into his head to marry a wife, and emigrate to Surrey, Tom Cobble, happening to meet the Duke in the Park soon after, offered himself as Head Keeper.

The Duke, who lived on the other side of the Park, five miles off from Southways, knew nothing of the queer things going on there, and did not suspect that Tom was the cause of his horned rabbits, and his winged deer, and his own golden boots, for which he had had to have a special wing built in the Castle; so he gave Tom the post, 'for,' said the Duke, 'I expect you know the ways of the Park by now.'

'I expect I do,' said Tom.

When he told the news to Sally Drake she sniffed and tossed and said nothing; she had her own opinions and she kept them to herself. When grapes began to cluster on the beech trees, and the primroses in the ash-copse grew twenty feet tall, and the squirrels in the King's Oak began to chatter in Chinese, it was none of Sally Drake's business if the Duke didn't know why. The village cronies over their cups told each other from day to day what new wonder had happened in the Duke's Park, and Ooney behind the bar heard everything, and had no patience with it.

'There's no sense in it at all,' said she, polishing the pint-pots. 'Why can't the boy do his work like an ordinary mortal?' And she put the pint-pots on the shelf, where they turned into Toby jugs.

Ooney, as you see, was very scornful of Tom Cobble, for he was trying to do the very things in Southways which she had run away from Fairyland to escape. And Tom, for his part, thought Ooney a little silly to object to all the things that made life different, and to prefer to cook the dinner on a stove rather than leave it to a magic table-cloth. So, during her seven years' service as maid-of-all-work at the Garland Inn, Ooney gave Tom the go-by, and he did the same to her. They had no use whatever for each other's ways.

Ooney was a good girl, and determined to make herself thoroughly useful; there was nothing she wasn't ready to turn a hand to, cooking or cleaning, dusting or sweeping, brewing or baking, or feather-bed-making. She helped in the garden, and looked after the chickens, and washed on Monday and ironed on Tuesday. She filled the lamps, and fed the dog, and served behind the bar; she was always sweet-tempered and never tired, and the Missus said she would have been a Treasure, but——

The fact is that, for all her willingness and busy-ness, there was *never* a job Ooney undertook that didn't end up different from the way it set out. If she put a cabbage into the pot, it came out porridge; when she cleaned the step, the customers who trod on it stuck fast until they had granted the Missus her first request; when she swept and dusted a room, there was always a litter of silver pennies left behind her broom and her brush; when she brewed the ale, it turned into golden syrup; when she baked a pie, it was sure to contain at least one singing blackbird; and when she made a feather-bed, it flew to Arabia with whoever next slept on it.

When she dug for potatoes, she turned up chocolate creams.

When she gathered the new-laid eggs, before she could get them to the house they changed into Easter-eggs with presents inside them.

When she washed the sheets they turned into table-napkins, and when she ironed the napkins they turned into pocket-handkerchiefs.

When she filled the lamp, it gave out moonshine.

When she fed the dog, he got a dragon's tail.

When she served the drink, you know what happened.

So at the end of the seven years the Missus said to her: 'Ooney, you must go.'

'Oh, Missus!' said Ooney, and her eyes filled with tears, 'couldn't you keep me?'

'Your time's up,' said the Missus, 'and your place is wanted. You're a good girl, Ooney, but Pharisees' ways aren't Southways' ways, and what between you and Tom Cobble we're getting the talk of Sussex.'

'Me and Tom Cobble?' cried Ooney, very hurt. 'Why, Missus, you'd never make a pair of us two? Tom never tried to do a useful thing in his life, and even his magic is left-handed, because my Father blew on his eye before he went away. But oh, Missus, I do try so hard to do jobs and be useful!'

'I know you do,' said the Missus, 'but your jobs are as left-handed as Tom Cobble's magic, and for all I can see there's nothing to choose between you. No, Ooney, my dear, I can't keep you any longer, and I'm sorry I ever stole you. You may take with you, for a present, anything you fancy that will go into your pocket.'

'Then I'll take the Garland Inn, Missus,' said

Ooney—and before you could say Jack Robinson! the Garland Inn had dwindled to the size of a money-box, with bar and kitchen and bedrooms all complete; and Ooney popped it into her apron-pocket and went back to Fairyland.

★

On the day of Ooney's departure Tom came in to tea at the Lodge as usual, and found the Missus of the Garland Inn sitting with Sally Drake by the fire, wringing her hands and telling her tale.

'And what I'm to do for a living, Mrs. Drake, I'm sure I don't know,' said she. 'The Duke'll never put me up another Inn to take its place. Ah dear, dear, dear! to think of him with his Castle ten times as big as any one man needs, even if he does have to house nine-and-ninety servants to see to his wants. There now, if he could only spare me a little bit of what he's got, I could set myself up again.'

'Wait a bit,' said Tom Cobble, 'and don't worry, Missus.' And he got out his book and buried his nose in it.

Sally Drake said sharply: 'Put that there reading away, uncle, and sup your tea.'

'There's no hurry,' said Tom Cobble, and poked the fire three times and said something to the poker. Then he had his tea, and when the Missus got back to the village she saw a quarter of the Duke's Castle planted where the Garland Inn had stood, and two or three villagers standing about it waiting for a drink.

Now the Duke had overlooked a good many things, such as the grapes and the primroses and the squirrels, and a fountain of wine that appeared one day in the middle of his ornamental lake; and when the stone Cupid there took to singing 'Ring-a-ring-o'-roses' at seven o'clock every evening and sat down with a splash at the finish, and when the white swans began to wear gold crowns on their heads, and every water-lily as it opened had a queen-cake inside it, he was really rather proud of it, though he couldn't understand it in the least; and he took all his best visitors to see the swans, and listen to the Cupid, and eat queen-cakes to their hearts' content. But when a quarter of his Castle, including the armoury, disappeared bodily one day, leaving his own suite of apartments open to the east wind, he felt that things had gone too far, and he must take steps.

He told his Steward to make inquiries, and a week later the Steward reported that he'd heard there was a rumour of a portion of a Castle, but of course he couldn't say whose, that had strayed by accident into Southways; so the Duke got on his horse and rode to see for himself, and sure enough there was the missing bit. It now had a nice sign hanging out, with a picture, and the words 'The Quarter-Castle' painted on it; and the Missus was serving drinks in the Armoury, using the helmets as pint-pots.

He called her out, and pointed at the building, and said: 'Where did you pick that up, Missus?'

She curtseyed and replied: 'Please, Your Grace, it's Tom Cobble's doing.'

'Send for Tom Cobble,' said the Duke; and when Tom came he asked: 'Is this your doing, Cobble?'

'Yes, sir,' said Tom Cobble.

'Is this your only doing, Cobble?' said the Duke.

'No, sir,' said Tom.

'Did you do the swans, and the lilies, and the fountain, and the squirrels, and all the rest of it, Cobble?' said the Duke.

'I did, sir,' said Tom.

The Duke frowned a mighty frown, and said in a voice of thunder: 'What do you think should be the fate of the man who spoils the Duke's Park and steals the Duke's Castle?'

'I think, sir,' said Tom, 'that he should marry the Duke's daughter.'

'I haven't got a daughter,' said the Duke. 'Take a month's wages, and go. You're spoiled as a mortal, Tom Cobble, and no use to Southways.'

He paid Tom his wages and rode away, and was so upset that he was quite half-way home before he discovered that he was riding on a large white kitten with blue eyes.

Tom pocketed his money, said good-bye to the villagers and Sally Drake, and left Southways for ever. He hadn't gone far before he heard a sound of sobbing on the high-road; and there was Ooney in her silver dress and check apron, crying her eyes out under a hedge. So he sat down in the grass beside her and said, 'What's up?'

'Oh, Tom!' wept Ooney, 'they've turned me out. I set up the Garland Inn so nice and proper, and did everything there as I'd learned how of the Missus, and tried to get them to come in regular for drinks like real human beings, and they didn't like it at all. I was spoiled for a fairy, they said, and no use to Fairy-land any more, so they gave me a wish and told me to go.'

'Where's the wish?' asked Tom.

'On the tip of my tongue,' said Ooney.

'It's better than nothing,' said Tom, 'so let's come along together, and see if we can't find a place in the world after all.'

He had hardly said this when there was a sound of drums and trumpets on the road, and round the corner, gorgeous in the sunlight, came the long procession of Carlo's Circus—black-and-white ponies, red-and-white clowns, ladies in spangles, boys in pink tights, Indians on elephants with feathers in their turbans, a Strong Man with a starry world upon his shoulders, and Prince Carlo himself in a golden chariot drawn by six white donkeys with red reins and tassels.

'Is it magic?' asked Ooney.

'No,' said Tom, 'it's the real thing.'

'Really real?' cried Ooney joyfully. 'Oh, I *wish* Prince Carlo would give us a job!'

No sooner had she wished than Prince Carlo said: 'Whoa!' to his donkeys, stepped down from his chariot, and said:

'Do you happen to be looking for a job?'

'Yes, we do,' said Tom and Ooney in one breath.

'Well,' said the Prince, 'my Strong Man's just leaving me to get married to my Lady Equestrienne, and if *you*' (he turned to Tom) 'think you could juggle with the world, and *you*' (he turned to Ooney) 'can ride a cream pony on one toe and jump through a paper hoop, I'll take you on.'

It was settled then and there, and Tom Cobble and Ooney joined the Circus. And before long, wherever it went, they became the chief attractions.

For Ooney in her silver dress and wreath of stars rode the pony like a moonbeam floating in mid-air, sometimes forgetting to stand on him even on tip-toe, and flying a few inches above his back all round the ring, so that the little boys and girls on the twopenny benches screamed for joy.

And Tom Cobble in pink tights and a gold belt

played with the starry world as no Strong Man had ever done before, and while he tossed and caught it, and walked on it and balanced it, all sorts of lovely things happened to it; skylarks and swallows darted from it as it rolled in the sawdust, and filled the tent with twittering, or violets and peardrops fell from it as it tossed on the air, and sprinkled the twopenny benches, and the stars would dance on its surface and turn all sorts of colours, so that the little boys and girls screamed louder than ever.

In time Tom Cobble married Ooney, and when Prince Carlo retired they took the Circus over entirely, for the life exactly suited them.

'Thank goodness,' said Tom, 'nobody minds *what* magic you play in the Ring!'

And 'Thank goodness,' said Ooney, 'I'm doing something real at last!'

If ever their Circus comes your way, don't miss it.

First Interlude

THE children fastened off their daisy-chains.
'Is that all?' asked Sophie.

'All,' said Martin, 'that I am going to tell. If I told all I should be lost in the growth of my beard, and still I'd be telling.'

'Right inside it?' asked Sally.

'So deep inside that you could not even hear me. You'd only see a mountain of white hair wagging, and wonder what the mouse was doing in there.'

'Are you a mouse then actually?' asked Sally.

'In the claws of six kittens,' said Martin.

'I'm sorry it's all for now,' sighed Sophie; to which Martin replied: 'I'm glad you're sorry.'

'You needn't look so pleased with yourself,' observed Stella. 'Sophie's sorriness has nothing to do with the goodness of the story.'

'You didn't like it?'

'I must say I thought it a bit far-fetched,' said Stella.

'If you must say it, you must. I would fetch a tale from the Antipodes to please you.'

Martin looked so downcast that Selina said gently: '*I* liked it, and I wish I had grass hair.'

'I wish I had that big brown book,' said Sylvia.

'*I* wish a circus would come by,' said Sue.

Sally said: 'Ow!'

Martin asked: 'What sort of wish is that?'

'My toffee's pulled my loose tooth out.'

'Let's look!' Selina, Sophie, Sue, Stella, and Sylvia crowded round, and peered with interest into Sally's mouth.

'It's a front one,' announced Sue. 'Shut tight, Sally, and let me look through the little hole.'

'What can you see?'

'Not anything. It's all black.'

'Black in my throat?' asked Sally anxiously.

'Black as night,' said Sue positively.

'Then you ought to be able to see Sally's stars,' drawled Selina.

'Do I have stars in my throat?' Sally looked happier, but Stella said: 'S'lina's moony.'

'She does go moony sometimes,' Sophie explained.

Martin. There's nothing to be done with them when they do. Let her moon, while I take you into a corner of the field and guess you.

Sophie (deaf as a post). Did it hurt much, Sally?

Sally. It didn't hurt a bit, but I can't get it out.

Stella. It *is* out.

Sally. It's out of my mouth but not out of my toffee.

Sue. Suck it out.

Sally. What would happen if I swallowed it?

Sylvia. You'd turn into a rhinoceros.

Sally. Would I, *would* I?

Sophie. Don't tease her, Syl.

Sally. I'd like to be a rhinocellos for a minute.

Sylvia. It wouldn't be a for a minute. It would be for ever.

Sue. Shall I——

Sylvia. How'd you like *that*?

Sally. I might. Shall you what?

Sue. Suck it out for you.

Stella. No, greedy. Let Sally swallow her own tooth.

Sally. I'll be fearfully careful.

Martin. Time's up, Sophie. Come. If I guess you right you shall give me your daisy, and if I guess you wrong you shall have mine.

Sophie. All right. Oh dear. All right.

She followed him into a corner of the daisy-field, where two elms stood like patient shire horses, their thick trunks fringed with leaves down to the root, as those best of horses' legs have manes to the hoof. Their shadows barred the grass. Between them lay the stump of a brother-tree, sawn flat, and lined like the page of a book with its own story. It made only a little block of shadow, and the sun streamed full upon it. Martin set Sophie there with her face in the light, and inspected her until she put her fingers over his eyes.

'That's enough looking. Now guess whose I am.'

'It is easier,' said Martin, 'to guess whose you are not. By elimination perhaps we shall come to it. You are not Jennifer's child, you laugh too much. Nor little Joan's, because you are too tall. Nor Joscelyn's, for you haven't an atom of scorn in you. Nor Jane's, because you are not matter-of-fact. Can you be Jessica's?'

'Is that your guess?' asked Sophie, so quickly that Martin smelt fire.

'Jessica had a very inquiring mind. You take the world for granted. No, not Jessica's. Therefore, you must be——'

Of the six milkmaids, laughing Joyce alone was left. Martin looked into Sophie's gay brown eyes, and saw a fringe of gold lashes, such as Joyce loved. Sophie looked into Martin's eyes, and saw a little bed, turned

down for the night. Her eyes kept their smile, but
behind it formed a tear, and for a moment they looked
at each other through a rainbow.

'Therefore,' said Martin softly, 'to bed with you,
for you must be *my* child.'

Rainbows vanish before you know where you are.
'Wrong! wrong! wrong!' cried Sophie heartlessly.

She snatched the daisy from behind Martin's left
ear, stuck it behind her own, jumped off the stump,
and raced like a colt down the daisy-field, shouting:
'He guessed me wrong! He thinks I'm his! Hurrah!
I'm never going to bed any more for ever!'

Martin followed slowly, to face the jeers. If you
will do good actions, you have to pay for them.

★

'And whose tale next?' asked Martin, when they had done with him.

'Mine!' said Sue.

'Mine!' cried Sylvia, Stella, Selina, one breath later.

'Mine,' said Sally, getting there last, because she often heard things long after they were said, and sometimes before.

'Five of one mind,' remarked Martin, 'and what a change of mind from an hour ago.'

'I'd get tired of my mind if I didn't change it sometimes,' said Sally.

'You don't really *change* it, you know,' stated Sue. 'You can't take it out of your head and put another one in, however you try.'

Sally sat very still, and looked intensely into the distance.

'She's trying,' whispered Selina.

'Is anything happening, Sally?' called Sylvia across a thousand miles and years.

'Let her alone,' said Martin, 'till she chooses to come back and tell us, or not. Meanwhile, Sue's tale.'

'Why Sue's?' demanded Stella.

'Because I said Mine! first,' said Sue.

'Only just first,' said Stella.

'So that Sue's tale should come next,' said Martin, 'is only just. Though I'm still cudgelling my brains to know why you are all so eager.'

'Well you see, it's safe now,' explained Sue. 'We were afraid you'd be able to guess us, and look at you!'

'I often try to, and I never succeed,' sighed Martin.

Selina (pityingly). You aren't very clever, are you?

Martin. Preserve me!

Sally (suddenly). Like jam?

Sylvia. Have you come back then, Sal?

Sue

Sophie. She's a long way off yet. She only popped that out without thinking.

Sue. Yes, because how *could* Martin be jammed?

Martin. Why not, if pippins can be preserved?

Stella. I hate and detest dried pippins.

Sylvia. Let's put Martin in soak.

She snatched up an old pan and started for the Murray River, but Martin pulled her back by her pinafore-strings. 'If Stella can't fancy dried pippins more than that, it wouldn't help though you soaked me in the Murray for seven years. What *does* Stella fancy, I wonder?'

> 'Plum, Apple, Raspberry Tart!
> Tell me the name of your Sweetheart!'

sang Sophie.

'She shall have all three if she tells,' said Martin.

'Nothing to tell, and that's only a silly skipping-rhyme,' said Stella.

'Do you know a sensible one?' asked Martin; and Stella recited:

> 'Lay the table, knives and forks,
> Bring me in a leg of pork,
> If it's fat, take it back,
> If it's lean, bring it in,
> And don't forget the—
> Salt-Mustard-Vinegar-Pepper!'

'That's *pretty* sensible, but skipping-rhymes don't have to be sensible,' said Sue.

'Stella's rhyme seems to me all that is required for sensible domestic training,' said Martin. 'I am sure she never forgets the vinegar when she lays the table.'

'Charley Parley
Stole some barley
Out of the Baker's shop,
The Baker came out
And gave him a clout
And made poor Charley hop!

is that a sensible one?' asked Sue.

'It was sensible of the Baker, no doubt,' said Martin, 'but not what I call nice of him. Poor Charley Parley.'

'Well he shouldn't of took the barley, did he?' said Sue.

'Boys take so many liberties they shouldn't of.'

'Barley's not a liberty,' said Sue. 'You make bread with it.'

'You can take a liberty with it,' said Martin, 'and make beer instead.'

'Grenadier,
Why comest thou here?'

(demanded Sylvia)

'For a bottle of Beer!
And what have you got to pay for the Beer?
Nothing! said the Grenadier.
Then go away and come not here!'

'What is all this?' asked Martin.

'It's another skipping-rhyme.'

'A horrid one,' said Stella.

Sylvia defended it. 'I like it, and it's *very* sensible.'

Stella slashed it. 'It's very vulgar, and where's the sense in it?'

'Because the Grenadier has to go away without the beer because he hasn't got any money.'

'He ought to have asked for a bottle on tick,' said

Martin. 'I agree with Stella that the Grenadier was a dunderhead.'

'I never said that,' snapped Stella. 'I do wish you wouldn't go on agreeing with me when I didn't say things.'

'There's no agreeing with you when you do,' apologized Martin.

Stella looked like answering back. Selina said soothingly:

> 'All in together
> This fine weather.
> I saw Peter
> Hanging out of window—
> Shoot! *Bang!* FIRE ! ! !

Ha, ha, Martin, you jumped!'

'That is the object of skipping-rhymes, sensible or silly. And as long as it's fine weather we're all together in, I'll jump in any direction you please. So while Sally, who has not yet skipped for us, goes on changing her mind, let me stick this daisy behind Sue's right ear, and let your lips jump to a vanilla chocolate cream, while mine jump where Sue tells them to.' Then Martin took from his pocket a paper bag containing six chocolate creams precisely, and once more the nestlings opened their beaks, even to Sally, who seemed to do it by instinct; and Martin slipped a chocolate into each. But at Sue, who came last, he halted, to ask: 'What would you like your tale to be about?'

'Skipping, of course,' said Sue.

'Of course,' agreed Martin. 'No more talking!'

He chose a daisy carefully from the grass, consulted it eye to eye, and repeated softly:

'Andy Spandy,
Sugardy Candy
French
Almond
ROCK!
Breadandbutterforyoursupper'sallyourmother'sGOT!'

Then he slipped the daisy into place behind his left ear, settled himself once more against the clothes-basket, and told the tale of

ELSIE PIDDOCK SKIPS IN
HER SLEEP

ELSIE PIDDOCK lived in Glynde under Caburn, where lots of other little girls lived too. They lived mostly on bread-and-butter, because their mothers were too poor to buy cake. As soon as Elsie began to hear, she heard the other little girls skipping every evening after school in the lane outside her mother's cottage. *Swish-swish!* went the rope through the air. *Tappity-tap!* went the little girls' feet on the ground. *Mumble-umble-umble!* went the children's voices, saying a rhyme that the skipper could skip to. In course of time, Elsie not only heard the sounds, but understood what they were all about, and then the *mumble-umble* turned itself into words like this:

> '*An*dy
> *Span*dy
> *Sugar*dy
> *Candy*,
> *French*
> *Al*mond
> ROCK!
> Breadandbutterforyoursupper'sallyourmother'sGOT!'

The second bit went twice as fast as the first bit, and when the little girls said it Elsie Piddock, munching her supper, always munched her mouthful of bread-and-butter in double-quick time. She wished she had some Sugardy-Candy-French-Almond-Rock to suck during the first bit, but she never had.

When Elsie Piddock was three years old, she asked her mother for a skipping-rope.

'You're too little,' said her mother. 'Bide a bit till you're a bigger girl, then you shall have one.'

Elsie pouted, and said no more. But in the middle of the night her parents were wakened by something going *Slap-slap!* on the floor, and there was Elsie in her night-gown skipping with her father's braces. She skipped till her feet caught in the tail of them, and she tumbled down and cried. But she had skipped ten times running first.

'Bless my buttons, mother!' said Mr Piddock. 'The child's a born skipper.'

And Mrs Piddock jumped out of bed full of pride, rubbed Elsie's elbows for her, and said: 'There-a-there

now! dry your tears, and tomorrow you shall have
a skip-rope all of your own.'

So Elsie dried her eyes on the hem of her night-
gown; and in the morning, before he went to work,
Mr Piddock got a little cord, just the right length,
and made two little wooden handles to go on the
ends. With this Elsie skipped all day, scarcely stopping to eat her breakfast of bread-and-butter, and her
dinner of butter-and-bread. And in the evening,
when the schoolchildren were gathered in the lane,
Elsie went out among them, and began to skip with
the best.

'Oh!' cried Joan Challon, who was the champion
skipper of them all, 'just look at little Elsie Piddock
skipping as never so!'

All the skippers stopped to look, and then to wonder. Elsie Piddock certainly *did* skip as never so, and they called to their mothers to come and see. And the mothers in the lane came to their doors, and threw up their hands, and cried: 'Little Elsie Piddock is a born skipper!'

By the time she was five she could outskip any of them: whether in 'Andy Spandy,' 'Lady, Lady, drop your Purse,' 'Charley Parley Stole some Barley,' or whichever of the games it might be. By the time she was six her name and fame were known to all the villages in the county. And by the time she was seven, the fairies heard of her. They were fond of skipping themselves, and they had a special Skipping-Master who taught them new skips every month at the new moon. As they skipped they chanted:

> 'The High Skip,
> The Sly Skip,
> The Skip like a Feather,
> The Long Skip,
> The Strong Skip,
> And the Skip All Together!

The Slow Skip,
The Toe Skip,
The Skip Double-Double,
The Fast Skip,
The Last Skip,
And the Skip Against Trouble!'

All these skips had their own meanings, and were made up by the Skipping-Master, whose name was Andy-Spandy. He was very proud of his fairies, because they skipped better than the fairies of any other county; but he was also very severe with them if they did not please him. One night he scolded Fairy Heels-o'-Lead for skipping badly, and praised Fairy Flea-Foot for skipping well. Then Fairy Heels-o'-Lead sniffed and snuffed, and said: 'Hhm-hhm-hhm! there's a little girl in Glynde who could skip Flea-Foot round the moon and back again. A born skipper she is, and she skips as never so.'

'What is her name?' asked Andy-Spandy.

'Her name is Elsie Piddock, and she has skipped down every village far and near, from Didling to Wannock.'

'Go and fetch her here!' commanded Andy-Spandy.

Off went Heels-o'-Lead, and poked her head through Elsie's little window under the eaves, crying: 'Elsie Piddock! Elsie Piddock! there's a Skipping-Match on Caburn, and Fairy Flea-Foot says she can skip better than you.'

Elsie Piddock was fast asleep, but the words got into her dream, so she hopped out of bed with her eyes closed, took her skipping-rope, and followed Heels-o'-Lead to the top of Mount Caburn, where Andy-Spandy and the fairies were waiting for them.

'Skip, Elsie Piddock!' said Andy-Spandy, 'and show us what you're worth!'

Elsie twirled her rope and skipped in her sleep, and
as she skipped she murmured:

> 'Andy
> Spandy
> Sugardy
> Candy,
> French
> Almond
> *Rock!*

Breadandbutterforyoursupper'sallyourmother'sGOT!'

Andy-Spandy watched her skipping with his eyes as
sharp as needles, but he could find no fault with it, nor
could the fairies.

'Very good, as far as it goes!' said Andy-Spandy.
'Now let us see how far it *does* go. Stand forth, Elsie
and Flea-Foot, for the Long Skip.'

Elsie had never done the Long Skip, and if she had
had all her wits about her she wouldn't have known
what Andy-Spandy meant; but as she was dreaming,
she understood him perfectly. So she twirled her rope,
and as it came over jumped as far along the ground as
she could, about twelve feet from where she had
started. Then Flea-Foot did the Long Skip, and
skipped clean out of sight.

'Hum!' said Andy-Spandy. 'Now, Elsie Piddock,
let us see you do the Strong Skip.'

Once more Elsie understood what was wanted of
her; she put both feet together, jumped her rope, and
came down with all her strength, so that her heels
sank into the ground. Then Flea-Foot did the Strong
Skip, and sank into the ground as deep as her waist.

'Hum!' said Andy-Spandy. 'And now, Elsie Piddock, let us see you do the Skip All Together.'

At his words, all the fairies leaped to their ropes, and began skipping as lively as they could, and Elsie with them. An hour went by, two hours, and three hours; one by one the fairies fell down exhausted, and Elsie Piddock skipped on. Just before morning she was skipping all by herself.

Then Andy-Spandy wagged his head and said: 'Elsie Piddock, you are a born skipper. There's no tiring you at all. And for that you shall come once a month to Caburn when the moon is new, and I will teach you to skip till a year is up. And after that I'll wager there won't be mortal or fairy to touch you.'

Andy-Spandy was as good as his word. Twelve times during the next year Elsie Piddock rose up in her sleep with the new moon, and went to the top of Mount Caburn. There she took her place among the

fairies, and learned to do all the tricks of the skipping-
rope, until she did them better than any. At the end
of the year she did the High Skip so well, that she
skipped right over the moon.

In the Sly Skip not a fairy could catch her, or know
where she would skip to next; so artful was she, that
she could skip through the lattice of a skeleton leaf,
and never break it.

She redoubled the Skip Double-Double, in which
you only had to double yourself up twice round the
skipping-rope before it came down. Elsie Piddock did
it four times.

In the Fast Skip, she skipped so fast that you couldn't
see her, though she stood on the same spot all the time.

In the Last Skip, when all the fairies skipped over
the same rope in turn, running round and round till
they made a mistake from giddiness, Elsie never got
giddy, and never made a mistake, and was always left
in last.

In the Slow Skip, she skipped so slow that a mole
had time to throw up his hill under her rope before she
came down.

In the Toe Skip, when all the others skipped on
their tip-toes, Elsie never touched a grass-blade with
more than the edge of her toe-nail.

In the Skip Against Trouble, she skipped so joyously that Andy-Spandy himself chuckled with delight.

In the Long Skip she skipped from Caburn to the
other end of Sussex, and had to be fetched back by the
wind.

In the Strong Skip, she went right under the earth,
as a diver goes under the sea, and the rabbits, whose
burrows she had disturbed, handed her up again.

But in the Skip like a Feather she came down like

gossamer, so that she could alight on a spider-thread and never shake the dew-drop off.

And in the Skip All Together, she could skip down the whole tribe of fairies, and remain as fresh as a daisy. Nobody had ever found out how long Elsie Piddock could skip without getting tired, for everybody else got tired first. Even Andy-Spandy didn't know.

At the end of the year he said to her: 'Elsie Piddock, I have taught you all. Bring me your skipping-rope, and you shall have a prize.'

Elsie gave her rope to Andy-Spandy, and he licked the two little wooden handles, first the one and then the other. When he handed the rope back to her, one of the handles was made of Sugar Candy, and the other of French Almond Rock.

'There!' said Andy-Spandy. 'Though you suck them never so, they will never grow less, and you shall therefore suck sweet all your life. And as long as you are little enough to skip with this rope, you shall skip as I have taught you. But when you are too big for this rope, and must get a new one, you will no longer be able to do all the fairy skips that you have learned, although you will still skip better in the mortal way than any other girl that ever was born. Good-bye, Elsie Piddock.'

'Aren't I ever going to skip for you again?' asked Elsie Piddock in her sleep.

But Andy-Spandy didn't answer. For morning had come over the Downs, and the fairies disappeared, and Elsie Piddock went back to bed.

If Elsie had been famous for her skipping before this fairy year, you can imagine what she became after it. She created so much wonder, that she hardly dared to show all she could do. Nevertheless, for another year she did such incredible things, that people came from far and near to see her skip over the church spire, or through the split oak-tree in the Lord's Park, or across the river at its widest point. When there was trouble in her mother's house, or in any house in the village, Elsie Piddock skipped so gaily that the trouble was forgotten in laughter. And when she skipped all the old games in Glynde, along with the little girls, and they sang:

'Andy
Spandy
Sugardy
Candy,
French
Almond
Rock!

Breadandbutterforyoursupper'sallyourmother'sGOT!'—

Elsie Piddock said: 'It aren't all *I've* got!' and gave them a suck of her skipping-rope handles all round. And on the night of the new moon, she always led the children up Mount Caburn, where she skipped more marvellously than ever. In fact, it was Elsie Piddock who established the custom of New-Moon-Skipping on Caburn.

But at the end of another year she had grown too big to skip with her little rope. She laid it away in a box, and went on skipping with a longer one. She still skipped as never so, but her fairy tricks were laid by with the rope, and though her friends teased her to do the marvellous things she used to do, Elsie Piddock only laughed, and shook her head, and never told why. In time, when she was still the pride and wonder of her village, people would say: 'Ah, but you should ha' seen her when she was a littling! Why, she could skip through her mother's keyhole!' And in more time, these stories became a legend that nobody

believed. And in still more time, Elsie grew up (though never very much), and became a little woman, and gave up skipping, because skipping-time was over. After fifty years or so, nobody remembered that she had ever skipped at all. Only Elsie knew. For when times were hard, and they often were, she sat by the hearth with her dry crust and no butter, and sucked the Sugar Candy that Andy-Spandy had given her for life.

It was ever and ever so long afterwards. Three new Lords had walked in the Park since the day when Elsie Piddock had skipped through the split oak. Changes had come in the village; old families had died out, new families had arrived; others had moved away to distant parts, the Piddocks among them. Farms had changed hands, cottages had been pulled down, and new ones had been built. But Mount Caburn was as it always had been, and as the people came to think it always would be. And still the children kept the custom of going there each new moon to skip. Nobody remembered how this custom had come about, it was too far back in the years. But customs are customs, and the child who could not skip the new moon in on Caburn stayed at home and cried.

Then a new Lord came to the Park; one not born a Lord, who had grown rich in trade, and bought the old estate. Soon after his coming, changes began to take place more violent than the pulling down of cottages. The new Lord began to shut up footpaths and destroy rights of way. He stole the Common rights here and there, as he could. In his greed for more than he had got, he raised rents and pressed the people harder than they could bear. But bad as the high rents were to them, they did not mind these so much as the loss of their old rights. They fought the new Lord, trying to keep what had been theirs for centuries, and sometimes they won the fight, but oftener lost it. The constant quarrels bred a spirit of anger between them and the Lord, and out of hate he was prepared to do whatever he could to spite them.

Amongst the lands over which he exercised a certain power was Caburn. This had been always open to the people, and the Lord determined if he could to close it. Looking up the old deeds, he discovered that, though the Down was his, he was obliged to leave a way upon it by which the people could go from one village to another. For hundreds of years they had made a short cut of it over the top.

The Lord's Lawyer told him that, by the wording of the deeds, he could never stop the people from travelling by way of the Downs.

'Can't I!' snorted the Lord. 'Then at least I will make them travel a long way round!'

And he had plans drawn up to enclose the whole of the top of Caburn, so that nobody could walk on it. This meant that the people must trudge miles round the base, as they passed from place to place. The Lord gave out that he needed Mount Caburn to build great factories on.

The village was up in arms to defend its rights.

'Can he do it?' they asked those who knew; and they were told: 'It is not quite certain, but we fear he can.' The Lord himself was not quite certain either but he went on with his plans, and each new move was watched with anger and anxiety by the villagers. And not only by the villagers; for the fairies saw that their own skipping-ground was threatened. How could they ever skip there again when the grass was turned to cinders, and the new moon blackened by chimney-smoke?

The Lawyer said to the Lord: 'The people will fight you tooth and nail.'

'Let 'em!' blustered the Lord; and he asked uneasily: 'Have they a leg to stand on?'

'Just half a leg,' said the Lawyer. 'It would be as well not to begin building yet, and if you can come to terms with them you'd better.'

The Lord sent word to the villagers that, though he undoubtedly could do what he pleased, he would, out of his good heart, restore to them a footpath he had blocked, if they would give up all pretensions to Caburn.

'Footpath, indeed!' cried stout John Maltman, among his cronies at the Inn. 'What's a footpath to Caburn? Why, our mothers skipped there as children, and our children skip there now. And we hope to see our children's children skip there. If Caburn top be built over, 'twill fair break my little Ellen's heart.'

'Ay, and my Margery's,' said another.

'And my Mary's and Kitty's!' cried a third. Others spoke up, for nearly all had daughters whose joy it was to skip on Caburn at the new moon.

John Maltman turned to their best adviser, who had studied the matter closely, and asked: 'What think ye? Have we a leg to stand on?'

'Only half a one,' said the other. 'I doubt if you can stop him. It might be as well to come to terms.'

'None of his footpaths for us,' swore stout John Maltman. 'We'll fight the matter out.'

So things were left for a little, and each side wondered what the next move would be. Only the people knew in their hearts that they must be beaten in the end, and the Lord was sure of his victory. So sure, that he had great loads of bricks ordered; but he did not begin building for fear the people might grow violent, and perhaps burn his ricks and destroy his property. The only thing he did was to put a wire fence round the top of Caburn, and set a keeper there

to send the people round it. The people broke the
fence in many places, and jumped it, and crawled under
it; and as the keeper could not be everywhere at once,
many of them crossed the Down almost under his nose.

One evening, just before the new moon was due,
Ellen Maltman went into the woods to cry. For she
was the best skipper under Mount Caburn, and the
thought that she would never skip there again made
her more unhappy than she had ever thought she
could be. While she was crying in the dark, she felt
a hand on her shoulder, and a voice said to her:
'Crying for trouble, my dear? That'll never do!'

The voice might have been the voice of a withered
leaf, it was so light and dry; but it was also kind, so
Ellen checked her sobs and said: 'It's a big trouble,
ma'am, there's no remedy against it *but* to cry.'

'Why yes, there is,' said the withered voice. 'Ye
should skip against trouble, my dear.'

At this Ellen's sobs burst forth anew. 'I'll never skip no more!' she wailed. 'If I can't skip the new moon in on Caburn, I'll never skip no more.'

'And why can't you skip the new moon in on Caburn?' asked the voice.

Then Ellen told her.

After a little pause the voice spoke quietly out of the darkness. 'It's more than you will break their hearts, if they cannot skip on Caburn. And it must not be, it must not be. Tell me your name.'

'Ellen Maltman, ma'am, and I do love skipping, I can skip down anybody, ma'am, and they say I skip as never so!'

'They do, do they?' said the withered voice. 'Well, Ellen, run you home and tell them this. They are to go to this Lord and tell him he shall have his way and build on Caburn, if he will first take down the fence and let all who have ever skipped there skip there once more by turns, at the new moon. *All*, mind you, Ellen. And when the last skipper skips the last skip, he may lay his first brick. And let it be written out on paper, and signed and sealed.'

'But ma'am!' said Ellen, wondering.

'No words, child. Do as I tell you.' And the withered voice sounded so compelling that Ellen resisted no more. She ran straight to the village, and told her story to everybody.

At first they could hardly swallow it; and even when they had swallowed it, they said: 'But what's the sense of it?' But Ellen persisted and persisted; something of the spirit of the old voice got into her words, and against their reason the people began to think it was the thing to do. To cut a long story short they sent the message to the Lord next day.

The Lord could scarcely believe his ears. He rubbed his hands, and chortled at the people for fools.

'They've come to terms!' he sneered. 'I shall have the Down, and keep my footpath too. Well, they shall have their Skipping-Party; and the moment it is ended, up go my factories!'

The paper was drawn out, signed by both parties in the presence of witnesses, and duly sealed; and on the night of the new moon, the Lord invited a party of his friends to go with him to Caburn to see the sight.

And what a sight it was for them to see; every little girl in the village was there with her skipping-rope, from the toddlers to those who had just turned up their hair. Nay, even the grown maidens and the young mothers were there; and the very matrons too had come with ropes. Had not they once as children skipped on Caburn? And the message had said 'All.' Yes, and others were there, others they could not see:

Andy-Spandy and his fairy team, Heels-o'-Lead, Flea-Foot, and all of the rest, were gathered round to watch with bright fierce eyes the last great skipping on their precious ground.

The skipping began. The toddlers first, a skip or so apiece, a stumble, and they fell out. The Lord and his party laughed aloud at the comical mites, and at another time the villagers would have laughed too. But there was no laughter in them tonight. Their eyes were bright and fierce like those of the fairies. After the toddlers the little girls skipped in the order of their ages, and as they got older, the skipping got better. In the thick of the schoolchildren, 'This will take some time,' said the Lord impatiently. And when Ellen Maltman's turn came, and she went into her thousands, he grew restive. But even she, who could skip as never so, tired at last; her foot tripped, and she fell on the ground with a little sob. None lasted even half her time; of those who followed some were better, some were worse, than others; and in the small hours the older women were beginning to take their turn. Few of them kept it up for half a minute; they hopped and puffed bravely, but their skipping days were done. As they had laughed at the babies, so now the Lord's friends jibed at the babies' grandmothers.

'Soon over now,' said the Lord, as the oldest of the women who had come to skip, a fat old dame of sixty-seven, stepped out and twirled her rope. Her foot caught in it; she staggered, dropped the rope, and hid her face in her hands.

'Done!' shouted the Lord; and he brandished at the crowd a trowel and a brick which he had brought with him. 'Clear out, the lot of you! I am going to lay the first brick. The skipping's ended!'

'No, if you please,' said a gentle withered voice, 'it is *my* turn now.' And out of the crowd stepped a tiny tiny woman, so very old, so very bent and fragile, that she seemed to be no bigger than a little child.

'You!' cried the Lord. 'Who are *you*?'

'My name is Elsie Piddock, if you please, and I am a hundred and nine years old. For the last seventy-nine years I have lived over the border, but I was born in Glynde, and I skipped on Caburn as a child.' She spoke like one in a dream, and her eyes were closed.

'Elsie Piddock! Elsie Piddock!' the name ran in a whisper round the crowd.

'Elsie Piddock!' murmured Ellen Maltman. 'Why, mum, I thought Elsie Piddock was just a tale.'

'Nay, Elsie Piddock was no tale!' said the fat woman who had skipped last. 'My mother Joan skipped with her many a time, and told me tales you never would believe.'

'Elsie Piddock!' they all breathed again; and a wind seemed to fly round Mount Caburn, shrilling the name with glee. But it was no wind, it was Andy-Spandy and his fairy team, for they had seen the skipping-rope in the tiny woman's hands. One of the handles was made of Sugar Candy, and the other was made of French Almond Rock.

But the new Lord had never even heard of Elsie Piddock as a story; so laughing coarsely once again, he said: 'One more bump for an old woman's bones! Skip, Elsie Piddock, and show us what you're worth.'

'Yes, skip, Elsie Piddock,' cried Andy-Spandy and the fairies, 'and show them what you're worth!'

Then Elsie Piddock stepped into the middle of the onlookers, twirled her baby rope over her little shrunken body, and began to skip. And she skipped as NEVER SO!

First of all she skipped:

> *'An*dy
> *Span*dy
> *Sugar*dy
> *Can*dy,
> *French*
> *Al*mond
> ROCK!

Breadandbutterforyoursupper'sallyourmother'sGOT!'

And nobody could find fault with her skipping. Even the Lord gasped: 'Wonderful! wonderful for an old woman!' But Ellen Maltman, who *knew*, whispered: 'Oh, mum! 'tis wonderful for *any*body! And oh mum, do but see—she's skipping in her sleep!'

It was true. Elsie Piddock, shrunk to the size of seven years old, was sound asleep, skipping the new moon in with her baby rope that was up to all the tricks. An hour went by, two hours, three hours. There was no stopping her, and no tiring her. The people gasped, the Lord fumed, and the fairies turned head-over-heels for joy. When morning broke the Lord cried: 'That's enough!'

But Elsie Piddock went on skipping.

'Time's up!' cried the Lord.

'When I skip my last skip, you shall lay your first brick,' said Elsie Piddock.

The villagers broke into a cheer.

'Signed and sealed, my lord, signed and sealed,' said Elsie Piddock.

'But hang it, old woman, you can't go on for ever!' cried the Lord.

'Oh yes, I can,' said Elsie Piddock. And on she went.

At midday the Lord shouted: 'Will the woman never stop?'

'No, she won't,' said Elsie Piddock. And she didn't.

'Then I'll stop you!' stormed the Lord, and made a grab at her.

'Now for a Sly Skip,' said Elsie ~Piddock, and skipped right through his thumb and forefinger.

'Hold her, you!' yelled the Lord to his Lawyer.

'Now for a High Skip,' said Elsie Piddock, and as the Lawyer darted at her, she skipped right over the highest lark singing in the sun.

The villagers shouted for glee, and the Lord and his friends were furious. Forgotten was the compact signed and sealed—their one thought now was to seize the maddening old woman, and stop her skipping by sheer force. But they couldn't. She played all her tricks on them: High Skip, Slow Skip, Sly Skip, Toe

Skip, Long Skip, Fast Skip, Strong Skip, but never Last Skip. On and on and on she went. When the sun began to set, she was still skipping.

'Can we never rid the Down of the old thing?' cried the Lord desperately.

'No,' answered Elsie Piddock in her sleep, 'the Down will never be rid of me more. It's the children of Glynde I'm skipping for, to hold the Down for them and theirs for ever; it's Andy-Spandy I'm skipping for once again, for through him I've sucked sweet all my life. Oh, Andy, even you never knew how long Elsie Piddock could go on skipping!'

'The woman's mad!' cried the Lord. 'Signed and sealed doesn't hold with a madwoman. Skip or no skip, I shall lay the first brick!'

He plunged his trowel into the ground, and forced his brick down into the hole as a token of his possession of the land.

'Now', said Elsie Piddock, 'for a Strong Skip!'

Right on the top of the brick she skipped, and down underground she sank out of sight, bearing the brick beneath her. Wild with rage, the Lord dived after her. Up came Elsie Piddock skipping blither than ever—but the Lord never came up again. The Lawyer ran to look down the hole; but there was no sign of him. The Lawyer reached his arm down the hole; but there was no reaching him. The Lawyer dropped a pebble down the hole; and no one heard it fall. So strong had Elsie Piddock skipped the Strong Skip.

The Lawyer shrugged his shoulders, and he and the Lord's friends left Mount Caburn for good and all. Oh, how joyously Elsie Piddock skipped then!

'Skip Against Trouble!' cried she, and skipped so that everyone present burst into happy laughter. To the tune of it she skipped the Long Skip, clean out of sight. And the people went home to tea. Caburn was saved for their children, and for the fairies, for ever.

But that wasn't the end of Elsie Piddock; she has never stopped skipping on Caburn since, for Signed and Sealed is Signed and Sealed. Not many have seen her, because she knows all the tricks; but if you go to Caburn at the new moon, you may catch a glimpse of a tiny bent figure, no bigger than a child, skipping all by itself in its sleep, and hear a gay little voice, like the voice of a dancing yellow leaf, singing:

> 'Andy
> Spandy
> Sugardy
> Candy
> French
> Almond
> *Rock!*

Breadandbutterforyoursupper'sallyourmother'sGOT!'

Second Interlude

ANOTHER six daisy-chains came to an end with the story. Even Sally's fingers had been busy while her mind was far away. Now she sat up very straight, making her eyes tiny, and pushing out her lips as far as they would go.

> 'Swish swash! barley wash!
> Turn the bucket right over!'

she burst forth, in a voice that was half a snuffle and half a snort. It became more like a little girl's voice, as she added: 'That's *my* skipping-rhyme.'

'Then you *did* hear us saying ours,' said Sylvia.

'In a way,' said Sally, opening her eyes a little wider, while her mouth grew less and less snouty.

'Are you out of the way now?' inquired Selina.

'Almost.' Sally's small face became her own again. 'Yes, now I quite am.'

'Did you get your mind changed?' asked Sue.

Sally nodded.

Selina. Oh, what to?

Sally. A pig.

Stella. How disgusting.

Sally. A little pig. A dearling. A pigwiggin.

Sue. Did you have a name?

Sally. I nearly did, but then Martin stopped talking so I had to attend again.

Martin. There's no better cover for one's attention than other people's talking.

Sophie. It's rather impolite.

Martin. Not if it doesn't show. I'm sure none of us suspected that Sally was attending to little Trot while I was talking about skipping.

Sylvia. Little Trot?

Martin. That was the name she would have had in another moment. It was lucky for Sally that I didn't talk a single second longer by the clock, for if you have a name, you must go by it.

Sylvia. How do you know her name would have been Trot?

Sally. It would. I just remember. But the skipping went on going on, and I wasn't un-mixed enough.

Martin. So nothing has come of it but a skipping-rhyme fit for a pig.

Sue. It didn't *come* of it, you know. It's one of our *real* rhymes. It was there before the pig.

Martin. I'll wager there were pigs in Eden before there were skipping-rhymes.

Stella. There simply couldn't have been pigs in Eden.

Martin. Fie on you, Stella. In Eden pigs are as beautiful as dappled fawns, and as dear to God and his Saints. But our attention is wandering from the main point. Sue!

Sue (*rapidly*). Let's talk about skipping some more. Let's talk about the story. I would like to have a rope with sugar-candy handles. I *could*, you know. I would like to know the way to do all those skips. I'd like to go to Mount Caburn and learn how from Andy-Spandy. Is Andy-Spandy real? Let's get our ropes and skip the new moon in.

Sylvia. Where *is* Mount Caburn?

Martin. On the other side of things, just like Sue's chatter. For she is talking as hard as she can against time and fate, so that she needn't attend to what she is thinking.

Selina. What is Sue thinking?

Martin. That it may be bedtime soon.

Selina. It may be never, if you aren't clever.

Sue. I would like to talk in poitry like Selina. I would like——

Stella. You would like too many things.

Sally. Can one?

Martin. One can't. I can like six little girls at once. But I would like only one of them to come with me to the Guessing Stump.

Sue (sighing heavily). Well then.

So heavy was Sue's sigh that Martin was afraid she would never get herself up with it inside her. To make short work of it, he picked her up and carried her to the far corner of the daisy-field, where the two grave elms stood as dignified as judges on either side of the stump. As soon as Sue found herself plumped on it, she sat down and squeezed her fists over her face.

'And what,' asked Martin, 'do you expect to gain by that?'

'So you can't see whose I'm likely to be,' whispered Sue.

'Now you are talking in poitry, just like Selina,' said Martin, 'and we agreed long ago that you weren't likely to be Jane's-and-John's.'

Sue took her fists away, and beamed on him. 'Yes, we did, you know. They were the only ones left, and it would of been funny if I *was* theirs all the time.'

'Almost as funny—but not quite—as if you had

been Jennifer's-and-Oliver's. But Jennifer could never
have had so matter-of-fact a child as you are. Almost
as funny—not quite—as if you had been Joscelyn's-
and-Henry's. But Joscelyn pretended so often to be
what she wasn't, and you never try to be anything but
what you are. Almost—not quite—as funny as if you
had been Joyce-and-Michael's. But Joyce had a
frivolous mind, and it's not to be thought of. Very
nearly as funny as if you were Joan's-and-Charles's.
But Joan was such a lot of things, and you are

all-of-a-piece. Now Jane, as a matter of fact, was as matter-of-fact as you are.'

Sue put her fists over her face again.

'Can it possibly,' mused Martin Pippin, 'come back to Jane after all?'

A muffled voice answered him through the fists. 'You *did* say the chances were against it. You *did* say you wouldn't be such a goose as to say Jane-and-John.'

'I did,' said Martin, 'but what's the alternative?' Between the brown dimpled fists, two round drops squeezed themselves, and Martin knew the battle was lost for good. 'The only alternative,' he sighed, 'is myself.'

The fists began very slowly to descend. Sue's round eyes peered cautiously over the knuckles.

'You, Martin?'

'Me.'

'For my father-and-mother, do you mean?'

'I'm awfully afraid so.'

'Is it your guess?'

'What else is there for it?'

'No, but I mean, do you *guess* it?'

'I shall have to, sha'n't I?'

'Go on, then, *guess* it.'

'I guess,' said Martin, throwing up the sponge, 'that I am your father and you are my very child.'

'GOOSE!'

The fists uncovered two wet cheeks and a laughing mouth. 'I'm Jane's-and-John's, I'm Jane's-and-John's!' Sue chortled. 'The chances were against it, but I'm Jane's-and-John's all the time! And I'm never never going to bed any more!'

She pulled the daisy out of Martin's ear, bumped

herself off the Guessing Stump, and marched across the daisy-field, chanting a Song of Triumph.

> 'Goose! Goose! Martin's a Goose!
> Martin-a-Goose, a-Goose!'

(sang Sue).

Martin Pippin had no option but to follow her, hanging his head.

★

The song turned into a chorus for a while. When it had sung itself out——

'Do not forget the old saw,' said Martin. 'No Goose without its Stuffing.'

'Onions!' scoffed Stella.

'And sage!' sniffed Sue.

'And sage,' said Martin Pippin. 'But faith is more than wisdom, and if Stella goes on looking scorn I shall cry on my Saint to protect me.'

Stella. A goose with a saint indeed!

Martin. Do not geese come into their glory at Martinmas? Why shouldn't a goose have its saint as well as a pig?

Stella. Pigs indeed!

Martin. You are too hard on pigs, who were beloved of Saint Anthony.

Sally. Was Anthony a nice saint?

Martin. Two of the best.

Sally. (*Lets out an unexpected wail.*)

Martin. Don't whine like a Tantony Pig, child. What's the matter?

Sally. I so nearly did have two of the best saints.

Sue. What's a Tan—— What's that sort of pig what you said?

Martin. A Tantony Pig is what I said.

Sue. Well what's *that*?

Martin. That's a saying.

Sylvia. Is a pig a saying?

Martin. Not all by itself.

Sylvia. Then what *is* it?

Martin. What is what?

Stella. He's just going round and round on purpose. Let's make chains.

The children thereupon picked daisies for six more chains; and Sue filled her pinafore with the exact number before she began, and Sylvia filled hers with too many, and Stella hers with too few; and Sophie strung hers as they came from the grass, and Selina plucked a handful, and when that was done plucked another. But Sally put two together, and stopped to consider whether that was a chain or not.

So Martin, left to his own devices, fell into a monologue, for he had to be talking, to himself if to nobody else.

'These sayings,' he mused, 'where on earth do they spring from, and where in heaven do they come from? My old nurse, as the saying goes, whose name was Aunt Parsley, though she wasn't old and she wasn't my aunt, and now I come to think of it may not have been my nurse, indeed, I am not sure I ever had a nurse, but if I did, Aunt Parsley had two ways with me when I was peevish. Her kinder way was to say: "Stop crying, child, and I'll give you a Silver New Nothing," her tarter way: "Now then, child, don't whine like a Tantony Pig!" And she never explained what she meant by either, which was as well. For what something could equal the boundless promise of a nothing, and a silver new one at that? And what

queer fate must I have suffered, had I whined myself
into one of Tantony's pigs? Both sayings stopped my
weeping and my whining, as a cobweb will stop a cut.'
Having come to the end of his thoughts for the time
being, Martin hummed to himself:

> 'A Crust of Bread for the Tantony Pig!
> He's not very strong and he's not very big.
>   With his bell on his cheek,
>   Week! week! week!
> *Give me some Bread!* whines the Tantony Pig.'

Sally looked up quickly from her two daisies.
'What is *that*?'

'A bit of an old ballad on the matter.'

'There's lots more of it,' nodded Sally.

'Seven verses in all. But I cannot hope the other six
will interest the six of you, concerned as you are with
your daisies.'

'I can do daisies and songs together,' drawled
Selina. 'D is for Daisies and D is for Downs.' She
strung a daisy, looked up at Rackham Hill, and sang:

> 'The Downs are ups as well as downs,
>   Down they run to the fields and towns,
>   But up they go to the endless sky
>   Where kites and clouds and peewits fly.'

Then she looked down, and strung another daisy.
Stella nipped a slit in a daisy-stem, saying: 'I can
do W for the Weald.

> 'Sussex Weald is flood and field,
>   Sussex Weald is wood and water,
>   I'll hew and drain the Sussex Weald,
>   And till it for my son and daughter.'

Then she slipped another daisy-stem through the slit, and drew the head close.

'Is it alphabets?' asked Sally.

'The very best sort,' said Martin, 'which is taking your favourite letter, and placing it where you please, and that makes literature. What is your favourite letter, Sally?'

'It's O today,' said Sally, undoing her two daisies to squint through the holes, north and south. 'O is for Ouse.

> 'Where does River Ouse steal forth?
> Near a greenwood in the North.
> Where has River Ouse its mouth?
> Near a haven in the South.'

Then she put north and south daisy together again.

Sue, who had been thinking hard, threaded a daisy announcing: 'K is for Kingcups, you know. The floods on Amberley Wildbrooks In Spring spread out for miles, And the Kingcups grow in the water Like clustering golden isles, is that a poem what I've made?'

'As good as many another,' Martin assured her. 'What question, Sylvia, will you ask in yours, eh?'

'A,' said Sylvia, making a mistake in her chain, 'is for Arundel.

> 'Run, Arun, run and tell
> How shall men know Arundel?
> A Castle Tower, a Cathedral Bell,
> By these all men know Arundel.

Bother! My chain's broken, that stalk was too thin.'

'You must choose thick ones like this, see?' said Sue.

'C is for Chanctonbury Ring,' said Sophie, and sang:

Sally

'Ring-a-ding, Chanctonbury!
What shall I sing?
Beeches on a hill-top
All in a ring.
Green in the morning,
Black in the night,
And burning in the autumn
Like a beacon light.

*The
King's
Barn*

There, we've all done one now but Martin. Martin,
what's *your* best letter?'

'He couldn't do X if he tried,' taunted Stella.

'Then I'll try,' retorted Martin. 'Two daisies,
Sally, do not make a chain, but they form a link. Put
one behind your left ear, put the other behind my
right, and I will say, and you shall hear, with a pepper-
mint all round to avoid interruptions.' Out of his
endless pockets came another paper bag, and out of
the bag six peppermints, which went the rounds. But
at Sally, who this time came sixth, Martin stopped to
say: 'I need not ask what your tale is to be about.'

'No,' said Sally, 'you needn't.' And she absorbed
her mint while Martin propped himself against the
clothes-basket, twisted the corners of his paper bag
into two little pig's-ears, and said, very thoughtfully,
'X.'

'Ha, ha!' scoffed Stella.

'Keep your tongue in its place,' said Martin, 'and
no more talking.

'X is Chichester Market Cross.
If you tell me it's not I am quite at a loss.'

And without more ado he launched upon the tale of

THE TANTONY PIG

A Tantony Pig! A Tantony Pig!
When he comes into market he's not worth a fig!
 The heart of a Saint,
 Both tender and quaint,
Alone knows the worth of a Tantony Pig.

A RARE hard life Little Trot had of it in Forage Yard where he was born. Twelve brothers had come into the world with him, for he was the thirteenth and smallest of the litter, the dearling as they say. 'There's the little bit over, wife,' said Farmer Gurly, dandling him, and the Farmer's Wife said: 'There now! the wee trot!'

'Don't go getting too fond of wee Trot,' said the Farmer, 'for when the time comes he must go to market like the rest.'

'That's not yet awhile,' said Mistress Gurly, and till Trot was old enough to know the taste of mash, she saw to it that he got as much milk as his brothers. When they nuzzled him out of place under the old mother-sow, the Farmer's Wife made it up with neat's-milk and water. But it did not fatten him or help him to grow. By the time he and his twelve brothers were gobbling out of the trough, Trot was still the weakling of the brood.

After that, he had no chance at all. He was always crowded out round trough and bucket, and never got his share of swill and mash. That poor little Trot! When the Farmer's Wife lost interest in her dearling, it was Forage Yard indeed for him. His scrubby flanks were hollow. He rootled all over the farmyard for any stray peelings he could find, but there was as little hope for him on the dung-heaps as in his own sty. All the scraps and droppings were pounced on by the five dogs, the seven cats, the three goats, and the army of cocks and hens who roamed where they would, and found everything before he did.

Run, Trot, run! Molly has spilled some milk from her milking-pail. It slopped over the brim as she carried her yoke to the dairy. Run, Trot, run!

How Trot ran! But when he reached the milk, there were the seven cats, lapping thirstily, Tib and Gib and Sib, grey Malkin, black Tom, Ginger, and Snowball.

'Is that some milk?' asked innocent Trot.

And the seven turned and spat on him, and hissed: 'Yes, that's some milk, and it's not for you!'

Run, Trot, run! Hodge is going through the pasture eating raw turnip, and throwing the rind behind him! Run, Trot, run!

How Trot ran! But when he came up with Hodge,
there at his heels were the three goats, Billy and Silly
and Tilly, eating the bits of rind as they touched the
ground.

'Is it turnip?' asked innocent Trot.

And the three turned on him, and lowered their
butting horns. 'Turnip it is, and it is not for you.'

Run, Trot, run! The Miller has been through the barnyard with a sack of meal, and there was a hole in the bottom corner of the sack. Run, Trot, run!

How Trot ran! But when he reached the barnyard, there was a flurry of hens from the gate to the granary, with ten cocks mounting guard about them.

'Would it be meal?' asked innocent Trot.

And the ten stretched their throats and flapped their wings at him, crowing: 'Meal it is, and it is not for you.'

Run, Trot, run! For baby Bet has flung her gravy-crust out of the window and into the yard. Run, Trot, run!

How Trot ran! But when he reached the yard, there were Spot and Tray and Bob and Toby and Towzer all fighting in a heap.

'Might it be a crust?' asked innocent Trot.

And the five disentangled themselves, and snarled: 'A crust it was, and it wouldn't have been for you!' And they sat there licking their chops, while Trot turned sadly away.

Run, Trot, run! Giles has gone to the sty with swill and mash. Run, Trot, run!

How Trot did run! For this was his own place, and his own food. But when he reached the sty, his twelve brothers were crowded round trough and bucket, and once again there was no corner for the dearling.

'Swill-an-mash! swill-an-mash!' squeaked Trot. 'Lemme in to my own swill-an-mash!'

And through their greedy gobbles the twelve grunted: 'Beautiful swill-an-mash, and it ain't for *you!*'

Is it to be wondered at that Trot grew up a weakling?

To Chichester Market the pigs they must go,
The tusky old boar and the wallowing sow,
        Load up the cart
        With stock for the mart—
To market in Chichester piglings must go.

The time had come for Trot and his family to say
good-bye to the farm. In the course of his short life,
he had seen other families of older pigs vanish from
the scene. Sheep, too, and calves had been driven
down the road or laid under nets in carts, and had
come back no more. Hens had been packed in baskets,
ducks and geese who had been Trot's daily compa-
nions had disappeared—who knew whither? Sometimes he ventured to put a question to one of the dogs
who, Trot noticed, went about with their master and
always came home again.

'What's come to Mammy Fleece, Towzer, and
where's little Bully-Boy?'

'Ask me no questions and I'll tell you no lies,'
yapped Towzer.

'What for *should* you tell me lies?' asked Trot.

But Towzer wouldn't say. So Trot ran off to Dapple
in his stall.

'I seed you go off this morning with Henny-Penny
and Cocky-Locky in the cart, Dapple,' he squeaked.

'Did ye then?' said Dapple.

'The cart comed back empty,' squeaked Trot.

'The better for me,' said Dapple.

'And for Henny-Penny too?' asked Trot. 'And
Cocky-Locky?'

'Where ignorance is bliss,' said Dapple, ''tis folly
to be wise.'

'But I want to be wise,' whined Trot.

'The more fool you!' whinnied Dapple. 'Don't

worry, little Trot. You'll be wise to it some day. You'll be in the cart yourself when the time comes.'

And now the time was come.

One fine morning, Farmer Gurly came with Giles and Hodge, and began catching the family of pigs of which Trot was the dearling. How they squealed, running hither and thither, twisting and turning, and making the men's task so hard that it was rough handling they got in the end. When the twelve were safe in the cart, Hodge addressed the Farmer. 'What about the dearling, master?'

'Up with him,' said Gurly.

'Will it be any manner of use?' asked Hodge.

'Trot's no manner of use where he is,' said Gurly.

'He bain't fit,' said Hodge.

'I'll take my chance of that,' said the Farmer, winking. 'It all depends whether Gregory Broyle or John Goodwood comes round. If 'tis John Goodwood, I'll tip him the wink to say Trot is as handsome a pig as his brothers.'

When Trot heard that, he stood still with delight. He hadn't grasped much else in the talk, and who John Goodwood was he hadn't a notion, but he hoped he would come round, instead of Gregory Broyle. Grand John Goodwood! who would praise him till he felt at last the equal of his family. So when Hodge made a dash at him, bawling: 'Now, then, come along, young skin-an-bones!' Trot allowed himself to be caught without any trouble, and bundled into the cart under a net with the rest. Then off they set, at Dobbin's best pace, though with such a cartful it wasn't his *very* best.

'Did you hear, Grunt?' he squeaked to his eldest brother. 'We're going to a show, for to be said which is the handsomest, and if John Goodwood comes round perhaps it might be me.'

'*I* heard, stoopid!' snorted Grunt. 'And *I* say, let it be Gregory Broyle, who tells the truth, it seems.' And he gave Trot such a gunt in his starved little belly that Trot said no more for the rest of the road.

At Chichester Cross, what a babel greeted their ears! Sounds they were used to hearing, to be sure— lowing and mooing, baaing and bleating, crowing and clucking, and squealing and squeaking—but mooings and bleatings and crowings and squeakings to such a degree that the thirteen little pigs couldn't hear themselves grunt, when they were tumbled out of the cart and driven into a pen. Chichester was full of such pens, crammed with livestock from all the farms around, their owners standing by them, while other men came to lean over and look and prod and pinch. One came to Trot's pen, and prodded Grunt, who was the fattest, and said to Farmer Gurly: 'What d'ye ask for *this* un?' And Farmer Gurly winked at him and pointing to Trot said: 'What'll ye give for *that* un?' And the man said: 'Ho-ho! *that* un looks like a Tantony Pig to me.'

'Hush!' said the Farmer, jerking his thumb over his shoulder. Two men with staves in their hands had come among the crowd, and were going about examining the animals. One was a small grim man, the other was tall and handsome. This one was friendly with everybody; he joked with the farmers, who slapped him on the back, saying: 'How do, John? How's the wife? Nagging for a new gown, I shouldn't wonder!' and John grinned, and after he had looked at the animals and had shaken their owners by the hand, his hand often went into his pocket. But nobody

cracked jokes with the little man, who went about
with a suspicious sort of scowl, and kept his hands
outside him.

'D'you see, d'you see!' squeaked Trot excitedly.
'They are saying which is the best in every pen, and
oh, how I hopes it's John, not Gregory, who comes
to *us*!'

'Hold yer snout!' muttered Grunt rudely, gunting
him again. So Trot contented himself with watching
eagerly out of his little pink eyes, to see which way
the two men were going. And it was Gregory, the
scowling one, who came to him.

> Fat pig and lean pig, they all must be viewed
> To see which is fit and unfit to be food.
> > Grunt shall be passed,
> > And Trot shall be last,
> When fat pig and lean pig they come to be viewed.

'What d'ye call this thing?' snarled Gregory Broyle.

He had examined the twelve fat brothers, and
twelve times had said sourly: 'He'll do. He'll do.
He'll about do,' and 'I s'pose he'll do.' And each time
he said it more grudgingly than the last. Now Trot's
turn had come, and he shivered as Gregory hauled
him out of the mass of piglets, and felt his ribs. Alas
little Trot! he knew from the start that the magic
words, 'He'll do!' would not fall from the lips of this
bitter man, who felt and fumbled and sneered at his
starved carcass.

'What is it? A rat?' he asked.

'A rat! ho-ho-ho!' guffawed the Farmer. 'That's a
good jest, that is. You were always a rare man at
a jest, Master Broyle.' His voice sounded hearty, but
his face was red and displeased.

'I never jest,' growled Gregory. 'I am City Officer for Chichester, and it's no part of an officer's duties to jest, Farmer Gurly.' He let his eye travel to a far spot where John Goodwood was laughing loud enough to cover any smaller sound, such as the chink of money. Who was to know if any chinked or not? But as Gregory Broyle did not laugh, a curious chink in Farmer Gurly's pocket was plain to hear. 'None o' that!' snapped Gregory Broyle.

'None o' what, man?' asked the Farmer gruffly.

'None o' your tricks.'

'I've no more tricks than you have jokes, officer,' said Gurly more respectfully. His voice even sounded a little nervous, Trot thought. For the first time in his life, the dearling felt sympathy for his big rough master, who, like himself, was being treated with contempt by the City Officer. When Grunt whispered sneeringly: '*You* won't do, Trot! you'll *never* do, *you* won't!' a tear squeezed out of his little pink eye, and he looked longingly across the market-place at John Goodwood's corner, from which that nice smiling man was moving away, with two or three farmers, towards the door of the *Pig and Whistle*.

Gurly was looking that way too, as longingly as Trot. He cleared his throat, coughed a little, glanced at Gregory, and muttered: 'Thirsty work and thirsty weather, officer!' and raised his hand carelessly to his mouth, like a man drinking.

'Stow it!' said Gregory. 'Are you looking for trouble?' He stooped and tied a cord round Trot's neck, adding: 'You'd no business to bring this miserable critter to market, and well you know it. He ain't fit for any good man's board. A case for Saint Anthony, *he* is!' And he led Trot out of the market, a disgrace to the name of pig. The little outcast went meekly, snout to cobble-stone. He felt dreadfully ashamed of himself.

> Tantony Pig, you must go with a bell
> That people may know you are not very well.
> Ting-a-ling-ling!
> Some provender bring
> To the Tantony Pig when he tingles his bell.

Cling! Clang! Clong!

The bell of Saint Anthony's Hospital rang out its summons, and the Porter went to the gate. There stood Gregory Broyle, with Trot, who trembled and wondered what was going to become of him. Rather to his surprise, Gregory had not been as rough with him as he had been with Farmer Gurly. Also to his surprise, as they left the market they passed the door of the *Pig and Whistle*, where John Goodwood was lolling on a bench with his friends; and seeing Gregory he grinned, saying: 'Another pet for St Anthony—no wonder you're no favourite with the farmers, Master Broyle.' Gregory had answered: 'Another quart for your gullet! No wonder you're fond o' the farmers, Master Goodwood.' And what it had all meant Trot couldn't make out, except that all of a sudden he began to like Gregory Broyle more, and John Goodwood not so much. Still, he could not help feeling anxious, as he waited for the Porter to open St Anthony's gate.

The Porter had by the hand a very small girl, with a tear-stained face and a bright smile. 'Run along home, Betsy,' said the Porter, patting her head. ''Twill be all right now, you'll see.'

Betsy nodded. 'Tantony'll find her, *I* know!' Then

she caught sign of Trot, and stared hard at the little
pig. 'Piggy, piggy, am you bacon?' cried she.

Both Gregory and the Porter laughed, and Gregory
said: 'No, missy, that's just what this starveling am
not.'

'Can I have him then?' demanded Betsy.

'No, missy,' said Gregory again, 'he's St Anthony's piggy now, but you can feed him as often as you like, same as sparrows.'

'Sparrows like bread,' observed Betsy.

'So do pigs,' said Gregory.

'I'll bring the Tantony Pig some bread tomorrow morning,' said Betsy, and she trotted across the road and went into a little house on the other side, chanting:

'Tantony Pig! Tantony Pig!
Tantony, Tantony, Tantony Pig!'

'Widow Bonny's baby, ain't she?' said Gregory.

The Porter nodded. 'Yes, that's Betsy Bonny. She came here crying for her lost dolly, so I let her into the chapel to ask Saint Anthony to find it.'

'They say he'll find anything,' said Gregory, 'but if he has to find all that children lose, he's got his work cut out. I hope he'll find Betsy's dolly, however, for her mother's a good sort of woman, and I was sorry last year to hear she'd lost her husband.'

'Maybe she has said a word to St Anthony about *that*,' winked the Porter. But Gregory said rather shortly: 'I've no more time to waste. Where is the Proctor?'

'What next?' wondered Trot, as he was led into a yard, where presently came a man who was the Proctor of Saint Anthony's Hospital.

'Is this pig sick?' he asked, fondling Trot's ear.

'Not to say sick,' said Gregory, 'but he was taken to market to be sold for food, a starved weak critter, unfit for pork and bacon. So I fetched him away.'

'And you did right,' said the Proctor. He took out his knife, and made a little slit in Trot's ear, and Trot let out a squeal that was longer than the slit. 'Come,

come!' said the Proctor, 'don't make such a fuss about
it. If you knew all, you'd be grateful for that slit in
your ear, my little pig.' Then he fastened a collar
with a bell on it round Trot's neck, adding: 'You
are safe now. No man will hurt you, for by the bell
on your neck and the slit in your ear they will know
you're St Anthony's own.' He led Trot to the dungheap in the yard and said: 'Bless you, little pig. Eat
what you like.'

And to Trot, this was the most surprising thing of
all.

> A Crust of Bread for the Tantony Pig!
> He's not very strong and he's not very big.
> > With his bell on his cheek,
> > *Week! week! week!*
> *Give me some Bread!* whines the Tantony Pig.

A fine life of it little Trot led now. He was allowed
to roam where he liked and feed as he pleased.
Nobody stopped him, nobody harmed him, nobody
kicked him or pushed him or pulled him. He was
St Anthony's own, and people treated him well—else
what might not St Anthony do? Only one boy,
Simon Croucher, who bullied children smaller than
himself, looked at Trot as though he would like to
bully him too. But he did not dare; only now and
then he flung a stone, as if by accident, and if it
chanced to hit Trot, he said: '*Poor* little piggy-wiggy!'
—so that St Anthony wouldn't think he had done it
on purpose.

But everybody else was kind to Trot. Children
with cakes of bread, men munching their snacks in
the street, women carrying baskets of broken victuals
for the poor, would hear Trot's bell, and turn to
throw him something. At first Trot was suspicious.

He had been rough-handled for so long that he could
hardly believe all this kindness was for him. But soon
he forgot that men had ever been rough, he gained
confidence, as all things will when they have no cause
for fear. He let strangers come near him as a kitten
or a puppy might, and people he saw every day he
knew to be his friends. He ran to them, whining for
food. He did not know it was whining, to him it was
just a joyous greeting, a way of saying: 'There you

are and here I am! where is bread?' · But he whined it
so vigorously that Widow Bonny, when Betsy was
in one of her peevish fits, slapped her smartly, saying:
'Now, now, don't whine like a Tantony Pig!'

Betsy was Trot's best friend of all. He took the
place in her heart of her lost doll. 'Stoopid ol' Tantony
couldn't find my dolly,' he heard her tell her mother.
So now she petted Tantony's pig instead.

Because of her, Trot never roamed far away. He
was sure of something from her hand every day, and
she made a rare pet of him, cuddling and chattering

to him by the hour together, until her mother came to
say: 'As long as Betsy is with the Tantony Pig, I
know she's all right.' This made Trot prouder than
ever, and the time when he had been despised passed

out of his piggy mind. Another thing that made him
proud was the flock of sparrows that hopped and
fluttered about him, sure of crumbs wherever Trot
was thrown a crust. He looked on them as his little
train of attendants. It was one of these pert gutter-
snipes, called Pip, who explained to him the good luck
that had come his way; for there isn't much a sparrow
doesn't know.

'My eye!' chirped Pip hoarsely, after Trot had
told him the story of his life, 'some is lucky, some is!
You kin jest thank your stars, Trot, that you've

grown up so bony. If your brothers had eat a little less, an' you a little more, you'd be where they are now.'

'Where's that?' asked Trot.

'Chimbley-corner in the smoke,' said Pip, 'turning into flitches of bacon an' shoulders of ham. Even St Anthony can't stop that, not if he *is* the Patron Saint of pigs. It's the ones like *you* he keeps an eye on, Trot, when the City Officers go round the markets, to see which pigs is good for ham-an-bacon. You wasn't.' Trot looked abashed at this, till Pip chirped: 'Cheer up! nothing to be ashamed of. It's all on account of your elegant figger.' Then Trot looked pleased with himself again. An elegant figure was something for any pig to be proud of.

He went off and rootled in Simon Croucher's father's dungheap, which was the richest in the neighbourhood. Simon Croucher, who teased Betsy Bonny till she cried, was no favourite of Trot's; but his father's yard had the best garbage he knew of, and Trot spent many a happy hour rootling in it. He unearthed numbers of things he couldn't eat, and had no idea what some of them could be; and once he found something so very curious, that though he couldn't eat it he hid it in a bottom corner of the heap, and rootled it out to look at now and then.

> A Tantony Pig gets the lean and the fat,
> The thinnest cannot remain thin upon that.
> > Piggy, take care!
> > Piggy, beware!
> It's bad to be lean, and it's worse to be fat!

One day Gregory Broyle came along the street to pay a call on Widow Bonny. He often did this, when

his duties as City Officer took him to and from the
Hospital. When he did, if Betsy happened to be in the
house, Widow Bonny would open the door, look up
and down the street, and give a whistle—and Trot
came to know that the whistle was for him. It always
meant some delicious titbit, such as yellow cabbage-
leaves. He came running to the Widow's whistle,
and she would say: 'There, Betsy, play with your
Tantony Pig till I've done talking with Master Broyle.
And here's a stalk for you to give your Tantony.'
Then in she would go, remarking: 'As long as Betsy is
with the Tantony Pig, I know she's all right,' and
then she and Gregory would talk of grown-up things.

On this particular day Trot chanced to be near the
Widow's door when Gregory came, and when Mistress Bonny opened the door Gregory said: 'Look at
the fat on him, will you?'

Widow Bonny stooped to fondle Trot's slit ear.

'Everybody feeds him,' she said. 'He is the most popular Tantony in the street.'

'So I can see,' said Gregory, 'and going by his figure he has no more right to be a Tantony at all.'

'What's the matter with his figure?' asked Widow Bonny.

'Why, he's lost it, that's what,' said Gregory, 'like a woman will sometimes do—though not always.' And they went inside joking, leaving Trot feeling uneasy, but he didn't know why.

'Hear that?' chirped a hoarse little voice, and there was Pip, picking crumbs out of the gutter. 'You better look out, you better!'

'Why?' asked Trot.

'You been an' lost your elegant figger,' said Pip.

'Well?' asked Trot.

'Ham-an-bacon!' was all Pip would answer; and he flew away as the door opened again, and Betsy Bonny trotted out with a beautiful big cabbage-leaf in her hand. 'Run along now,' said her Mother's voice behind her, 'and play with your Tantony till I call you.'

Betsy sat down, and Trot lay down beside her. Betsy tore big bits off the cabbage-leaf for Trot, and little bits for herself. As she tore, she chattered.

'I'm goin' to have a new daddy,' she confided to Trot, 'but I'd rarver have a new dolly. My new daddy's goin' to give me a new dolly, but I'd rarver have my old dolly. Tantony's a stoopid old Saint an' never found my old dolly, my new daddy's cleverer 'an Tantony becos he's goin' to give me annuvver dolly, but I'd rarver have my old one but stoopid old Tantony can't find her.'

Betsy chewed the juice out of the coarse ribs of the

leaf, and spat out the chewed bits, which Trot snuffled up with relish. The world was all sunshine, and he forgot his anxiety entirely, till Gregory Broyle came out of the house, and laughed to Widow Bonny: 'Look at 'em, will you! Betsy had better make the most of her pet while he lasts.'

'Oh, you wouldn't!'' smiled Mistress Bonny. 'Not Betsy's Tantony, would you? Any other Tantony, but not *Betsy's*!'

'He's a disgrace to the Hospital, and a credit to the market,' said Gregory good-naturedly, for lately he had lost his scowl and become quite pleasant-looking. 'I'm afraid I must do something about it, now that he has put on fat and lost his figure.'

''Twill break Betsy's little heart,' cried her Mother.

'Little hearts soon mend,' said Gregory.

'I shouldn't wonder,' smiled Widow Bonny.

Then they joked some more, and parted, and Betsy ran into the house. Widow Bonny shut the door, and Trot blinked his little pink eyes, and Pip chirped in his hoarse voice: 'Lost your figger, did you hear? You better speak to St Anthony about it.'

> Anthony, Anthony, hark to my prayer!
> You find what is lost, be it here, be it there.
>> What I have lost
>> Will be to my cost,
> If you don't answer a little pig's prayer.

'Please, St Anthony, I've lost my figure! Please, St Anthony, find my lost figure for me! do, dear St Anthony, *please*!'

So prayed Trot, standing in St Anthony's chapel before the picture of the Saint himself in his cave in the wood, with a pig beside him for company. The chapel door was always left ajar, a little snout could easily thrust it open, and that night, when the lights were out in the streets, and the Hospital was quiet, Trot pushed his plump body through the opening he had made for it. Had not Betsy come here to pray, the very first time he saw her? Alas! the Saint had not found her lost dolly for her, and perhaps he would be no cleverer for Trot—even if so great a fellow would stoop to listen to so humble a petitioner. Still, it was better than nothing, it was at least worth trying before Gregory Broyle came again and sealed Trot's fate. But would St Anthony hear him?

He whined again, a little louder than before. '*Dee*-ar St Anthony! you find things what are lost. Please, St Anthony, find my figure for me, plee-ee-ee-*eeeeee-se*!'

'Now then, child, don't whine like a Tantony Pig!'

It was the Saint in the picture who spoke! It was St Anthony himself.

'Saint Anthony!'

'Well, child?'

'I whine like a Tantony Pig because I *am* one.'

'Yes, of course, child.'

'I'm *your* pig, aren't I?'

'Yes, of course, child.'

'Then will you find my figure for me, please!'

'Yes, of——' St Anthony stopped short, and a shadow crossed his brow. 'It's the same tale over again,' he sighed, 'but bless me! I never had a request like *that* before!' He leaned out of the picture to pass his thin hands over Trot's fat sides. 'Why,' said he, 'you've got plenty of figure! lots of it! What do you want any more for?'

'I want some less,' said Trot. 'I've lost mine like a woman will sometimes do. I want the one what I had, not the one what I got.'

St Anthony pushed his halo to one side, and scratched his head.

'Can't you do it?' asked Trot. 'Are you really a stoopid old saint?'

'What's that?'

'You couldn't find Betsy Bonny's dolly,' said Trot, 'so I dessay you can't find my figure for me neither.'

'Nonsense!' said St Anthony. 'Of course I can find your figure—if I try. Though I am *not* St Antony of Padua.'

'Who?' asked Trot.

'The other St Antony, the one who finds lost things.'

'Is there two of you then?' asked Trot.

'Yes, of course, child. But stupids will get us mixed up. It's *my* job to look after little pigs like you, and *his* job to find lost dolls like Betsy Bonny's. And all for that, I've lost my reputation.'

'What is a reputation?' asked Trot.

'It is people thinking well of you,' said St Anthony.

'When did you lose your one of that?' asked Trot.

'When Betsy Bonny called me a stupid old saint. It isn't as though,' said St Anthony, 'I don't know where her dolly is. I do.'

'Then why don't you give it back to her?' asked Trot.

'Because it is where I wouldn't touch it with a barge-pole. It is in Simon Croucher's father's garbage-heap.'

'Ow!' squealed Trot. 'Is it a wood ball, an' some red-and-black paint on, and some more wood with bendy bits, an' a rag with blue dots on?'

'That is it,' said St Anthony.

'*Ow!*' squealed Trot again. 'I would not touch it with a barge-pole neither, I would touch it with my snout.'

'Would you, my piglet?'

'And then,' said Trot, 'Betsy would find her doll, and you would find your reputation.'

St Anthony leaned out of the picture again, and fondled Trot's slit ear. 'Well, piglet, suppose we strike a bargain. If *you* rootle Betsy's dolly on to her doorstep, *I'll* see to it you wake tomorrow as lean as when you went to market. Only—just this.'

'Just what?' asked Trot.

'You mustn't eat so much ever again. You must only rootle garbage-heaps once a day, and you must turn away from everything people offer you.'

Trot blinked his little piggy eyes and said: 'I just could *not*. It aren't my nature, St Anthony.'

'You'll lose your figure again in no time, then!'

'Not if you put it back again every night, then!'

'That fat of yours,' said St Anthony, 'is going to keep my hands full.'

'Not the little teeny bit what I get every day,' wheedled Trot. 'And for that, I will rootle in all the heaps for lost things, whenever stoopid people mix you up. I will be your Tantony Pig for evermore. I will rootle for dolls, and pearls, and barge-poles, and peelings, and never grow fat however much I eat of everything there is!'

'That would be a miracle,' said St Anthony.

'What is Saints *for*?' asked Trot.

And as Trot wished it to be, so it was.

In the morning, Betsy Bonny ran crying to her Mother, 'Clever ol' Tantony's found my dolly, look!' And at noon, when Gregory Broyle came calling and wooing, all he saw in the way of pigs in the street was Trot, as flat as a pancake, rootling in Simon Croucher's father's garbage-heap. By the bell on his neck and the slit in his ear, Gregory knew him for a Tantony Pig, but not for the plump little porker he had seen yesterday. 'There's a misery for you!' said Gregory. 'For all the world as if a giant had trod on him.'

But Trot was no misery. For the rest of his days he

gobbled his fill, and remained as thin as a lath. What better fate can any pig ask than that?

A Tantony Pig! A Tantony Pig!
When he comes into market he's not worth a fig.
    The heart of a Saint
    Both tender and quaint
Alone knows the worth of a Tantony Pig.

Third Interlude

FIVE daisy-chains came full circle with Martin's story. But Sally slit the tail of her last daisy, so that it had two points instead of a hole, saying: 'This is my Tantony Pig, with a split in its ear. Nobody can eat *this* pig for dinner, see?'

'I'm going to be a vegetablearian anyhow,' said Selina dreamily. 'Suppose if we ate a dearling by accident. Except bacon.'

'I'll be a vegeltarian too,' said Sue, 'only for sausages.'

'No more pigs for me for evermore,' vowed Sophie. 'Just the crackling.'

And Sylvia was as firm on the matter of pigs, but had always wondered what a trotter tasted like, and meant to know that, though nothing more, one day.

Stella swore never to touch pig again, bar a slice of home-cured ham.

Sally said: 'Not even chitterlings.'

Sylvia. What's chitterlings?

Selina. I think they're the part pigs sing with.

Sue. Pigs don't, you know. They honk.

Sophie. Honking's a sort of singing.

Sally. You couldn't honk with your chitterlings.

Sylvia. How do you know?

Sally. I do know.

Stella. What do you do with your chitterlings then?

Martin. It is one of the unsolved riddles of the animal kingdom.

Sue. I know a very good riddle I made up.

Selina. Perhaps Sally made up chitterlings, did you, Sally?

Sally. No I did *not*, chitterlings is the bits pigs are afraid with, I chittered fearfully when I was nearly little Trot, and when I'm a veginarian and it's pig I'm only going to have the apple sauce.

Martin. That settles it nicely. Between the six of you little vegetarians, the pig will come to a perfect end. Am I mistaken, or is Sally looking sleepy?

Sally. You are a lot mistaken, I am never sleepy at this time of the evening, only at this time of the morning. Why are there *two* Saint Anthonys?

Martin. Because a kind providence has given birth to more saints than names to go round. But only Saint Anthony of Egypt protects pigs, while Saint Antony of Padua finds lost things.

Sally. If it was a lost pig, what?

Martin. Sally, you are a very artful one. I see you may be going to be too much for me. So I will go to the Guessing Stump without losing any more time and pray to Antony of Padua to find my memory for your parents' names.

But when they were kneeling at the Guessing Stump, Sally looked so lost that Martin felt like praying to Saint Antony for *her*. He tried to harden his heart as he reminded her: 'One of us most lose the day, you know.'

'All this going to bed and going to bed,' grieved Sally. 'Why must anyone lose the day while it's shining? But p'raps' (she brightened) 'I'll be as lucky as Sophie and Sue.'

Martin shut his eyes tight on her, and prayed:

'Saint Antony of Padua! help me to find the name of Sally's father and mother.'

'Saint Antony of Padua!' prayed Sally, shutting her eyes still tighter, 'find me the day if I lose it!'

Then they opened their eyes, and stared at each other across the Guessing Stump. But they had shut their eyes so tight, that neither could see the other one exactly.

Martin Pippin set her on the stump, saying: 'Sally, you artful one! how do you manage to look like nobody's child?'

'Not even like Jane's?' asked Sally, trying to.

'Jane had no arts whatever.'

'Then don't I look the weeniest bit like Jessica's?'

'Jessica? The least sly creature on earth.'

'Jennifer's, do you think?'

'Jennifer wasn't subtle.'

'Well, Joyce's mightn't I be?'

'Joyce teased without cunning.'

'Joscelyn's?' asked Sally shakily.

'Joscelyn's? Not you! Would Joscelyn's voice have trembled, though her heart thumped?'

Sally thumped her chest, to make the tell-tale stop.

'No good! I hear it thumping *Joan-Joan-Joan*! Or can I be mistaken?' said Martin Pippin.

Sally cast one desperate look at the day, shut her eyes, and knelt on the Guessing Stump, while her lips moved breathlessly.

Martin. What have you lost now, Sally?

Sally (out of the darkness darkly). Hope.

Martin (shutting his eyes again). Saint Antony of Padua! I've lost the day. Be a dear kind Saint, and find what Sally has lost.

'I was mistaken,' he said, opening his eyes. 'That you are my child and nobody else's, Sally, is as plain as day.'

Sally unstuck her two eyes one by one. 'The day isn't fearfully plain yet.'

'It never is when one has been in the dark.'

'Did *your* black have queer patterns on it too?'

'Such queer patterns that nothing looked like itself. Nor does it yet. For you still look like my child.'

'I'm not,' said Sally sorrowfully.

'It can't be helped now. The Gentleman of Padua has restored your lost hope, and I have lost the day. There's nothing to cry for.'

'Nothing's what I do cry for,' Sally explained.

'Here's something to cry for instead.' Martin gave her his daisy, and Sally bedewed it all the way back to the clothes-basket.

★

'He's guessed her!' shouted the five in consternation. 'He's guessed she is Joan's-and-Charles's.'

'No, he slipped,' said Sally.

'Then what are you blubbing for?' asked Sue reprovingly. 'You'll never have to go to bed in the dark any more.'

'There are worse things than that,' sighed Sally.

'One learns it too late,' sighed Martin.

'I'd very much like to know what they are,' said Sylvia.

Martin. There's going to bed in the light.

Sue. I *am* glad I'm not a kangaroo.

Stella. Kangaroos don't go to bed in the light, you owl.

Sue (*argumentatively*). Yes they do, you owl, in *our* light.

Martin. We can only speak according to our lights.

Stella. Who's the owl now?

Martin.

> The Owl calls Who,
> Who? as he goes.
> Is it me? Is it you?
> Nobody knows.

Stella. Don't be a cuckoo.

Martin. There are two camps about cuckoos.

Stella. They're bothers.

Sophie. They're darlings.

> Cuckoo's going like a bolt
> Over hollow, hill, and holt.
> All round Sussex far and near,
> Cuckoo-flower comes up to hear.
> Cuckoo! cuckoo! happy hour
> Of cuckoo-call and cuckoo-flower.

Sue. Can I do one about a water wagtail?

Martin. The question is, can you?

Sue.

> Water water wagtail,
> Hippity hippity hop,
> Somebody wound the wagtail up
> And he—can't—stop!

Yes I can. Am I getting rather good at poitry?
Martin. Rather!
Sylvia. My turn next. Mine is a chaffinch.

> Where I hoe my row
> Chaffinch hops behind,
> Following my hoe
> To pick what he can find.
> > He does not heed
> > Potato-seed,
> He likes a worm the best
> To carry to the chaffinch-wife
> Mothering his nest.

Selina. Here's a linnet.

> I passed a nest with six eggs in it,
> And on the eggs there sat a linnet.
> When I came back in twenty minutes
> There were no eggs, and seven linnets.

Sylvia. Seven linnets out of six eggs?
Martin. One must have had a double yolk.
Selina. The answer is, there couldn't be six at all
without the seventh.
Sue. Why couldn't there? I like asking riddles.
I know a good one.
Stella. We're doing birds, not riddles. Mine is
swallows.

> When swallows fly high
> The day will be dry.
> When swallows fly low
> The rain will flow.

Sue. Why do swallows fly low when it's going to rain?

Martin. To get as far away from it as they can.

Sally. If I was a swallow, I'd fly high and get on top of it.

Martin. There are two ways of looking at everything.

Sally. Like blue tits do.

> White is coco-nut's inner,
> Coco-cut's coat is brown,
> Where Mr Blue Tit takes his dinner
> Up-side Down.

> Brown is coco-nut's upper,
> White is coco-nut's cup,
> Where Mrs Blue Tit takes her supper
> Down-side Up.

'I expect that's about all the birds there are,' remarked Sue.

'There's still the one,' said Martin, 'you are all bent on turning me into.'

'What bird?' asked Stella.

'A gull. Between you, I've been three already.'

'You *are* a gander!' said Stella.

'The sea is my goose-pond. Who'll risk the next voyage with me?'

'I'm not afraid,' said Stella.

'You will need all your courage,' Martin warned her. 'The sea is full of perils.'

Stella boasted: 'When I went to Selsey I swam out of my depth.'

Martin selected a very tall daisy from the grass. 'Did you by any chance run across my friend Bill there? That famous old salt could swim farther out

of his depth than anyone I ever saw. Sometimes his
adventures carried him so far that I feared he would
never get back.'

'Was Selsey Bill a Pirate?' asked Sylvia.

'Did he ever find a Treasure on an Island?' asked
Sue.

'The very two questions I put to him the first time
we met. Take a daisy, Stella.'

Stella held out her hand for the tall one, but Martin
picked a very short one and gave it to her instead.
'This other,' said he, placing it behind his ear, 'I
shall need for myself, for Selsey Bill's answer to our
questions was the tallest yarn I ever laid ears on.
Luckily I have six brandy-balls in this bag. Stick one
in each of your cheeks, while I stick my tongue in
mine and spin you the yarn that sailor-man spun me,
when I asked him if he had ever been a Pirate and
found a Treasure.' Out came the bag and in went the
brandy-balls. This time it was Stella who came sixth
and last, and as the big sweet went in she mumbled:
'You needn't think you can gull *me*.'

'I'll have a jolly good shot at it,' said Martin. 'No
more talking!'

He lolled back on the clothes-basket, looked Selsey-
wards, and chanted:

> 'The hungry gull
> Who follows the hull,
> Swoops to the sea
> For what he can cull,
> And sometimes his dish
> Is a *very* queer fish!'

Then Martin raised anchor, and letting the wind
swell the sails of his thoughts, he told them in the
Sailorman's own words

Stella

THE TALE OF SELSEY BILL

Have I ever been a pirate? No, I have not. The Union Jack was good enough for me. But that's not to say I never sailed with a Pirate, for you never know your luck on the High-Seas. And Treasure? My word, Treasure! I've took Treasure, and I've lost Treasure; I've buried Treasure, and I've dug it up. I've looked for it and not found it, and found it when I wasn't looking for it. Treasure? I should say so! And the Treasure I remember more than any other was that I was forced to go looking for with Rico da Costa, the most notorious Pirate on the Spanish Main, when he captured the good ship *Cuckoo* with all hands aboard.

We'd sailed from Worthing City bound for Lima, with a cargo of soda-water-syphons. They were wanted bad in Lima, where the Lime-juice was plentiful, and the water not fit to drink with it. Those South American rivers are full of python, and they don't do the water no good. It brings the Limen out in bumps. Pythonitis they call it, and if you scratch it's fatal. They always did scratch, and died off like flies. So one voyage when we were drinking Lime-juice-cordial neat with the Head Liman, our Cap'n, A. B. Gander, Master Mariner, tossed off his third pint, put down his tankard, and said: 'You can't go on like this.'

'We have to,' said the Head Liman. 'Or die of thirst. Or Pythonitis.'

'No Have-to about it,' says Cap'n Gander. 'The cure for Pythons is syphons. I'll get you some.'

'You shall have their weight in rubies if you do,' said the Head Liman.

'Done!' said Cap'n Gander. He had a Second Cousin who ran a soda-water-syphon factory on Cissbury, and that's how our crew for the return trip came to be picked up in Worthing.

Of course, Cap'n Gander had the best part of his crew already. He stuck to us, and we stuck to him. There never was a deserter from the *Cuckoo*, but now and then one of the crew fell out of step for a voyage, for one reason or another. At such times a Master Mariner couldn't do better than the Worthing district, where the Old Salts and the Young Salts run their farms. Ships' masters from all parts would come to see what the farmers had smoking in the chimney corner in the shape of a well-cured Old Salt or a promising green Young 'Un. We'd had one of each sort along that trip, good seamen and better husbands, which is a rarity. As it happened, we were fitting out the *Cuckoo* for her return voyage during the Spring-Cleaning Season, and these two were lending their missuses a hand at home in the meantime. The night before we sailed they come aboard and the Young Salt said to Cap'n Gander: 'Very sorry, Cap'n, but we can't come along this voyage.'

'That's right,' said the Old Salt.

'Can't come along?' said Cap'n Gander. 'You've got to come along. D'ye suppose I can sail to Lima two hands short?'

'I don't see what's to be done about it,' said the Young Salt. 'Our missuses aren't through yet, and I've promised to whitewash the kitchen tomorrow,

and Old Jack here pro-
mised his wife he'd stain
the parlour surround.'

'That's right,' said
the Old Salt.

'Well, that *is* a
nuisance,' said Cap'n
Gander.

'A British Seaman
can't go back on his
word to a woman,' said
the Young Salt.

'No, I see that,' said
Cap'n Gander.

'That's right,' said
the Old Salt.

There was nothing
for it but to let
the men go, and

they went. And the Cap'n sent for me and told me the
news and said: 'Come along o' me, Bill, and see what
we can find in Worthing to take the lubbers' places.
But I'll smash my Toby-Jug,' said he, 'if I take
another married man along, if he were the best seaman in Britain. Bachelors and widowers, Bill, that's
what we're after.'

So we went ashore to look for bachelors and
widowers.

Well, we found seamen who were married men
with wives; and bachelors and widowers who weren't
seamen. It's a peculiar thing how married sailors are.
In the end we found but two who answered to the re-
quirements. One was a long, thin, pale-faced fellow,
who looked as though he couldn't say Bo to a goose.
The other was a thick, dark, greasy ruffian, who looked
as though he'd swallowed both goose and gander.
We didn't fancy the looks of either of 'em, but Cap'n
Gander put to each his two main questions:

'Are you a seaman?' he asked, sharp and short, so
as to startle the truth out of 'em.

And they both said Yes they were.

'Are you a lawful married man?' he popped out
next.

And they both said No they weren't.

Then Cap'n Gander drew me aside and said: 'What
do you think, Bill?'

'I think,' I said, 'it's a pity they ain't found some
good woman to take 'em on. But you can't be surprised at it, and they being the only single sailors left
in Worthing, you'll have to have 'em, or smash your
Toby-Jug.'

'I don't want to do that,' that Cap'n Gander. 'It
was a legacy from my Grand-Aunt. She filled and

emptied it twenty times a day until she died. A grand
aunt, Bill. Pity she died so young.'

'How old?' I asked.

'I don't remember,' said Cap'n Gander. 'I wasn't
born at the time. By all accounts she died the week
after she bought the Toby.' Then he turned to the fair
and sickly and the dark and stout one. 'Sign on, my
lads,' he said, 'or make your mark.'

The fair one signed, and the dark one made his
mark. Their names were Simon Sugar and Orinoco.
I leave you to guess for yourselves which man was
which. The crew being complete, we sailed next day,
and for the first time in my recollection we sailed with
an uncomfortable feeling. We didn't like Orinoco, and
we couldn't love Simon Sugar. We were sorry for the
latter, because of a nasty cough he'd been considerate
enough to keep under during the signing on. Once

aboard, he coughed fit to shake the *Cuckoo* out of her course. Cap'n Gander went in and rubbed him night and morning till the camphorated oil gave out, but it didn't do him any good, though he was grateful. He was the most pathetic sailor I ever sailed with; and he hated Orinoco like poison. Orinoco used to mimic his cough when Cap'n Gander was out of hearing. If he'd done it in his hearing he would have been sent to Coventry.

It looked as though the *Cuckoo* was going to make a tame trip; nothing out of the common happened to us till we got within a day or so of Lima. Then one morning, as I was giving Simon Sugar his eleven o'clock gruel, he sits up in bed, looks through the port-hole at the sea-water, and says in an anxious sort of voice: 'Whereabouts are we, mate?'

'Two days off Lima,' I told him.

'Lima!' cried Simon, going as white as granulated. 'And I thought we were bound for Lyme Regis. If I'd ha' known, I'd never ha' signed on.'

'You ought to have asked then,' I said. 'Or looked.'

'I did look, and it looked like Lyme,' said Simon, rather obstinately.

'If we'd been bound for Lyme,' I observed, 'we'd ha' been there and back forty times by now, starting from Worthing as we did.'

'It's not the starting-point that counts,' said Simon Sugar, 'it's which way round you go. Anyways, a man with a cough like mine don't take no heed of time. Bill,' says he, 'go to the Captain and say I want a word with him.'

I went up to the Bridge and told the Cap'n; and Cap'n Gander said: 'I've thought for weeks that Sugar had something on his mind, Bill,. for it's certain he's got something on his chest.'

'Meaning his cough?' I inquired.

'It's before you come to his cough,' said Cap'n Gander; 'It's a parchment map he keeps there, taking it off before I rub the oil in, and putting it back when I've done.'

'P'raps he keeps it there for consolation,' I suggested.

'Well, since he's sent for me,' said Cap'n Gander, 'I'll have you there as a witness. Only somebody must mind the Bridge while I'm away.'

He cast his eyes about and every man Jack of the crew seemed to be doing something he couldn't be took off doing, except Orinoco and the Bosun.

'Bosun's your man,' I said.

'I wish it might be so,' said Cap'n Gander, 'but it's his birthday. No, there's nothing for it but Orinoco.' And he gave the dago a hail.

'It's only for five minutes, after all,' I said, as Orinoco came up, showing his teeth in the sort of smile that reminded me of crocodiles.

'Just keep an eye on the Bridge while I'm gone,' said Cap'n Gander. 'I shan't be long.'

'Take your time, Cap'n,' says Orinoco, affably.

Then me and the Captain went below to Simon Sugar; and as soon as we got inside the cabin he declares: 'Cap'n Gander, I want to go back.'

'Back where?' asked Cap'n Gander.

'Worthing City,' said Sugar. 'Turn the *Cuckoo* round and take me home.'

'Now, Simon, be reasonable,' said Gander soothingly, 'I can't do that without letting the Limen down. What's your objection to Lima?'

'It isn't Lima,' said Simon Sugar, 'it's the latitude. I never meant to sail these latitudes again.'

But before Simon could tell him why not, the *Cuckoo* got a bump. Next moment the air was full of shouts

and grappling-irons. The shouts might have meant anything from Land-ahoy to waterspouts; but grappling-irons on the High Seas mean one thing, and one thing only. Pirates.

Pirates it was. A moment later Cookie knocked at the door and said: 'Excuse me, Cap'n, if you're engaged, but we've just been captured.'

'I thought as much,' said Cap'n Gander. 'Who's responsible?'

'Rico da Costa,' said Cookie, 'the most notorious Pirate on the High Seas.'

'Who says so?' asked Cap'n Gander.

'He does,' says Cookie. 'And he says, will you be so good as to come on deck, along of anybody else as may be below.'

'Come along, Bill,' says Cap'n Gander, 'and you too, Sugar.'

'I can't get up today,' said Simon Sugar, 'my cough's too bad. It'd be the death of me.'

'All right,' said Cap'n Gander, 'I'll tell him.' So he and I and Cookie went up aloft, and I knew by the set of the Captain's mouth that there was dirty weather ahead.

The sight on board the *Cuckoo* was enough to make you pipe your eye. The deck was black with Pirates, and we was hitched up to the side of as foul a looking craft as ever I want to set eyes on. The *Marrowbone*, that was the name on her, and her figurehead was a Buccaneer gnawing a monstrous bone like a mouth-organ. But dirt! You never saw so much dirt on a ship in your born days! Enough to make an able-bodied seaman sick, who kept a ship like a pin, as we did the *Cuckoo*.

But we hadn't much time to take these details in, because we found ourselves confronted by Rico da Costa himself; he was seven foot high, and his mouth was so full of teeth that he couldn't shut it.

'Cap'n Gander,' he barked, as soon as we appeared.

'And no other,' said the Cap'n.

'Al Bert of that ilk?'

'The same.'

'You're my prisoner,' said Rico.

'So I understand,' said Cap'n Gander, rather stiffly.

'Stay put,' roared Rico, 'till I've done questioning you; and you!' he turned to me, 'go over there.'

He pointed aft, where all the crew was gathered except the Bosun who was sitting thinking on a bale of rope.

'Ain't Bosun coming too?' I asked.

'I told him to,' said Rico, 'but he says it's his birthday, and he's off duty.'

'It *is* my birthday,' says Bosun, looking up, 'and I wish you would not interrupt my thoughts. I am a triplet, and I spend every birthday thinking of my brothers, and they do the same by me. It's a family fixture.'

'Get on with it then,' says Rico, 'but if I find you're deceiving me, I'll slice you into eight!'

'My sailors speak the truth,' said Gander proudly. 'I never shipped but one I couldn't trust. That one there!' And he turned like a flash of lightning on Orinoco, who was standing all this while in Rico's shadow.

Orinoco swaggered a little and tried to brazen it out. 'What, me, Cap'n?' he said.

'Yes, you,' said Cap'n Gander. 'You were a Pirate all the while! You signed on for this purpose; you took advantage of your control of the Bridge to run the *Cuckoo* into Rico's grapnel.'

'Right three times!' retorted Rico da Costa. 'And now we know where we are. So, Cap'n, we'll come down to brass tacks. What's your cargo?'

'Soda-water,' said Cap'n Gander.

'Drat it!' cursed Rico. 'Are you certain sure?'

'Dead certain,' said Cap'n Gander; 'you'll find nothing but syphons in the hold, Mr Pirate.'

'Then all I can say is, it's a blind!' said Rico. 'Whoever heard of a Prize Ship sailing the Spanish Main with syphons of soda? Ah, Cap'n, you're a clever one, you are! it's Treasure you're after, and you've loaded up with soda-water to discourage me. Now then! what Buried Treasure do you know of? What Island are you bound for? Out with it!'

'Stuffy-nonsense,' said Cap'n Gander.

'I'll show you if it's stuffy-nonsense,' bellowed Rico. 'If you don't produce your treasure-island-map before I count three, I'll brain you with your own anchor.' And he picked up the anchor with one hand, as easy as if it was a toothpick, and cried:

'ONE!'

Cap'n Gander stood firm, every inch a man.
'Two!' cried Rico da Costa.
Still Cap'n Gander didn't flinch.

Then Rico da Costa opened his jaws to shout
'THREE!' and swung the anchor above his ugly head;
but before the sound got past his teeth, Simon Sugar's
pasty face appeared in the hatchway, and he held
up his finger at Rico, while he finished a fit of coughing.

Rico da Costa put down the anchor and stared at

him. 'Hello!' he said. 'Who are you? That's a nasty cough you've got.'

As soon as he could speak, Simon agreed, 'It is. A very nasty cough. I want to go home.'

'Where's that?' asked Rico da Costa.

'Worthing City. Now listen to me,' said Simon Sugar gently. 'You can see for yourself how it is with me. Not fit to lift my finger to a fly. Weak as a new-born babe. You've no call to fear me.'

'I hadn't thought of doing so,' said Rico da Costa.

'Very well then. By rights I oughtn't to be put out of my bunk; but when I heard you threaten Cap'n Gander it wasn't in me to think of myself. That man has rubbed me night and morning, back and front. It's up to me to do what little I can for him. Now listen to me,' said Simon Sugar again. 'Cap'n Gander has told you the level truth; the object of this voyage is soda-water, and nothing but. Only, though *he* doesn't know it, there *is* a map of an island on this ship, where a Treasure is to be found; and only I can tell you where it is.'

'I'll make you tell me at the point of the cutlass,' blustered Rico, flourishing his cutlass.

'There's no call,' said Simon Sugar, 'for you to point your cutlass *or* to laugh in that nasty little way. I'm going to tell you without any making. All I want is to go home after I've told.'

'How'll we manage that?' asked Rico da Costa.

'Easy,' said Simon Sugar. 'Put me and Bosun into the jolly-boat. He'll row me to Lima where we'll take ship for Sussex. *I'm* no good to you, and *he's* no good to you, so you might as well let us go.'

'Oh, I dare say,' jeered Rico, 'and let you tell the Limen all about me.'

'I'll tell them nothing,' said Simon Sugar. 'I only want to be quit of you. As for Bosun, he isn't, in a manner of speaking, here at all.'

'I am not,' said the Bosun. 'I'm in Bognor, catching shrimps with Alfie and Alf. I don't know who you are and I don't want to know. Leave me be.'

Rico da Costa left the Bosun be and turned his attention again to Simon Sugar. 'There's something in what you say,' he remarked, 'and I'm inclined to agree. Only first I want to know about this Treasure. Is it a big one?'

'Enormous,' said Simon Sugar.

'Why did you leave it on the Island?' asked Rico.

'It was more than I could bear,' said Simon Sugar. 'All I thought of was getting away with a whole skin. One night an empty boat was tossed upon the shore. It was my first and only chance of escape. My Treasure would have sunk the boat; so I just went. I rowed and rowed until I got to Lima; and when I got there I made a chart of the Latitude and Longitude of the Island, so that I should never forget where my Treasure was.'

'How come you to be on the Island?' asked Rico da Costa.

'I'd been marooned by the Captain of my ship,' said Simon.

'What for?' asked Rico.

'I wasn't popular with the crew,' said Simon.

'And what about this Treasure on the Island?' asked Rico. 'How many men would it make rich for life?'

'It would do for any fifty men,' said Simon.

The eyes of the Pirates shone with greed at his words. There were exactly fifty of them, you see.

'Well, where's that map?' asked Rico da Costa.

'Here,' said Simon Sugar. He laid his hand on his chest. Rico da Costa made a movement towards him; but Cap'n Gander held up his hand and checked him.

'Rico,' he said, 'the map is this miserable man's sole chest-protector. There's two yards of Welsh Flannel in my cabin; you'll find it in the deep end of my writing-desk.'

'What do you keep it there for?' asked the Pirate.

'I have to keep it somewhere,' said Cap'n Gander. 'Don't I?'

'I admit it,' said Rico, and sent Orinoco for the flannel. Meanwhile he got the jolly-boat unshipped. By the time Orinoco returned, everything was ready; the boat was launched, Bosun was at the oars. A box of biscuit and a dozen of soda was provided, and Simon Sugar coughing by the taffrail. Rico let Cap'n Gander himself apply the flannel, as soon as Simon had removed the map; which he gave into the Captain's hands with a tear.

'Here you are, Cap'n,' he said, 'and thanks for all. Dear knows if we shall ever meet again.'

Then he was lowered carefully into the jolly-boat, and Bosun bent to his oars like one in a dream. As they pulled off, Cap'n Gander leaned over the rail and called through his megaphone: 'Bosun! what's your other name?'

'Alfred,' answered the Bosun.

'I somehow thought it might be,' said Cap'n Gander. Then he delivered Simon Sugar's map into the hands of Rico da Costa.

There was a shout and a rush forward from the Pirates; but: 'No, you don't,' grins Rico. 'This is *my* pigeon. Nobody sets eyes on this map but me. You'll sail under my orders.'

'You ain't goin' to keep the Treasure to yourself, Rico?' inquired Orinoco, with a nasty look.

'Didn't you hear Simon Sugar say it'd do for fifty of us?' asked Rico da Costa. 'What d'ye take me for? No, boys, it's share and share alike. But we've got to get there first.'

'And what about these?' asked Orinoco, waving his hand at the crew of the *Cuckoo*. 'Shall we make 'em walk the plank?'

'That wouldn't be playing fair by Sugar,' said Rico. 'As I understand it there was a sort of understanding that their lives should be spared. So we'll take 'em along, and when they've helped us to load the Treasure up, we'll just maroon 'em and leave 'em to their fate.'

Then Rico da Costa divided us up, with some of the *Cuckoo*'s crew and some of the *Marrowbone* Pirates aboard each ship; and he commanded the *Marrowbone* and left Orinoco in command of the *Cuckoo*. I was in our ship with Cap'n Gander, and I could hardly bear to see that greasy dago cock of our walk. I said as much to the Cap'n, but he replied: 'Bill, there's points about this I don't yet grasp. When Sugar parted from me he whispered: "Just you keep hold of this, and trot it out when required. The *Marrowbone* was once the *Mary-le-bone*. I knew her again as soon as I set eyes on her." So I'm not fretting, Bill.'

I didn't see myself how Rico's changing the name of a ship he'd captured was going to help us; but as long as Cap'n Gander kept his pecker up I could keep up mine. We hadn't a ghost of a notion where we were bound for, but it took us a week to get there; because Rico da Costa would only sail by night, so that none of us should see the way we were going. And about dawn after the seventh night we fetched up on a rocky beach, and Rico da Costa said: 'Well, here we are!'

As far as we could see that Island kept itself inside a ring of rocks; over the tops of them we saw the green heads of palm trees, so we knew there must be vegetation inside. What did strike us was that we had never seen rocks anywhere with such a high polish on them. Another thing that struck us was the neatness of the beach itself; there wasn't a scrap of seaweed or litter of any sort to be seen, the pebbles, where there were pebbles, lay as even as setts in a road, and the sand, where there was sand, was as smooth as a carpet.

However, these were not things to occupy the minds of men set on finding an enormous treasure. When we had disembarked, the pirates came crowding round Rico da Costa, crying: 'The map, Rico! show us the map. Where does it say the Treasure is to be found?'

Rico saw that he must let them into the game a bit, so he took out the map and said unwillingly: 'It says the Treasure is mostly in the middle of the Island, but works outward in every direction.'

'Hurrah!' cried Orinoco. 'Then it doesn't matter which way we go in! We're sure to trip over some of it on the way, till we reach the main hoard. Come along, lads!' And he started across the sands to an opening in the rocks, followed by half a hundred shouting pirates.

They hadn't gone three yards when a loud shrewish voice cried: 'Get off! get off! Making footmarks all over my new-swept sand!'

Over the top of the rocks appeared the half of a woman, red in the face with anger. She was the most

enormous figure of a woman you ever set eyes on, her
arms were as thick as hams, and her huge hands brandished a broom that would crack a man's head.

'Get off!' she cried again.

The pirates were so startled that they got off the
sand at once, jumping sideways on to the rocks and
pebbles. And then the Woman shouted: 'Get off those
pebbles! get off those rocks *at once*. Scratching my
nice polish with your great ugly boots! Ugh! Look
how you've messed the pebbles up. Put them back,
every one of them, *do you hear*? Put them back this
instant, just as they were!'

All the pirates stooped immediately, and tried to

replace the pebbles as they had found them. We of the *Cuckoo* had stayed beside the ship; and we stood looking on, wondering what next.

What next was the Woman herself. She pushed herself through the widest gap in the rocks, and that was none too wide for her; and she bore down on Rico da Costa, shouting: 'Take that pipe out of your mouth! take it out, I say! D'you think I'm going to have tobacco-ash all over my Island? Slave, slave, slave, from morning till night, and that's all the thanks I get for it! A woman's work is never done!' she cried, and flourished her broom over Rico's head, much as he flourished his cutlass over Simon's.

When he could get his breath he began to say: 'Look here, ma'am! I never asked you to slave for me. I don't know who you are.'

'And I don't know who *you* are,' retorted the Woman tartly. 'But since you *are* here, pushing your way in at Spring-Cleaning time, you'll just turn to and help.'

'I'm sure,' said Rico, 'we don't mind lending a hand to oblige a lady, do we, lads? But whatever do you find to do in the way of spring-cleaning on a desert island, ma'am?'

'Just like a man!' the Woman snapped again. 'Nothing to do, you say? With the sea messing up the beach twice in every twenty-four hours; and the wind blowing the coco-nuts down, and coco-nuts themselves all matted, and scratches on the rocks to get out, and the tree-trunks needing varnishing, and what not! Nothing to do, indeed! Why, there's more to do here even than there was at home in Worthing City, where I wore myself to a bone keeping the place fit for Sugar to live in.'

'For WHO?' cried Rico da Costa.

'Simon Sugar. Now what's wrong with you?'

'Who are you?' asked Rico da Costa in trembling tones.

'Sarah Sugar, that's who I am.'

'And Simon Sugar is——'

'My husband, of course. Well do I remember our wedding-day. "You've got a Treasure in Sarah," my mother said to Sugar. "If ever man married a Treasure, you have today." And that's what I tried to be. I kept his house like a pin. I cleaned and scoured and scrubbed from morning to night. And was he grateful? No!'

'When did you see him last?' asked Rico da Costa; and if ever a Pirate spoke with his heart in his boots, Rico was that pirate.

'Ten years ago,' said Sarah. 'He was sailing from Worthing City in the good ship *Mary-le-bone*.'

'The *Mary-le-bone*,' said Rico da Costa.

'The *Mary-le-bone*,' said Sarah Sugar. 'It was Spring-Cleaning time, and some of the men, he told me, were staying at home to see their wives through. "Ho!" I said, just like that.'

'Why,' asked Rico da Costa, 'did you say "Ho!" just like that?'

'Because it was just like the men, and just like the women! Catch *me* with my house not cleaned half-way through Spring-Cleaning time. "Well," I said to Sugar, "if you're short-handed on the *Mary-le-bone*, I'll sail with you. I'm as good as fifty men any day when it comes to scrubbing." Sugar said something about having to make it right with the Captain, but "*I'll* make it right with the Captain," I said; and so I did. We sailed the very next day for Lima.'

'For Lima,' said Rico da Costa.

'For Lima,' said Sarah Sugar. 'And you never saw such a mask of dirt on any ship in your life as I saw on the *Mary-le-bone* when I got aboard. My word! I set them working! Before we got to Lima I had that ship as clean as a new pin. But we never did get to Lima.'

'How was that?' asked Rico.

'Why, one fine day we sighted this very Island; and the Captain of the *Mary-le-bone* said: "There's Lima!" and I believed him. Then he turned very politely to me and asked: "Wouldn't you like to be the first ashore, marm?" I'd small opinion of the Captain, but it went up a point at that; and I said I wouldn't mind. Next thing I know, Simon and I and the Bosun were bundled into the jolly-boat, and rowed to this very beach. "Out you hop!" said the Bosun, which, with Simon's help, I did; and as soon as we'd landed, the Bosun turned the jolly-boat round and rowed back to the *Mary-le-bone*; and then the *Mary-le-bone* sailed away. Now, why did they do that?'

'Ask me another!' groaned Rico da Costa wearily.

'Well, never mind,' said Sarah Sugar. '*I* didn't. There was plenty to do on the Island, as *I* soon found. It looked as though nobody'd tackled it since Creation; so I set to, and made Sugar set to with me. It was almost more than one pair of hands could manage. Then *he* disappeared.'

'How?' asked Rico da Costa.

'I've never found out. Perhaps it was a tarantula.'

'You have tarantulas?' said Rico da Costa.

'Thick as cockroaches. Nasty teasing creatures. But *I* don't stand any of their nonsense. They fly when they see me coming!' Sarah Sugar flourished her broom again, and I fancy the thought in all our minds was thankfulness that we were not tarantulas seeing her coming.

'Well, that's the story,' said Sarah Sugar.

'Not all of it, surely, marm,' said Rico da Costa. 'Haven't you left out the Treasure?'

'What Treasure?' asked Sarah Sugar.

'The Treasure on this Island,' pleaded Rico da Costa. 'The enormous Treasure that one man couldn't bear. The Treasure that would do for fifty men for life. The Treasure that is mainly in the middle of the island, and works outwards. Simon Sugar's Treasure, marm! you've omitted to mention it.'

'I've omitted nothing,' snapped Sarah Sugar, 'and if there'd been any treasure messing up my Island I'd have found it long ago. Now then, you men! I've no use for idle hands. Just come along and I'll show you where to begin.'

'Excuse me, Mrs Sugar,' said Cap'n Gander. It was his first remark to her, and to tell you the truth she had been so surrounded with pirates that she hadn't seemed to notice us. But now she came sweeping through their ranks and looked us up and down. 'And who may *you* be?' she asked.

'Cap'n Gander, commanding the good ship *Cuckoo*,' said he, saluting. 'And there she is.'

Sarah Sugar turned a critical eye on the *Cuckoo*. She raked it fore and aft looking for dirt; and could she find a speck? No, she could not. 'A very tidy ship,' she admitted, grudgingly.

'Can you say the same of that?' asked Cap'n Gander; and he pointed to the good ship *Marrowbone*.

Sarah Sugar let out a piercing shriek. 'As I'm alive,' cried she, 'it's the *Mary-le-bone*!'

'It was the *Mary-le-bone* till took by pirates,' said Cap'n Gander. 'And then its name was changed, for deception's sake.'

'If you changed its name a dozen times you'd never deceive me,' said Sarah Sugar. 'I've scoured and polished that ship from top to toe. And look at it now! worse than when I came aboard her with Sugar. Who's responsible?' She rounded on Rico da Costa, who cowered before her. '*You*? Then all I've got to say to you is this: that ship's a disgrace to the Piracy!' She turned up her sleeves.

'Don't hit me!' cried Rico da Costa.

'Hit you!' she said witheringly. 'I wouldn't touch you with a marlinespike—not till you've had a bath. Now then, all aboard!'

'What for?' asked Rico.

'To clean the *Mary-le-bone*, of course,' said Sarah; 'a month's charring, as I see it.'

'And what about the *Cuckoo*, missus?' asked Cap'n Gander.

'The *Cuckoo*?' She looked it over again. 'There's nothing to do for *that*. You can take yourselves and your ship off my island. Now then, pack off with you!'

We didn't need telling twice; and while Sarah Sugar bustled the pirates aboard their dirty craft, the crew of the *Cuckoo* manned her once again, and prepared to set sail. Only just as we veered about, Cap'n Gander called through his megaphone from the Bridge: 'Mrs Sugar!'

'What is it *now*?' she asked from the Bridge of the *Marrowbone*.

'What was the name of the Bosun who landed you and Simon on this Island?' asked Cap'n Gander.

'Alfie,' said she.

'I somehow thought it might be,' said Cap'n Gander.
And we sailed away, leaving the pirates up to their
elbows in soapsuds.

We landed three days later in Lima, where all the

Limen were waiting for us on the shore, with sacks
of rubies. The Head Liman ran to meet us with open
arms.

'We thought you were never coming!' he cried joyfully. 'We're so sick of Lime-juice-cordial neat that
it's all I can do to stop the folk from drinking the
water again. We've got one case of Pythonitis as it is.
Have you brought the soda-water?'

'I have,' said Cap'n Gander, 'it's in the hold.' In a
jiffy we had it out, and the Head Liman weighed it
fairly and gave us its weight in rubies. After this
he invited us all to an evening celebration, which

Cap'n Gander accepted for everybody; and then he asked about the Pythonitis case.

'He's not as bad as he might be,' said the Head Liman, 'for he hasn't scratched once, and the bumps are past the danger-zone.' He took us along to the wharf, and there we saw Simon Sugar and our Bosun. Bosun was sitting on Simon Sugar's hands; and Simon was looking out to sea, where a ship lay at anchor, with the jolly-boat just putting out. I must say Simon looked another man. The bumps had filled him out, in a manner of speaking, and he had lost his cough.

'How's that?' asked Cap'n Gander, after the greetings and mutual rejoicings were over.

'You can't have Pythonitis *and* a cough,' said Simon Sugar; 'according to the doctors'-books they don't agree. I really owe my life to Alfred here; to stop me scratching, he's been sitting on my hands for three days, saying never a word.'

'He has a contemplative nature,' said Cap'n Gander, stroking Alfred's head. 'And now I suppose you're ready to go back.'

'Alfred will go back with you, but not me,' said Simon Sugar. 'I've booked a berth on the good ship *Demerara* over there. She sails for Bognor Regis in half an hour; and there's the Bosun coming to fetch me now.'

'Before you go,' said Cap'n Gander, 'I'd like to know two things. Why did you bother to make a map of that Island, latitude and longitude and all?'

'Because if I hadn't,' said Simon Sugar, 'I might have mistook the latitude and longitude.'

'I see,' said Cap'n Gander. 'The second thing is: why did you tell me you weren't a lawful married man?'

'I'm not,' said Simon Sugar. 'I'm a bigamist.'

'*I* see,' said Cap'n Gander again; and then the Bosun of the good ship *Demerara* fetched alongside, and Alfred got off Simon Sugar's hands, and handed Simon Sugar into his care. The Bosuns gave each other a thoughtful look, and parted. As the jolly-boat rowed back to the *Demerara*, Cap'n Gander called through his megaphone: 'Bosun! what's your name?'

'Alf!' yelled the Bosun.

'You know, Bill,' said Cap'n Gander, as we strolled into the city, 'I somehow thought it might be.'

That night the crew of the *Cuckoo* joined the Limen in a great celebration of Lime-juice-cordial and Soda, than which there are few prettier tipples.

'They say, Cap'n,' said the Head Liman, tossing off his third pint, 'that a good woman's worth is above rubies—but *I* say, give me Soda-Water.'

'Quite so,' said Al Bert Gander.

Fourth Interlude

Six more chains were rounded off in the daisy-field.
'That,' said Stella, as she fastened hers, 'is the
silliest tale I ever heard in my life.'

'Your life is young,' said Martin Pippin. 'With
luck you will hear sillier tales yet.'

'With luck indeed!' repeated Stella scornfully.

'He might mean bad luck, you know,' explained
Sue.

Stella rejected this. 'He never means anything so
sensible.'

'You call bad luck sensible?' asked Martin with great
astonishment.

Stella (annoyed). You know I didn't.

Sue. It did sound like it, you know.

Sally. Talk is jumpy sometimes.

Martin. Like the Knight's move in chess. You hardly know how you've landed where you've jumped from. A sophist's trick.

Sophie. Mine?

Martin. Oh, dear me, no. You move as straight as a Castle.

Sylvia. How straight is that?

Martin. As the rook flies.

Sue. Do *I* move straight?

Martin. Like a Pawn, a step at a time.

Sue. That's the sensiblest way, isn't it?

Martin. When it leads to the Eighth Square, which is the vision of every Pawn on the board, you know. Too many fall by the way, and most of the rest end in a blind alley, where they find themselves face to face with a Pawn of the other colour, and there they have to stick till the kingdom falls.

Sue. Then what?

Martin. The game starts all over again.

Sue. Well, if I see the other colour coming, I'll get out of its way.

Martin. Easier said than done. When Fate sets the board, there was never a white Pawn yet that hadn't a black one fixed in her way.

Sally. Or a black one a white one.

Martin. You have jumped to the fearful truth. I suspect you of being the Knight.

Selina. How do *I* move, Martin?

Martin. You, Selina, glide sideways, now on the dark tide, now upon the light.

Sylvia. He means you're one of the Bishops. He's only being poetical to please you, aren't you, Martin?

Martin. I wouldn't dream of contradicting Your Majesty.

Sylvia. Oh! am I the Queen?

Stella. You might be the feeble old King.

Martin. Sylvia is far from feeble. She sweeps in all directions, any distance, inquiring into everything and keeping her eye on the game.

Sylvia. I *am* the Queen!

Martin. Yes, you danger! One of these days I shall sweep you off the board.

Sylvia. Just try it! Who's the feeble old King then?

Martin. Stella remains.

Stella. I never heard anything so silly in my life.

Martin. What did I tell you? You are already a little older, life is already a little sillier—and of all silly things, commend me to a King! The King, dear Stella, is merely a puffed-up Pawn. He is his kingdom's menace, the vulnerable point of attack. He is a figure-head, weaponless, indefensible. The Pawn that falls in his service is the better man, for its inconspicuous death does not dissolve a nation. This feeble creature whom we call the King shirks every issue. He gathers his band about him for protection. He dare not venture into open country. He even pretends that he is *not* the King, in order to escape the consequences. He——

Stella. If you think I'm afraid——!

She walked very haughtily across the meadow to the elms, and refusing Martin's respectfully-offered hand, mounted the Guessing Stump and faced him with defiance. 'Afraid indeed!' said she.

'I never saw a hero yet,' said Martin, 'who tried to look like one.'

'You do annoy me,' frowned Stella.

'I try my best,' said Martin modestly. 'Will you

really pretend you aren't shaking in your shoes? Do you not fear that bedtime is at hand? Aren't you terrified of my guessing the names of your parents? Good heavens! you haven't a spark of courage left. I defy you to name them yourself.'

'Joscelyn and Henry!' Stella proclaimed boldly. Then she turned very red.

'Spoken like a king!' said Martin heartily. 'Joscelyn and Henry!' (Stella turned very white.) 'But stay,' mused Martin. 'Kings have the privilege of side-stepping. Have you gone straight, or side-stepped?'

'I've said enough.' Stella shut her mouth tight.

'Perhaps you've said more than enough. If I could trust you! Whose daughter *can* you be, if you aren't Joscelyn's! Joan's child could never have looked so unkindly on her adversary. Joyce's would have gone on playing the game. Jennifer's would have thrown up the sponge at once. Jessica's would have fought it out to the finish. Jane's—ah, Jane's child *would* have faced the facts. Can Jane be your Mother?'

'Jane indeed!' exploded Stella, and went red again.

'That sounds like a straight move,' said Martin. 'But if it is, it leaves us only Joscelyn.' (Stella went white.) 'A rather horrid person, on the whole.'

'She *isn't!*' (Stella went red.)

'One speaks as one finds.'

'She's worth *ten* of Aunty Jane!'

'Is *that* a straight move, I wonder. I wish you would stop going white and red by turns,' complained Martin. 'One doesn't know where to have you, Joscelyn's daughter—or Jane's.'

Stella's fingers stole to her eyelashes. She turned her head aside so sharply that Martin looked at her with concern. 'Something in your eye? Only a fly?

Or are you bluffing? You needn't think you can put it across me, you know. Joscelyn's child, indeed! I can bluff too—and if you are not *my* child, you are nobody's.'

'Yours?' Stella turned her face to him again; she looked as though she couldn't believe her ears. The red rushed back to her cheeks. 'Yours indeed!' Her colour changed to its own wild-rose and stayed there.

'Not mine?'

'As if I could!'

'What, Joscelyn's after all?'

'You might have known it.'

'You never side-stepped once?'

'I wasn't afraid. I handed it out to you. But you were much too stupid to take it. Me your child! I *never*,' said Stella, 'heard *any*thing so silly in all my life!'

'You are young yet,' murmured Martin, handing her out his daisy. But she was already half-way to the clothes-basket, and didn't hear him.

*

The children had taken hands, and were dancing in a circle. When Martin came within earshot, they sang at him:

'One is staying up for good-an-all!
Two are never going to bed at all!
Three are staying up,
Four are staying up,
Four are staying up for good-an-all!'

'Don't go on at me,' said Martin Pippin. 'I've already had as much as I can bear.

Sue. Well, I tell you what, I'm *all* Body and *no*

Tail, But give me to your Cat, I'm *no* Body and *all*
Tail. And what d'ye make of that, it's a riddle, what
am I?

Martin. A Mouse?

Sue. A Mouse has *got* a Tail to begin with, you
know.

Martin. I didn't know, I thought he had a Tail to
end with.

Sue. Um. Well, I'm a Ball of String, see?

Martin. You are much more like a Mouse.

Sue. I mean, the *answer* is a Ball of String.

Martin. If you say so. When anyone asks me a
riddle, I always say what springs into my mind. It's
no use thinking.

Stella.

> Little Miss Pit-a-Pat, quick as a mouse,
> Walks without feet on the roof of the house.
> Thousands of footprints she leaves on the street—
> How can she do it without any feet?

What springs into your mind *now*?

Martin. Another Mouse.

Stella. Oh, you are STUPID! You don't LISTEN.

Martin. I do listen, and I distinctly heard you say
a Mouse.

Stella. Yes, but you wouldn't *say* it right out, if
someone had to *guess* it.

Martin. I had an idea you would. Your daisy, Stella.

Stella. We're not talking about that, and the
answer to my riddle is the Rain.

Martin. I expect you're right. Has anybody ever
guessed a riddle yet without being told?

Sylvia. Here's one with lots of clues. Now try
hard, Martin.

> I have a Tick, yet am no Clock,
> I bear Clothes, yet wear no Frock,
> I'm turned by day without a Handle,
> And used in the Dark without a Candle.

What am I?

Martin. A Birthday Cake.

Sylvia. Why?

Martin. Because of the Candle.

Sylvia. Oh, deary-deary-me! I'm a Mattress.

Martin. There's no accounting for tastes.

Sylvia. You *are* a bad guesser.

Martin. It is becoming more and more evident.

Sylvia. I mean, there were lots of things to go by without the Candle.

Martin. I couldn't remember one of them.

Sylvia. And even the Candle, I mean, is '*without* a Candle,' so a Birthday Cake's *all* wrong.

Martin. From the pink sugar name on top to the currant in the middle, a Birthday Cake's all right.

Sylvia. But it's *got* to *have*—a cANdle!

Martin. Haven't I been saying so all the time?

Sophie. He's just being aggravating. Now do listen carefully:

> I'm long, I'm short,
> I'm every sort,
> I'm under your feet
> But I can't be caught,
> I'm thin, I'm fat,
> I'm round, I'm flat,
> And wherever *You* are
> *I* am at.

What am I?

Martin. I haven't a shadow of an idea.

Sophie. Ha-ha! I'm a Shadow. Ha-ha!

Martin. How long does this sort of thing go on?

Selina. Oh do let me say mine. I've got a very nice one for you:

> When it is warm
> With a stir in the air
> I hide my white form
> In my shivering hair.
> When it is cold
> I stand without care,
> Slender and bold,
> Silver and bare.

What am I?

Martin. A Chimney-pot.

Selina. Were you *listening*? I said my white form.

Martin. Three thousand years ago in Athens, my chimney-pot was made of pure white marble——

Selina. My shivering hair——

Martin. —— wreathed in a trail of smoke.

Selina. The smoke would make the marble black.

Martin. Realizing this in time, I never lit the fire again, and stood without care, slender and bold, silver and bare, till the Glory that was Greece died off the face of the earth.

Selina. Ought we to count that for the answer?

Stella. Of course not. There weren't any chimney-pots in Athens, and the answer's a Birch Tree. Anybody but him could see it.

Sally. Can I say mine before I forget what it is? It's a fearfully hard one. Listen!

> When I am Two I'm only One,
> Break me in half, and I am none.
> None did I say? No, that's not true!
> Break me in half, and I am Two.
> One to hang upon your ear,
> Two to pop in your mouth, my dear.

What am I?

Martin. Give it up.

Sally. Oh don't.

Martin. But you've muddled me so.

Sally. Yes, I've muddled me too.

Martin. What is the answer?

Sally. I've forgot again.

Martin. If you remember, I'll give you a cherry earring.

Sally. The answer's a Cherry Earring!

Martin. You astonish me.

Nobody was more astonished than Sally herself.

'This,' said Martin, 'has been one of the most tiring half-hours of my life. I have pursued your identities from the rain in the sky to the shadow on the earth, and you are still enigmas to me. It would be easier to solve the riddle of the Long Man of Wilmington than to say who and what you are.'

'Who and what was the Long Man of Wilmington?' asked Selina.

'We can only make a guess at the truth,' said Martin. 'But since you are curious enough to inquire, I am prepared to say whatever springs into my mind. I have here precisely six Thirst-Quenchers. You will need them, as we pant after knowledge; and the starter of this hare shall wear the daisy.'

So saying, Martin produced his fifth paper bag, and provided the little girls with a Thirst-Quencher apiece. To Selina, who came last, he also gave a daisy, which that absent-minded child put into her mouth, sticking the Thirst-Quencher behind her right ear. When this little mistake had been rectified, Martin picked himself a left-ear daisy, and asked himself the riddle he was about to solve:

Selina

'You Long Long Man of Wilmington,
How long have you been there?—
Before your grandsire's grandsire's grandsire's
Grandsire's sire was seen there.

You Long Long Man of Wilmington,
How long will you be there?—
Until your grandson's grandson's grandson's
Grandson's son see me there.'

Then, making himself comfortable against the clothes-basket, Martin plucked the petals off his daisy till only seven remained, stuck it behind his left ear, and began the strange enigma of

THE LONG MAN OF WILMINGTON

A VERY long time ago, a very little man called
Wilkin lived in the village of Wilmington on
the last lap of the Downs to the east. Where he was
born nobody knew. He was found at the age of five
or thereabouts by the Seven Sisters of Wilmington,
when they took their daily walk up Windover Hill
to look at the sea. They looked at the sea for two
reasons: the first, because their one and only brother
had run away to it: the second, because it had no
dust on it, and dust and dirt were what they could least
abide. Dust, thought the Seven Sisters, was one of
the little mistakes when the world was made. Autumn
was another. The falling of the leaf was a perfect
bugbear to them. They spent the day fighting the
dust in the house and the litter in the garden; and
when they needed a respite from work, they took it
by climbing the north side of Windover, and gazing
on the dustless water to the south. They thought
of their brother, but they never mentioned him. If
they spoke, it was only to express regrets that the
waves were not as smooth as they might be (the
Eldest Sister would have liked to iron them out), and
that the ships were scattered rather untidily about it
(the Youngest Sister would have liked to place all
the boats in a straight line on the horizon, and keep
them there). But on the whole the sea came nearer
to their ideas of perfection than anything else in the
world. Until Wilkin.

One clear evening, as they walked on the ridge of the hill, they saw an old fish-kettle lying under a juniper bush. The Youngest Sister spied it first. She pointed and cried: 'Look, girls!' 'What negligence!' exclaimed the Eldest Sister. One of the others remarked: 'It is badly in need of a clean.' The Seven Sisters rushed in a body upon the fish-kettle, and there lay Wilkin, aged five or thereabouts.

'A child!' breathed the Seven Sisters as one. They lifted up the fish-kettle: it had a hole in it, and they all looked at one another with the same two thoughts in their eyes. The second thought was that a fish-kettle with a hole in it is of no more use in this world.

They were spinsters, and had never had any children of their own. They were born to be Aunts, not Mothers; and they knew it. But aunthood for six would mean marriage for one, and marriage was worse to them than the dust on the road and the fall of the leaf. And here, like a gift, was a child for them to aunt.

Without even discussing the question, they buried the fish-kettle decently under the bush, and bore Wilkin downhill to their chalk house in which neither speck, spot, nor smut was to be seen. The doorstep was kept so spick-and-span, that visitors looked down at their boots, and jumped over the threshold. The Seven Sisters, hands, face, and hair, were as white as their own chalk house; and they always dressed in long white linen pinafores, which they were for ever washing and starching. The first thing they did with Wilkin, when they got him inside the house, was to wash him too; and he needed it.

(*Sue.* How dirty was he?

Martin. Hold up your hands.

Six pairs of hands went up, with fingers spread.

Martin. Splendid. And yet those hands are driven snow compared with the dirt on Wilkin's little body. The Seven Sisters hardly knew where to begin.

Sally. What was their names?

Martin. They went by the names of Monday, Tuesday, Wednesday, Thursday, Friday, Saturday, and Sunday. Not that those were their real names, but, as I say, they went by them, and in time their real names were forgotten. Even I cannot tell you what they were. I can only tell you that Monday was the eldest and Sunday the youngest of the Sisters. No more talking!)

When the Seven Sisters had washed their nephew seven times, till he was cleaner than he had ever been in his life, they asked him his name. He thought very hard and said:

'Wilmington Hill.'

The Eldest Sister shook her head and said: 'That isn't a name for anybody.'

'And if it were,' said the Second Sister, 'it's no name for him. He is much too little for a long name like Wilmington.'

'Will, if you like,' said the Third Sister, 'but never Wilmington.'

'Will Hill sounds funny to me,' said the Fourth Sister.

'Then Will without the Hill,' said the Fifth.

'Or Hill without the Will,' said the Sixth.

'Neither the one nor the other,' said the Youngest Sister. 'We will dispense with the Hill, and call him Wilkin, for that's just what he is, the tiniest Wilkin that ever I did see.'

And so it was settled. The Seven Sisters were overjoyed, and loved their charge all the more dearly, because he was so tiny and they were so tall.

★

The only fear was, that between them they might wear him out with taking care of him.

On the very first night, after each of the Seven Sisters had given him a bath, every one of them insisted on giving him supper, hearing his prayers, and having him sleep in her room.

Little Wilkin passed a very bad night. Let alone that he had found seven baths very tiring, seven suppers very filling, and seven sets of prayers very boring, he did not find sleeping in seven beds as restful as sleeping in one. A different Aunt waked him up each hour and a half of the night and bore him off to be cuddled. As a consequence, he looked so worn out in the morning, that the Seven cried with one voice:

'Wilkin shall have his breakfast in bed for a treat!'

But when they marched into the room in single file, carrying a breakfast tray apiece, Wilkin gave one look, scrabbled his way under the blankets to the foot of the bed, and refused to come out.

In vain they coaxed and pleaded.

'Such lovely thick porridge!' said one.

(*Seven platefuls*, thought Wilkin.)

'Such rich cream!' said two.

(*Seven jugfuls.*)

'Such a beautiful brown egg!' said three.

(*Seven beautiful brown eggs.*)

'Such nyummy marmalade!' said four.

(*Seven pots of nyumminess.*)

'Such crisp toast to make Wilkin's teeth sharp! Such yellow butter to make Wilkin fat! Such black tea to make Wilkin strong!' cooed five, six, and seven.

But clutching the bedclothes round him as tight as a cocoon, Wilkin in the dark at the bottom of the bed saw with his mind's eye seven toast-racks, seven butter-dishes, and seven steaming teapots. He shuddered so violently that the Seven Sisters thought he was suffocating. They dropped the trays in alarm, and rushed to unroll him; but when he heard the seven smashes, little Wilkin unrolled himself. Sitting up with tousled head and blinking eyes, he pointed his first finger at each of his Aunts in turn, and said:

'You, *and you only*, shall bring me up on Monday. You, *and you only*, shall bring me up on Tuesday. You, *and you only*, on Wednesday. You, *and you only*, on Thursday. You, *and you only*, on Friday. You, *and you only*, on Saturday. And you, *and you only*, shall bring me up on Sunday. What's today?'

'Tuesday,' said the Second Sister quickly. 'Do you feel like breakfast-in-bed today, Wilkin?'

'Yes, Aunt Tuesday. I *do* feel like breakfast-in-bed.'

'And what sort of breakfast do you feel like, Wilkin?'

'I feel,' said Wilkin blissfully, 'like porridge-and-cream, and toast-and-butter, and egg-and-marmalade, and a pot of black black tea.'

Tuesday hurried away delightedly to fetch these things, and the other six sisters remained as delightedly behind to clear up the messes, for they knew their turns were coming in due course. They were born caretakers, but had never learned that Too Many Caretakers Spoil the Charge. Wilkin taught them more than they suspected; for one thing, that there are exceptions to every rule. Wilkin was their exception to the rule of law and order. He could do no wrong in their eyes. They let him bring his dirty boots into the house, and wiped up after him without a murmur. They let him leave his toys all over the floor, and put them away without a sigh or a tear. If Thursday found his thumb-marks on the newly-washed paint, she washed it again, and never breathed a word of it to Monday. If Saturday found one of the best tea-cups smashed on the hearth, she brushed it up, and Friday never knew. They had not really changed their minds about things; but they had given little Wilkin their hearts.

*

Of course, he had to go to school. That's fate. It was a Dame School in those days, so after keeping Wilkin to themselves as a precious secret for one month, the Sisters reluctantly decided to see Dame

Dewberry about their nephew's education. They hated to let another woman have the say in Wilkin; but they themselves could neither read nor write. Their hands were made for dustpans and brushes, not pens and rulers; their eyes were made for spying out cobwebs, not for reading print. In their opinion, ink was a blot upon civilization, and perhaps they were right. They never saw a printed page without wanting to scrub the nasty little marks off the fair white paper. However, all children, it seemed, had to get their schooling, so one Sunday Sunday knocked on Dame Dewberry's door.

'Yes?' said Dame Dewberry, waking up from her nap. Sunday noted with disapproval that the table wasn't even cleared.

'It's about a child,' she said awkwardly.

'Has one of the little varmints been being bothersome?' asked the Dame comfortably; for the Sisters had complained before now of mud-throwing, window-breaking, and other natural phenomena of the sort.

'Not at all,' said Sunday. 'It's *our* child. It's time he went to school.'

'Bless me!' ejaculated Dame Dewberry. 'Which of your child's—I mean, of your children—might it be?' She was quite flustered by Sunday's unexpected announcement, and wished she had been able to peep into her grammar-book before she spoke. But Sunday hadn't noticed, and grammar wasn't her strong point anyhow. She too was in difficulties, for Wilkin had to be explained somehow; and the one thing the Sisters had determined on was that nothing and nobody should take him away from them. She looked over Dame Dewberry's head, so that she need not meet her eye, and said:

'It's none of ours and all of ours. A nephew.'

'Bless me!' cried Dame Dewberry again. 'Your long-lost brother's son, then?'

Sunday had never told a fib in her life. The Sisters were as strict about clean tongues as about clean faces. She nodded.

'Well, let him come tomorrow, the little dear,' said the Dame.

Sunday went home, and told her Sisters all about it; and she looked anxiously at old Monday when it came to the end, and said: 'I nodded a lie.' But Monday primmed her lips and said: 'It was a white one.' Then Sunday felt justified.

The next morning Wilkin walked by himself into school. He was very independent, and preferred to go alone. The school-bell had stopped ringing, the classroom was full, and every child turned to look at him when he opened the door. He was a bit of a surprise to them, and to Dame Dewberry too, as she came forward, took him by the hand, and lifted him on to a stool.

'This is our new scholar, children,' she said.

With one voice the children cried: 'He's too little!' Wilkin gave them a hurt look. Dame Dewberry stooped over him and asked: 'How old are you?'

'I'm five I dare say,' said Wilkin.

'Two he means!' shouted the children.

'I do not mean,' said Wilkin indignantly.

'Well, well,' said Dame Dewberry.

'Put him in a high chair and give him some pap,' giggled Tabby Bunch, yet she was quite a nice little girl.

'Give him some pap! give him some pap!' shouted the children, but they weren't bad children really.

Wilkin got down off his stool and went to the door without a word. That was the end of his schooling. Nothing would induce him to go back. He couldn't bear Tabby's teasing, and he wouldn't go to school, he said, till he was the tallest one in Wilmington. He stayed at home with his Aunts, waiting for it to happen. But it never did.

Wilkin came to Wilmington sixty months old and thirty inches high. Year by year he added twelve months to his age, but not an inch to his height.

*

When Wilkin was ten years old, the Wilmington Chimney-sweep spotted him, and said to the Seven Sisters: 'By your leave, I'll have that nevvy of yours to goo up my chimbleys.'

'That's as *he* likes,' said the Seven Sisters in a single breath.

Wilkin was sent for, and the Chimney-sweep put it to him. 'Howdee like to be my boy, an' goo up chimbleys with a black brush an' a green branch, an' find last year's swallow-nestes, an' see stars by day-light, an' get a farthing a day for it all?'

'I *would* like it,' said Wilkin promptly.

'There's a brave 'un,' said the Sweep. 'You can start tomorrow morning, in your ancientest clothes, and us'll stick together man and boy till I give up. Then you can have the business and my blessing.'

He went away, leaving eight happy people behind him.

'Think of it, Wilkin!' said Aunt Saturday. 'A farthing a day. Now you're a wage-earner.'

'Quite a little man,' chorused the Seven Sisters, beaming.

Wilkin beamed back. He was proud to be a little man so young.

The next day he began going up the Wilmington chimney-stacks. He did very well, got his farthing pay, and rushed home to show it to his Aunts. They were spreading the shining damask cloth for tea when he burst in; the white eggshell china was set just so round the table, the white loaf was ready to cut, the white sugar-lumps gleamed in the white bowl, the White Wyandottes' eggs were jigging in the pot. But Wilkin was too full of his doings to think about tea.

'Look, Aunt Tuesday! Look, Aunt Thursday!' he shouted. 'I went up-and-up-and-up, like rabbit-tunnels, some chimbleys is big as rooms, and some has cricks in their necks and bends in their backs, like Gaffer Friston. I got two nestes, look-see! I saw stars twinkle at noon-time! I said *Boo* to a Nowl, and the Yowl said *Whoo* to me! Oh, but best was when I poked my head out, an' Tabby Bunch stopped playing hopscotch faraway-down, and she scritched: "Hello Wilks! how *long* you are today!" Aunt Monday, here's my first farthing, it's for you because it *is* Monday. I'm going to make a nole in it to wear round your neck.'

'Thank you, Wilkin,' said Aunt Monday faintly. She hardly knew how to take the farthing from his hand. None of the Seven Sisters knew what to do. The print of Wilkin's sooty boot lay on the doorstep like a little nigger-foot, Wilkin's five sooty fingers left a little nigger-hand on the shining cloth, and Wilkin's face was as black as Sambo's. His hair, his clothes, every scrap of him was clotted with soot. He stood on the white drugget in the white room like a smoking lamp; and whenever he moved up flew the smuts, to walls, and chairs, and curtains, even to the ceiling. But he looked so happy, and they loved him so much, that they could not bear to upset him by letting him see how very upset they were.

Aunt Monday said gently: 'Come, Wilkin, come and have a lovely bath, and bring your first farthing with you.'

She led him away, and the other six sisters dealt with the smuts and soot as best they could, but it took them all night to get their darling white house clean again. And while they squeezed the drugget and wrung the curtains in the tub full of suds, Wednesday whispered to Friday: 'Oh Sister! we should have apprenticed him to the Miller.'

But it was too late to think of that now. Wilkin went on being a chimney-sweep, and the Seven Sisters gave up their daily walk. They gave up their nightly sleep. They gave up everything but trying to cope with the blacks Wilkin brought into the house. And they did not tell him what they suffered for his sake, for they saw that he was happy.

Day after day he followed his master with the long-handled brush with its fuzzy black head, and the stout

black sack for the soot; and he climbed up wide chimneys and swept their walls with a bough of green leaves. He found old mud nests with broken egg-shell sticking to them, he talked with owls and swallows, and each chimney-pot he climbed

was a tunnel of adven-
ture, leading to the
stars. The best joy of
all was coming out at
the top, and looking
down on the streets of
Wilmington, where the
children were playing
their games in the road.
What midgets they

looked, to be sure! Wilkin chuckled to think that any
human beings could be so tiny; and then he called out:
'Hello, Tabby! Hello, Bobby! See me!'

And Bobby and Tabby looked up and yelled with
laughter. 'Hello, Wilkin, how long you've grown!
Come and look at Wilkin up the chimbley? Isn't he
long!'

Then Wilkin's heart was ready to burst for pride.

But when he came down again, he was as little as
ever. By the time his master gave up, and turned the
business over to Wilkin with his blessing, Wilkin was
a child no more, but a man.

'*Quite* a little man,' his Aunts had said. And quite
a little man Wilkin remained. He was now the chimney-sweep of Wilmington, but he needed no boy to
go up his chimney-pots. He could still swarm up them
himself. And his happiest moments were still those
when his black face peered over the top, and he heard
one child call to another down below: 'I say, come
here, and look at Long Wilkin up there!'

★

The Seven Sisters got older and older and older.
The older they got, the more set they got; set in their

love for Wilkin, and set on keeping their house as
white as white.

Alas! while the love grew brighter the house grew
dimmer. Wilkin's walk in life proved too much for
them. Their nightly cleanings only touched the surface
of the trouble, and the blacks of the Wilmington
chimney-pots became ingrained in the bricks and
boards of their home.

One night, when Wilkin was abed, and Monday had been hard at it on her knees for three hours, there was a great fall of soot on the hearth which she had just whitened. Old Monday looked around at her sisters, bending and striving and straining like herself, and suddenly, she rose up and walked straight out of the house. Her sisters walked after her. The moon was bright on Windover Hill, and for the first time in twenty years the seven tall women, in their long white pinafores, climbed the Down to look at the sea.

It was a calm still night; the moon was like a polished plate, the sky was clean of everything but stars, the sea was stretched as smooth and tight as the undersheet on a well-made bed.

When the Seven Sisters had looked their fill upon it, they walked on with one accord. They did not stop until they reached a headland on the beach. There they took up their stand.

*

Wilkin was not used to waking himself up. That was the first duty of the Aunt who had charge of the day, and she did it before the sun had reached his east window. By the time the sun rolled into it, Wilkin had dressed himself, gone downstairs, found his porridge smoking on the table and his teapot steaming on the hob, made his meal, and was on his way to his first chimney-pots. Outside the house Wilkin raised his hands and arms in many another's service; but inside it he had never lifted a finger for himself. He had never had to. This system had gone on all his life, and your own lifelong system is deeper-rooted than one which has merely gone on for a billion years or so before you were born. So when, on the morning after the Seven Sisters had left the house, Wilkin awoke and saw the sun rolling out of the east window into the south, he scratched his head and said: 'The sun's got up early today!' For it never occurred to him that his Aunts had got up late. Aunt Wednesday still asleep at five in the morning? Impossible!

He lay on a bit, waiting for her to come. How long he would have waited it's hard to say, but that thing happened which moves us all to do something about it, if nobody else will. In short, Wilkin was hungry.

The little man sat up in bed, rubbed his eyes, and bawled: 'Aunt Wednesday!'

No answer.

He slung his knees over the edge, stretched his arms, and bawled a little louder: '*Aunt Wednesday!*'

No answer.

He got up, smothered a yawn, poked his tousled head through the door, and bawled with all the strength of his little lungs: 'AUNT WEDNESDAY!'

Still no answer.

'What's up?' wondered Wilkin. 'Am I a naddlepate, and is it *not* Aunt Wednesday's day today? But even if it's not, what about the rest of 'em?' And now the grimy walls of the chalk house resounded with his cries: 'Aunt Thursday! Aunt Friday! I'm hungry, Aunt Saturday! I'm ravenous, Aunt Sunday! Aunt Monday, I'm starving! I want my breakfast, Aunt Tuesday! Aunt Wednesday, where are you! I want *two* breakfasts, Aunt Wednesday!'

Dead silence.

Suddenly Wilkin cocked his head, and sniffed. The house was full of a smell he knew by heart. Not bacon-smell, or toast-smell, not pot, pan, or kettle-smell.

Soot-smell. Wilkin smelled soot. Oh lordy, lordy! the chimbley was on fire! And he remembered that his first chimney that day was to have been his Aunties'. It hadn't been done since dunnowhen. He had promised to do it before he left the house, and Aunt Wednesday had promised to call him extra early.

Wilkin hurried downstairs in his night-shirt. Nobody met, stayed, or called to him. The sitting-room was full of smoke. A lot of rubbish had been stuffed into the grate, yesterday's cinders had smouldered beneath it, and the fall of soot had settled the question. Nobody knew better than Wilkin what to do in an emergency like this; but when he had done it, and the fire in the chimney was extinguished, you *never* saw such a state as the house and Wilkin were in. But he hadn't time to clean up, to wash, to snatch a mouthful of bread, or to find his Aunts. He jumped into his blacks, shouldered his broom and his bough, and hobbled off to the first house on his list. There were nine on the list that day, and Wilkin caught nine scoldings from nine cross cooks. Nothing so puts cooks out as the lateness of sweeps. He explained as best he could that he had overslept himself because his Aunts had gone calling; but what explanation is that for a cross cook? It was the most fretful day of Wilkin's life; and at the end of it, he went home, long after sundown, with a bad headache and an empty stomach. He had never been so ready for a warm bath, a comfortable supper, and a nice go-to-bed.

There was no supper, no warm bath, and the go-to-bed was unpromising. Bed, table, and stove were just as he had left them. No fire lit, no kettle heating, no soup sizzling, no pillows plumped. Worst of all, nobody to greet him, nobody to tell things to. All the

way home he had treasured up the one splendid happening of the day; a little boy in Wannock had gazed up at him open-mouthed as he was emerging from the top of his fifth chimney, and cried excitedly: 'Daddy! Mammy! look at the giant up there!' 'The Longest Man in Sussex, that is what I am!' Wilkin had chuckled to himself, as he waggled his brush at the child. But his pleasure was chopped in two by the emptiness at home.

Wilkin took the cheese out of the larder and got into bed with it just as he was, dragging the sheet and blanket up anyhow. It wasn't comfortable, but he was past caring, and however hollow you are you can't put more than a certain amount of cheese inside you. Wilkin dropped off to sleep with his cheek on the Cheddar, and seven shrew-mice came up the stairs and finished it for him. No mouse had ever ventured in the Seven Sisters' house before. When he woke up to find the cheese all gone, Wilkin wondered why he still felt hungry.

*

Soon it was all over Wilmington that Wilkin's Aunts had vanished from man's sight. Search parties went forth all day from the villages of that reach of the Downs, from Folkington, Jevington, Willingdon, Littlington and Lullington; and after his work was done, Wilkin made a search-party by himself, all night. At the end of the month the villagers gave it up, and urged Wilkin to do the same; but the little man said: 'First I was and last I'll be. Thankee kindly and goo you home. I'll give my Aunties one more chance.'

On the last night of the year he trudged once again up Windover, and saw the cold moon shining on a distant blade of silver that was the sea. It was cold on the hill-top, and as the wind went over him he crouched under a juniper bush with his elbows on his knees and his chin in his palms, staring at the horizon, wondering which way to go.

'Straight on, little man,' said a voice that seemed to come out of the sky, 'and up to your neck in it, for you could do with a bath more than anyone I ever saw.'

Wilkin raised his eyes, and saw the tallest man in the world standing over him. Many a cottage in Wilmington was shorter than he. He wore the haphazard clothes of a gypsy, picked up from anybody, stolen from anywhere, a scarecrow's cast-offs, or a lord's losings. His toes peeped through his boots, and his beaver hat looked like a concertina that has lost its breath, but he had a thick gold ring on his finger with a king's ruby in it; his jacket had only one sleeve, and one of his knee-breeches was shorter than the other, but round his waist was a belt of red leather studded with cut steel, and his shirt-ruffle was of Mechlin lace. He was leaning on a spade as broad as a door, and chewing a sapling as another man chews a straw.

Little Wilkin was little in size only; he had the courage of ten, and returned the giant's stare with one of fearless admiration, tinged with envy.

'You are about the longest man I ever saw,' said he.

'And you,' said the giant, 'are about the shortest. What brought you stumping up Windover this cold winter night?'

'I'm looking for my seven Aunts,' said Wilkin.

'I,' said the giant, 'am looking for my only son.'

'What sort would he be?' asked Wilkin. 'As long as you?'

'Longer,' said the giant.

'That wouldn't be possible,' said Wilkin.

'It's certain,' said the giant. 'He was the biggest babe ever rocked on Cradle Hill. Why, when he was born he was as big as you are.'

Wilkin's eyes danced as he asked: 'Would you call me big?'

'For a full-blown man, no,' said the giant, 'for a new-born baby, yes.'

Wilkin's eyes stopped dancing. 'I suppose so. But why,' he asked, 'do you look for your son here?'

'For this reason,' said the giant. 'My wife was always complaining of the boy's weight on her back, and one day when I was down to Cuckmere, doing a bit of smuggling, she fell in with the gypsies from Pinchem. "That's a fine brat you've got there, missus," said they. "How old is he?" "Six weeks to the day," said she. "He's more like six months," said they; "a brat like yon is worth his weight in gold." "I'd sell him for a clothes-peg an inch," said she. "Done," said they. I *was* vexed when I got back and she showed me thirty clothes-pegs instead of my child. That was five and twenty years ago, and I've been tracking the Pinchem gypsies ever since. Last week I found their Great-grandmother smoking a pipe in a ditch, and "What's become of my brat?" I asked her. She sucks at her clay and says: "Which one would that be?" "The one you got for thirty pegs five-and-twenty year gone by." She sucks at her pipe some more and says: "Whisky-pegs?" "Wood," I tells her. She goes on sucking a bit, and presently nods. "I remember him now. He disappointed us, and we left him in a fish-kettle under the juniper bush on Windover." "When was that?" I asks. "A score of years ago," she says. "How did he disappoint you?" I asks. "He didn't turn out to pattern," she says; "that's all I shall tell, so leave me to smoke in peace." She'd told me enough, and I made tracks for Windover, and I looked under the bush where you're sitting now, and he wasn't there. I digged and I digged, and I found not him but the fish-kettle full of dust. So I began to raise his grave over there, look-see, to bury the kettle in. I'm raising the longest

barrow ever seen on the Downs, for if he'd lived he'd
be the longest man.'

Little Wilkin looked where the giant pointed, and
beheld a mighty barrow newly made.

'That's a grand tomb, to be sure,' he agreed. 'But
it's too big.'

'Not for the man my baby would have grown to,'
said the giant.

'Your son got all his growth the day of his birth,'
said Wilkin.

'How do you make that out?' asked the giant.

'Because I'm him,' said Wilkin.

The giant flung down his spade, threw back his
head, and roared with laughter.

'I am indeed,' said Wilkin. 'I am exactly thirty
inches long, just twenty-five years old, and was found
a score of years back in a fish-kettle under this juniper
bush.'

'Well!' exclaimed the giant. He went flat on his
stomach, stared into Wilkin's face, and said: 'The
gypsies were right. You've disappointed me.'

'You should see me looking out of a chimbley-pot,
dad,' said little Wilkin. 'Look at the Long Man!
that's what the childer call then.'

'Chimbley-pot be hanged!' cried the giant. 'My
son should ha' grown tall enough to sweep the smoke
off the moon!' And he rose up and strode away, leaving his spade behind him. He only paused once by
Long Barrow, to call over his shoulder: 'Goo take
that bath, you brat, goo take that bath.'

*

Little Wilkin sighed and shook his head, as he
saw his new-found father disappear down Tenantry

Ground; but it was the first time he had had a chance to be an obedient son, and he took it. He walked straight on, up Down and down Bottom to the seashore, pausing once only beside the mighty mound his dad had raised to bury him in. He knew it was all a mistake, and yet it was a matter of pride to the little man. Somebody had once thought of him as big as that, anyhow. He took comfort in the notion as he trudged through the icy night, and felt quite warm in his heart when he stood on the shingly beach of Birling Gap. It was high tide, but Wilkin did not know it, for this was the first time he had ever been within paddling distance of the sea, or had seen the chalk-white cliffs whose feet it washed. He sat down against them, and began to unlace his boots.

The night was as still as it was chill. Except at the very edges where the waves were frilled, the ocean looked like a solid block of grey ice, and the air seemed frozen from the water up to the moonlit sky. Yet as Wilkin set about removing his clothes, a breath tickled his ears, and he heard seven murmurs seemingly out of nowhere.

'What is Wilkin doing?'

'He's going to paddle.'

'On a night like this?'

'The boy is daft!'

'You know what boys are.'

'He'll certainly catch his death.'

'Tell him to put on his socks and boots at once.'

'Who? . . . You . . . you . . . you . . . you . . . you . . . you . . .'

As sure as he had ears, those were the voices of his seven Aunts! Wilkin jumped up and looked on all sides of him; but in front was the empty sea, right and left the empty beach, and at his back the tall white empty cliffs. Not a sign of the Seven Sisters, he thought, as his eyes travelled the stiff chalk cliffs from foot to peak, standing over him like seven white giantesses in long starched overalls. Now a confusion of murmurs sighed in his ears, and the voices he had heard singly breathed together: 'What day is it, sisters? Whose turn is it? Who'll tell him what to do and what not do so? You, Monday? Tuesday? Friday? Wednesday? Saturday? Thursday? Sunday? What day is it, sister? I do not know, I have forgotten time.'

As sure as he had ears, the voices came out of the cliffs.

'Aunt Sunday! Aunt Monday!' cried Wilkin joyfully. He ran from one to another of the cliffs, calling to them, knocking on them, listening at them, kissing them, caressing them. 'Is it here you've hidden yourselves so long a day? Come home to me, Aunties, the house is lone without you. It's Saturday night, Aunt Saturday, and my bed's not made, and my supper is uncooked. Come home and look after me, like you used to do.'

Were they too old and ossified to hear? No answer came to him out of the heart of the chalk. The night slipped by while Wilkin knelt and implored the Seven Sisters to come home. When the cold moon gave place to the colder dawn, he gave it up as a bad job, laced his boots sadly, and turned to go. As he did, seven sighs fretted his ears again.

'Look at my pinafore!'
'All over finger-marks.'
'His coat-sleeve has dirtied me.'
'You can trace his footprint on me.'

'And his lips too.'

'Will we never be done with cleaning up after him?'

'Wait, sisters, wait. The sea will wash us white.'

Little Wilkin stood stock still. For the first time in his life he knew the truth. He had blackened the snow-white lives of his seven Aunts. With soot he had driven them out of their own chalk house into a fortress of chalk that he could not assail. Those trifling marks of his on the cliffs were nothing. The print of his foot and his hand and his mouth would soon be bleached by the sun, washed by the sea, and worn by time. Suppose he were white, wouldn't his Aunts come home?

He set his jaw and turned due north again, by Friston, Snap Hill, and Windover; and as the sun came up, he dropped down to Wilmington, where he heated water, filled a tub, and scrubbed himself from top to toe with a bar of yellow soap. Alas! he had lived too long in the chimney-stacks; now he was so ingrained that ebony was ivory and a crow was a swan to him. He came out of the water as black as he went in.

'Well,' said the little man, 'it's no use grieving. I wish I was long enough to bury in Long Barrow, and I wish I was white as the chalk cliffs at Birling Gap; then I would be at one with my Aunts again. But black I must be, and my Aunts will never come back, and as for Long Barrow, tomorrow I'll let Sexton measure me for the littlest plot of earth in Wilmington churchyard, and till my time comes to lie there I'll sweep chimbleys.'

For five and seventy more years it was so. He swept chimneys till he had to use two sticks to hobble to work; yet up the chimney-stack he was as nimble as ever, for there it was that he felt most at home. Now it was Tabby Bunch's great-granddaughter who called: 'Look at the Long Man!' when Wilkin's black face topped the chimney-pot. Black he remained to the last, and as brief as when he was born. When in his hundredth year he came to die, it might have been a piccaninny that was to be laid in the littlest plot of earth in Wilmington churchyard.

*

Not so quick with your pocket-hankies, please! Are you really such sillies as to think that a man ends with his life? The end of life was the beginning of wonders for Wilkin.

The night before he was to go to grass, a miracle happened, seen by no man's eye. Four miles away the cliffs shook in Birling Gap, and the Seven Sisters stepped out in their pure white pinafores. Over the Downs they went, and under the moon. Wilmington was fast asleep when they came into it, and entered the chalk house that now looked like coal. Up the stairs they went, into Wilkin's room, and there they stood around and gazed down on him.

'Dear dear!' said Sunday, 'how he do need a bath!'

'Dare we?' said Thursday.

'Waste labour,' said Wednesday. 'Nothing'll make him white.'

'What a baby he is,' said Friday, gazing on him fondly.

'So little,' said Tuesday.

'And he did so long to be long,' said Saturday.

'He *shall* be long,' said Monday, 'and he shall be

white. He shall be known as the longest and the whitest man in Sussex. Fetch me his sweep's brush and bag.'

When they were brought, she lifted Wilkin out of his bed, and laid in his place his brush with its fuzzy black head. Up the handle she slipped the sack he carried the soot away in. 'Like as two peas!' said she, and laid over all the last green bush Wilkin had cut for the open chimneys.

The Seven Sisters took up their tiny charge, and went the way they had come. On the top of Windover Hill they stood from sheer habit of old, and gazed at the dustless sea four miles away.

'Look!' said Tuesday.

'What is it?' said Wednesday.

'Something coming in with the tide,' said Thursday.

'What sort of a thing?' asked Friday.

'A boat,' said Saturday.

'And a man in the boat,' said Sunday.

'Our long-lost brother,' said Monday.

A hundred years and more they had waited for him. Possessing their souls with the patience of the cliffs which have watched the tides for centuries untold, they waited for the man to beach his boat and join them on Windover. It was not long, for he, like his seven sisters, was a giant and took each hill at a stride. He knew them, and they knew him, at the first glance.

'Well, sisters,' said he, 'fresh from the wash as ever.'

'Well, brother,' said they, 'needful as ever of washing. Why did you run away?'

'To be honest,' said the giant, 'I couldn't abide your everlasting soapsuds. There's such a thing as overdoing it.'

'And underdoing it too,' said Saturday, fixing her eyes on his neck-line.

'It's too long ago to quarrel about,' said the giant. 'I'm not here to be scolded after all this time; I'm here because I felt in my bones you had need of me tonight.'

'We have,' said Sunday softly. 'We want you to raise the longest barrow from end to end of the Downs.'

'Why, I began it five and seventy years ago,' said the giant.

'Then finish it now,' said Monday.

The giant looked about for his spade and found it under the juniper bush where he had thrown it three-quarters of a century back. He heaved up seven spits of the soil on Long Barrow, and fished out the old fish-kettle he had flung there. The Seven Sisters laid little Wilkin inside it, where he lay as peaceful as in his cradle. 'Bless me,' said the giant, 'if that isn't my son.'

'Are you sure, brother?' asked old Monday.

'Did you ever see another like him?' asked the giant.

The Seven Sisters shook their heads. 'There was never another like him.' And Sunday said: 'Then he really was our nephew all the time. Cover him in.'

The giant covered Wilkin safe and snug under Long Barrow, and raised above him a mound fit for the son he had hoped to have.

When the work was done, the giant asked: 'What next?'

'For you, nothing,' they answered. 'For us, much.'

'Shall we meet again?' asked the giant.

'As long as you sail the sea we will stand and watch you come and go.'

The giant took four steps to Birling Gap, and sailed away under the moon.

But the Seven Sisters came down from the brow of the hill, and against the grassy side above Wilmington they outlined Wilkin's picture with the chalk-stones of their hearts. It was the picture of a giant they laid out on the grass, a huge man supported on two sticks as bleached as bone. They knew his wish was to be long and white. Yet oddly enough, because his Aunts were no draughtswomen, the picture they made was the enormous picture of a dwarf.

When it was done, they went with one accord over the Downs. Just as they reached Birling Gap a cheery voice overhead called: 'Thankee, Aunties!' And there in high heaven was Wilkin looking over the top of the moon as it might be a chimbley; and he was busy sweeping the smoke off its face, so they knew he had got the right job.

'Look at Wilkin, sisters!' cried Sunday. 'Isn't he *long!*'

'Quite a little man,' said old Monday complacently.

Then the Seven Sisters took up their stand again among the cliffs, and there they have been ever since.

*

Next day, Wilkin's brush and sack were buried with due solemnity in the churchyard; and the Sexton shook his head as he dropped the green bough, thinking: 'There, little man! Never again will the childer wonder at you.'

But even while he thought it, Tabby Bunch's great-granddaughter was scampering round-eyed to fetch all the children out of school with her screams—

'Oo! come quick! come and look at the Long Man of Wilmington!'

They came to the hill-side, saw the white figure and wondered; and then their elders came and wondered too; and presently folk came from the farthest boundaries of Sussex to see the Long Man. In time his fame spread so that travellers came on purpose from Kent and Surrey and Hampshire and America. By this time, nobody could even guess who the Long Man was, but the wiseacres said he was a giant who was buried in Long Barrow. And little Wilkin, looking over the moontop, heard them, and chuckled, for in men's minds he was long enough and white enough at last.

Fifth Interlude

ANOTHER six daisy-chains came to a finish. 'Is Wilmington far?' asked Sylvia.

'It all depends,' said Martin Pippin. 'When my Granny came in with the trug full on June the Fifteenth and said: "Just run down the garden, child, and find me my spectacles where I must ha' dropped 'em," I grumbled that I was so tired and the bottom of the garden was so far. "How 'm I to see to shell the English Wonders then?" said my Granny. When I saw the trug full of pea-pods, and knew the English Wonders had ripened a fortnight earlier than usual, the tiredness went out of my legs, and I cried: "*I'll* find your specs for you, Granny!" like the good little boy I was. It had seemed a long way off to the lost spectacles, but no distance at all to the young pea-pods at the bottom of the garden.'

'Is Wilmington far?' asked Sylvia again.

'From Rackham in West Sussex,' said Martin, 'to Wilmington in East, is as far as from North to South America.'

Stella. That gets one nowhere.

Martin. Or anywhere.

Sylvia. How *long* does it take to get from North to South America?

Sue. A hundred days, about.

Sally. About a second.

Martin. You see? It all depends. Even the Long Man looks a midget to Atlas, as he holds up the globe, and to the cricket in the chimney-corner Little Wilkin looks a giant bigger than Atlas.

Stella. That's nonsense!

Martin. Not if seeing is believing. The cricket could just see Wilkin, but he couldn't see Atlas at all.

Sylvia. Why not?

Martin. There's too much of him.

Sylvia. Could we see and believe the Long Man if we went to Wilmington?

Martin. Like any other Sussex-born child, East or West.

Sally. Could we see and believe the sack and broom they buried for Little Wilkin in the churchyard?

Sue. Not unless they unburied them. Why don't they bury more sorts of things than they do?

Martin. What would you bury first?

Sue. Slugs.

Stella. They'd only come up again, silly.

Sue. Jellyfish then. What would you?

Stella. Boiled milk.

Sophie. I'd like to bury the last day of the holidays.

Sally. I'd like to bury nuts.

Sue. But nuts are *nice*.

Sally (*looking like a squirrel*). Yes.

Sylvia. I'd like to bury all the stinging-nettles in the world.

Stella. They're all right if you grasp them.

Sylvia. Go on then, grasp them.

Stella. Why should I?

Sylvia. To prove it.

Stella. It's been proved. One doesn't have to go on proving things all the time.

Sylvia. Then one oughtn't to go on saying things.

Stella. If one knows things, one says them.

Sylvia. If one says things, one ought to prove them.

Stella. One *can't* go on proving everything all the time!

Martin. We've been here before. Before we get giddy, let's bury the hatchet. Selina is now the only one who hasn't told us what she would bury if she could.

Selina. If I tell you, you'll know what I'm thinking.

Martin. I have known by your silence, since the end of my story. You are thinking that you would like to bury bedtime in oblivion, which is deeper than the grave. Yet even oblivion isn't deep enough when the clock strikes. Bedtime, Selina!

Selina. It all depends.

Martin. On what?

Selina. You.

Martin. Let's prove it.

Selina was as docile as a dove. She twined her finger in Martin's, and side by side they ambled to the Guessing Stump. As he lifted her up: 'You know,' she drawled, 'I sometimes forget who my parents are myself.'

'That makes things doubly difficult,' said Martin. 'Do you happen to know whose child you are at the moment?'

'Yes,' said Selina.

'Hang on to it tight, while I consider you. Too gentle for Joscelyn's child,' said Martin Pippin, 'too dreamy for Jane's, too languid for Jessica's. The moon is your planet; if you were Joyce's child, it would be the sun. You must be Joan's, or Jennifer's.'

'How about Joan's?' suggested Selina, looking at him limpidly with her chicory eyes.

'Shall we say Joan's then?' mused Martin.

'I wish you would,' drawled Selina. 'She's my favourite Aunt.'

'Your favourite *What*?'

Selina's lip trembled, and Martin discovered that when chicory holds the dew it is twice as blue as before.

'This seems, alas, to reduce us to Jennifer,' he muttered, greatly bothered.

Selina asked wistfully: 'Mightn't I have been leading you astray?'

Martin shook his head. 'You might not—on purpose.' Selina gazed at him through two wet blue flowers, and Martin went astray all on his own. 'I know you now,' he said. 'You're my child, aren't you?'

The dew is doomed when the sun rises. The flowers dried like magic. Selina said: 'My mother is Jennifer,' and looked round the daisy-field like a reprieved prisoner. She added: 'Oblivion *is* deep enough after all. You can't dig my bedtime up out of it ever again. Oblivion is the deepest thing there is.'

'The duplicity of man,' said Martin, 'is deeper.' He offered her his daisy.

'I don't know what that means,' drawled Selina.

'And you never will,' said Martin, 'for you are kind to the fallen.'

Selina twined her fingers in his again, and held him up all the way back to the clothes-basket.

*

'She's been crying,' observed Sue.

'But not very much,' said Sophie.

'She's lolling against him,' said Sally.

'That needn't mean anything,' said Stella. 'S'lina always lolls.'

'It's all right,' said Sylvia, 'she's wearing both daisies.' Making a trumpet of her hands she called: 'Is it all right?'

'Yes,' Selina called back. 'It almost wasn't, because my tongue tripped over an aunt. But you mustn't tease him,' she added, as they entered the circle. 'One ought to be kind to the crestfallen.'

Martin looked crestfallen in the extreme. Sophie said kindly: 'When I used to fall and graze my knee, Mother used to laugh and say "Bad luck! up you jump!" Jump up, Martin! Bad luck.'

'*My* mother just went and got the iodine,' said Sue.

Sally. Iodine doesn't do for a graze on your feelings. He's looking fearfully depressed. We ought to talk about some other things, I think.

Sylvia. Martin, did you find your Grandmother's spectacles?

Martin. I was too busy eating peas to remember to look.

Sue. I like chewing the pea-pods afterwards.

Martin. So did I.

Sue. It's a pity about that shelly bit in the lining though.

Martin. One of the few mistakes made on the Third Day.

Stella. What did your Grandmother say when you got back without them?

Martin. Nothing. She was wearing them on her nose. Haven't you noticed that nobody ever finds anybody else's spectacles, because nobody's spectacles are ever really lost?

Sophie. Where were your Granny's?

Martin. At the bottom of the trug.

Selina. How did she shell the peas and find them then?

Martin. You don't really shell peas with your eyes. That was a little bit of cunning on her part, to get me to go and look at the bottom of the garden where the pea-pods were and her spectacles weren't.

Sally. P'r'aps she knew all the time, and was a very kind old lady who knew what little boys would like, and your Mother was in the kitchen so she couldn't give you handfuls of peas out of the trug, and just pretended her spectacles was lost.

Martin. The kindness of Grandmothers is limitless. No graze on the feelings can stand up against it. One of these days you will make a first-class Grandmother.

Sally. Are your feelings cured now?

Martin. I've quite forgotten I ever had any.

Sally. Then would you please mind telling me did you ever see an Indian Chief in Sussex?

Martin. Alas, I never have. How much does it matter?

Sally. Only then I could do I is for Indian Chief.

Martin. In that case it matters not at all. For in the realm of poetry, the poet has the choice of writing about either what is there or what isn't.

Sally. Like this?

> As I walk Sussex, hill and shore,
> I meet shepherds by the score,
> Fishermen and tramps as well,
> And gypsies more than I can tell.
>
> But what I really long to meet
> In country lane or village street,
> And what I've never never met,
> Is an Indian Chief in Sussex yet.

Martin. That's it exactly!

Sally. No, that isn't it, exactly.

Martin. Exactly.

Sue. *I* like things what is. A gypsy is.

> The gypsy peddles by Sussex day
> And sleeps by Sussex night.
> 'Come, Willie, buy my lantern pray,
> To keep your stable bright;
> And buy my clothes-peg, Mary May,
> Lest your pinafore blow out of sight!'

Gypsies always do have lanterns and clothes-pegs, don't they, why do they?

Martin. To look for mushrooms with on the Downs at night, and to pin them down when they

Sylvia

find them. Mushrooms have a habit of disappearing
like magic.

Sophie. They grow like magic, too.

> The cream-headed mushrooms
> With pinky-brown gills
> They grow on the Pharisees'
> Dancing-hills.
> From Bepton Down
> To Willingdon Hill
> When the Pharisees dance
> You can pick your fill.

Martin. Unless Jerry gets ahead of you.

Sylvia. Who's Jerry?

Martin.

> Jerry was an old man
> And lived in a pond,
> With Firle at the back of him
> And Five Lords beyond.
> He dined with the tadpoles,
> With newts made his bed,
> And all the year round
> Had a cold in his head.

Stella. He was a silly to live in a pond. He ought
to have lived on the chalk, like a proper caveman.

The Caveman of Sussex he lived on the Chalk,
And 'Umph! Umph! Umph!' was his manner of talk.
His tools and his weapons he fashioned of Flint,
Which said as he chipped it, *Chint! Chint! Chint!*
The Caveman of Sussex is long ago dead,
But you'll find if you're lucky his Flint Arrow-head.

Sylvia. Was that the one they shot Harold with?

King Harold, King Harold, he ran out of town,
And hastened to Hastings to fight for his crown;

But an Archer let fly and King Harold fell down,
And King William the Conqueror put on his crown.

Selina. No, Syl, it was a much longer-ago sort of
arrow than that. It was longer ago than Julius Caesar,
I think. It was longer ago than a Tumulus.

Sylvia. Would you find a flint arrow-head in a
Tumulus?

Martin. More likely a Roman spear-head. Yet
even that's not certain.

> All round the Tumulus
> The four winds do blow.
> Whom did they bury there,
> 'Twas long long ago?
>
> Was it the Roman
> Who came as our foe
> And tried to conquer Sussex,
> 'Twas long long ago?
>
> But the Downs took his heart
> Into their heart, so!
> And turned it into Sussex dust,
> 'Twas long long ago.

That's what the chalk does to a fellow.

Selina. The chalk's anything you like.

> When along the Downs you walk
> You'll find Quarries in the chalk.
> Some are caves with treasure strewn,
> Some are like a white half-moon.
> Some are forts and kingly halls,
> Some are Moorish city walls.
> And one's the cliff of the world to me,
> With tides of grass instead of sea.

Sue. That's what does *bother* me so, in poitry.

Martin. What does?

Sue. Calling the grass the sea when it isn't.

Martin. It is one of the Muse's favourite tricks. But don't let your little head be bothered by it. Go on calling the grass the grass until you find a winkle in a cornfield.

Sylvia. A winkle in the *corn*? You mean a snail, don't you?

Martin. I mean what I said. Don't look so unbelieving.

Sylvia. I'm not unbelieving, I'm only asking.

Martin. Then sit down and I'll give you the answer. Only you mustn't interrupt me more than you can help. And to help you not to interrupt me, I will supply you each with a stick of Rock, of which, praise the stars, I have just six lengths left. May they fill the bill till my story is done, and my Mermaid has come to the end of her tale.

Sylvia. What Mermaid?

Martin. If I stop to answer your questions, the tale will never begin.

He produced six pink and white truncheons from his shirt-front, stuck one in each of the little girls' mouths, and tucked a daisy behind Sylvia's right ear. While he was finding another for himself, Sylvia removed the sugar truncheon, and spelt out the cherry name imprinted on the end. 'W-I-N-C-H-E-L-S-E-A R-O-C-K. I didn't know Winchelsea *had* any rocks.'

'Winchelsea had a lot of things you don't know about,' said Martin, 'but you very soon will.' He twiddled his daisy reflectively. 'I wonder,' he mused, 'if she *was* any better off, when it came to the point.'

'What point?' asked Sylvia.

'The point of the pin that picked her out of her

shell. No more talking.' Martin leaned back against the clothes-basket, closed his eyes, and murmured:

'Mermaid, Mermaid in the Rye,
On the hill left high and dry,
How much happier would you be
Swimming in the Winchelsea?'

And without more ado he began the tale of

THE MERMAID OF RYE

S HE was born in a winkle.
    (Sylvia. A winkle?
Martin. A winkle.
Sylvia. Are mermaids born in winkles?
Martin. This one was, alas.
Sylvia. Why alas?

Martin. Because the Winkle Mermaids are the poorest of their species. The Pearl-Oyster Mermaids don't know they exist. The Mussel-Men ignore them, and even the Cockle-Babies look down on them. For the winkle ranks lowest among shell-fish, whelks excepted. No whelk has ever produced a mermaid yet. They try, but they can't. Shall we get on?
Sylvia. No, go back. I've forgotten. You talk such a lot.)

She was born in a winkle in the salt marshes of the east.

(*Sylvia.* The east of what?
Martin. The east of Sussex, of course. Where else is there?
Sylvia. I don't know.
Martin. Then don't ask unnecessary questions.)

The sea was flat and grey, not very interesting, and chock-full of winkles. All the hundred thousand winkles of Sussex congregated in that sea. She was an ignorant little thing, and she called them winchels, because she knew no better. Nobody had ever taught her to talk properly, not even Old Limpet, who was supposed to know everything. But she was perfectly happy, as those who know no better always are. She flopped about in the marshes, she combed her brown seaweedy hair with her skinny fingers, and on moonlight nights she slid along the moonglade, from the edge of the tide to the horizon and back again, singing:

> 'Look at me
> In the Winchel-Sea!'

And the hundred thousand winkles peeped out of their shells to listen, and chitter to each other: 'That child is a Wonder!'

For they also knew no better. This was *their*
mermaid. What if her voice was a little tinny?
Winkles are not remarkable for their ears. What if
her verse was not especially inspired? Winkles have
very little soul for poetry. What if her hair was like
the worst brown seaweed, instead of the best green,
and her eyes like cold grey pebbles instead of bright
blue sapphires? Winkles have no colour-sense at all.
What if she did comb her tresses with her fingers
because she hadn't been born with a golden comb in
her mouth? Winkles have no manners. All they
knew was that mermaids swim and sing and comb
their locks, and charm men young and old. Here was
their mermaid behaving according to pattern, and
with one voice they chittered: 'She is a Wonder!'
From the beginning of time mothers have chittered
thus over their infants, when they too behave according to pattern. They know it is a pattern, but they
think their babies make it better than it has ever been
made before. Don't ask me why, Sylvia. I am not
your mother.

(*Sylvia.* You might be my father, though.

Martin. I know I might. Am I?

Sylvia. Go on about Miss Winchel.

Martin. How did you know that was her name?

Sylvia. I had to call her something, hadn't I?

Martin. That is how the best names come about.)

Miss Winchel, then, did all the things she had been
born to do, but one; she was not yet of an age to
charm men young and old.

'How is it done?' she sometimes asked Old Limpet.

'Bide your time,' he mumbled. 'It'll come natural
to you when you open out.'

She bided her time, grew up a little, and wondered

if it was her opening-time, but it's never any use
asking limpets to speak twice about any one thing, so
she began to ask the winkles: 'How is it done, this
charming?'

The question threw them into a state of agitation.
'Don't ask, don't ask!' they clippered and cloppered.
They knew what they knew, but they didn't know
this: winkles charm men in ways that are not mermaids'. The charm of winkles is not man's doom,
but theirs. They had agreed among themselves never
to tell her, though every winkle is warned of its fate
at birth. One day Miss Winchel cornered a very
young one in a pool, and threatened it with her little
finger, crying: 'If you don't tell me about charming
men young and old, 'I'll throw you high-and-dry.
How is it done?'

The young winkle clecked with fright, and said:
'With a pin.'

'What's a pin?' asked Miss Winchel. But the
young one had said its little say, and got back into its
little shell, as far down as it could.

So Miss Winchel bided a bit more time, and went
on doing rather badly the things mermaids do, in the
flat grey water which she thought was the most
wonderful ocean in the hemispheres.

'Isn't it? isn't it?' she cried one day to Old Limpet.

But Old Limpet mumbled in his beard: 'There's
the Red Sea and the Yellow Sea, there's icy seas and
spicy seas, there's the peacock seas of Cornwall and
the wine-dark seas of Greece, there's the tropical
Pacific where the pigment is terrific, there's emerald
seas, and silver seas, and seas like the Golden Fleece.'

'Oh,' said Miss Winchel. 'Well, mine is a very
nice sea, anyhow.'

'Good enough for a mermaid the likes o' you,' mumbled Old Limpet.

'But what other likes *is* there?' asked Miss Winchel, very much surprised, for she'd thought, as we're all apt to, that she was the only kind there is.

'There's Nereids and there's Sirens in unusual environs,' mumbled Old Limpet, 'but there's none to match the Mermaids born in oyster-shells like pearls, and when those ones start tooning up, their listeners start mooning, and young men and old forget the faces of their girls.'

'I'd like that,' said Miss Winchel, and for the first time she wondered if being born in a winkle is Ultima Thule.—That'll do, Sylvia! I'll tell you afterwards.

Miss Winchel also asked questions. 'A pearl is what?'

'Round silky thing, like the moon by day,' yawned Old Limpet. Then he shut up.

Miss Winchel swam away with her noddle full of pearls and peacocks and men and the Golden Fleece. She hadn't the faintest conception what any of these things were. She cornered Young Winkle again and asked: 'What's a Terrific Pigment in a Pacific?'

Young Winkle answered promptly: 'The Giant Swineherd of the Tropics!' for you have to say these things quickly or not at all.

It didn't get Miss Winchel any farther.

Then one fine shining evening in late summer, as she swam and sang in the marshes, she happened to lift her eyes and look inland. And there she saw a hill of golden water rising afar, as high as a waterspout and as still as a pool. For the first time in her life, Miss Winchel knew there was something more.

(*Sylvia*. More than what?
Martin. Than what she'd got. How inquiring you are.
Sylvia. Well, I prefer to know.
Martin. Who doesn't prefer the impossible?)

'Oo! oo! oo!' cried Miss Winchel, and burst into tears. The hundred thousand winkles flocked to the scene.

'What is it? what is it, what is it?' they chittered. 'What is the matter with our poppadoodalums?'

'Nothing's the matcher with *me*,' wailed Miss Winchel, 'but our sea-water's all the wrong colour.'

'It's the same colour it's always been,' said a great-grandmother winkle, wrinkling as she said it.

'It's not the right shape,' whined Miss Winchel, 'and it's a very low highness. Look there, look up there!' She pointed her two skinny first fingers at the flood of gold on the hill. 'I want to be in *that* sea, I do.'

'Take care, take care,' chittered the winkles. 'It's a dangerous thing to change one's waters before one knows what's What.'

'How can I know what What is till I'm At?' demanded Miss Winchel, spreading her bony arms upon the air.

'Take care and beware!' twickled the winkles.

'Be where?' asked Miss Winchel, and plunged forward.

She soon found out where, in her attempt to swim overland to the gold on the hill. The comfortable water ceased to enclose her, the unstable air let her down, and she fell with a flop on the harsh marsh grass, and couldn't get up again.

(*Sylvia.* Harsh—marsh——

Martin. Grass.

Sylvia. Harsh-marsh-grarsh! Ha, ha! Harsh-marse-garsh!

Sue. He-he-he!

Sylvia. You say it then.

Sue. Harsh-marse-garse—it's easy.

Sophie. You said it wrong. Harse-marsh-grass, there! No, bother, but almost. Harsh——

Selina. Harsh-ur-marsh-ur-grass.

Sue. S'lina said it.

Stella. So can anybody that urs.

Sally. Harsh! . . . *marsh!* . . . GRASS!
Sophie. That's right, Sally.
Stella. Anybody can if they stop ten minutes
between each word.
Sophie. You say it quick then.
Selina. And no urr-ing.
Stella. I sha'n't try. It's silly.
Martin. Too silly for words.
Stella. Then what did you want to begin it for?
Martin. I can't think what came over me.)

There lay poor Miss Winchel, flipping and flopping
on the rough salt herbage, while all the winkles in
Sussex chittered and clittered at her from the edge of
the sea.

'Come in, Miss Winchel, come in from the out!'
cried the winkles.

'Come out and fetch me, my winkles, come out from
the in!' cried Miss Winchel.

But they could no more come out than she could
come in, and at last they had to leave her there to die
of high-and-dryness. They chickled and chackled back
into the sea, and sent a jelly-fish to the Mediterranean
for a cuttle-fish to paint their shells black. But jelly-
fish have no sense of direction, they go where they're
taken, and this one was taken to the Baltic instead.
Luckily, as it transpired.

Miss Winchel was nowhere near dying, for the
time being. She had fallen on a nice damp place,
where she had all the night to lie and wonder in,
before the sun came up and dried her. The light went
out of the sky, the gold faded on the hill, and the
starfish came out on the shore. A wind from the
Weald blew poppy-scent over her. She heard an

owl. It was all very nice indeed. She hadn't stopped wondering, when two people came by quarrelling. It was one of the nights that skip a moon, and starfish don't give much light, so Miss Winchel couldn't see what the quarrellers looked like, but by their voices one was a Him and the other was a Her.

(*Sylvia*. Isn't it a He and a She?
Martin. I sometimes say a Him and a Her.
Sally. I always do.
Martin. Bless you, Sally.)

What they were quarrelling about didn't matter. They'd got by that long ago, and had come to the part where you just call names and say things.

'Booby!' cried the Her.
'Gaby!' cried the Him.
'I'd be sorry for myself if I was you!'
'I'd be sorrier for myself if I was *you!*'
'Copycat! I'll go at my fortnight!'
'Good riddance!'
'To *you!*'
'Who's a copycat now?'
'Yah!'
'Yah!'

Yah is the low-water mark of bickering. After Yah there is no more to be said. The Him smacked the Her's cheek, and the Her stamped on the Him's toe, and there was a scuffle. Presently they scuffled away, almost treading on Miss Winchel, but not quite. It was all very exciting.

'So that's how it's done,' said Miss Winchel happily. 'Booby! Gaby! Yah, Copycat, yah!'

And must she die, now that she had learned the way to charm? Never! said she to herself. Before sun-up dried her, she would be back in the sea. Where there's a will there's a way, she said to herself.

Lashing her tail, she lifted her top half, dug her little pointed elbows into the ground, and very slowly, but with determination, wormed her way across the shore. At the second elbow-dig she squeaked 'Ooch!' as something pierced her right arm, and at the fifth dig she squealed 'Eeech!' when another thing stuck in her left. She pulled out the prickles, clenched one in either fist, and wiggled and wriggled herself to the edge of the water. When she had passed high-tide mark, she lay still and waited. The sun came up, the sea came in, and soon Miss Winchel was washed back to safety.

All the winkles in Sussex clattered about her, chippelling for joy. While they did so, Miss Winchel carefully undid her right fist till it was fingers again, and there on her palm lay a long thin thing with a round white thing on the top. The round whiteness gleamed, and Miss Winchel could not take her eyes off it. But the winkles took no heed of it; *they* only saw the long thinness, and their joyful chippelling changed to a fearful cruttering.

'Throw it away, throw it away!' they cried.

'Whatever for?' asked Miss Winchel.

'For good,' implored the winkles.

'It *is* good,' said Miss Winchel.

'It is disaster,' cruckled the winkles. 'It is doom. It is death. Little do you know. That is a Pin.'

'It is a Pearl,' said Miss Winchel, and she stuck it in her hair.

Then she undid her left fist into fingers, and it also held a long thin thing, but thicker than the Pin. Instead of a pearl, it had a point of gold.

'Is this a pin too?' asked Miss Winchel.

The winkles wrinkled a good deal as they considered it. Finally a great-great-uncle winkle said: 'I am not perfectly sure, but I *think* it is a Pen.'

'A Pen!' the winkles shivered.

'That's almost as bad as a Pin,' said the great-grandmother.

'In an emergency,' said a second cousin, 'it could be fatal.'

But Miss Winchel wouldn't throw that away, either. She tried to stick it in her other hair, but it wouldn't, and slipped down behind her ear; and she left it there, though the unaccustomed pressure made her ear ache. Finding the winkles unable to share her pleasure, she swam to tell the good news to Old Limpet.

'Look!' said Miss Winchel.

'That,' mumbled Old Limpet, 'is beyond me.'

'It's a pearl, then.'

'What is?'

'What I found on the foreshore. I'm a pearl-maid now, and the winkles don't like it a bit.'

'Howjer know it's a pearl?' asked Old Limpet.

'It's like the moon by day.'

'Biggun?'

'Big's the blob on the end of my nose.'

'How big's that?'

''Bout as big as a winkle.'

'Then your pearl's worth a forchune,' mumbled Old Limpet. 'Stick to it, me girl, and don't part with it for nothing to nobody.'

'I won't,' said Miss Winchel.

'On thother hand, remember,' yawned Old Limpet, 'you can always part with it for something to somebody.' And shut up.

'We'll see,' said Miss Winchel. She wasn't set on parting with her pearl to anybody for anything. She turned her eyes inshore, where the sun glowed on the land and on the sea, and the golden hill of her heart was in full flood. But she did not venture a second attempt to reach it. When the sun went down, she contented herself with floating on the swell, and pretending her pearl was the moon. She held the pale round thing above her nose, and saw it like a milky ball of phosphorous; this was another dark night, and there was nothing in the sky to compete with her treasure.

Presently, as she lolled and lounged on the tide, she heard soft fretful sighs blow out from the shore. 'Oh dear, oh dear! It's too bad, reelly it is. Oh dear, oh dear! it reely *is* too bad.'

The voice of the Her. Miss Winchel would have known it anywhere. 'My one-and-only, and me soon out of a place,' moaned the voice. 'I can't afford another sixpence, not yet I can't. Oh dear, oh dear! where *did* I drop that pin?' (Miss Winchel clutched it fiercely in her fist and turned upside down in the sea.) The voice of the Her became suddenly vindictive. 'It's all His fault!' Then it became defiant. 'Not if He arsked me on his bended knees I wouldn't stay.' Then derisive. 'Ho, not much I wouldn't, you needn't flatter yourself!' Then it grew fretful again. 'Oh dear, my pearl!' And then the voice of the Her trailed away up the shore.

When the sound of sighs and steps had died on the air, Miss Winchel turned right side up and played with her pearl again.

Every night for a fortnight the Her came back, between ten and eleven at night, to look for the pin.

Miss Winchel kept herself dark, for the moon was
visiting the stars again. By its light Miss Winchel,
peering through the water, beheld the face of the
Her, beautiful as the pearl. Part of her face was much
the same colour indeed, and so were her milky hands;
but her lips and nails were coral, and her hair was as
gold as the water on the hill. A pearl-maid, past all
doubt, one born to charm. Miss Winchel felt twiddly
sensations that surprised her. She hastened to consult

Old Limpet about them. When she had put the case to him, he mumbled:

'Jallasy, jallasy. That's all it is, me girl. Just jallasy.'

'Is that a bad sickness?' inquired Miss Winchel.

'One of the worst.'

'If I went close to the Her, would she catch it off me?'

'Not a hope,' said Old Limpet, 'and you with a blob like a winkle on thend of yer nose. But there, she'd not see you however close you got. Her eyes aren't right for it, not if they're bluer than sapphires. *She's* no pearl-mermaid, walking about on two feet.'

'Yes, well,' said Miss Winchel, flicking her tail a trifle, 'and I've got her pearl too, haven't I?'

After this talk with Old Limpet, she wasn't afraid to be seen, and that night came out in the open, under the stars. But the Her did not put in an appearance. So Miss Winchel drifted about on the moonglade, turning her pearl in its gleam, and dreamed she was born in an oyster-shell in the South Pacific, and had silver hands and coral lips and sapphire eyes and hair like the Golden Fleece, whatever that was; her song was sweeter than the screel of seagulls, and men young and old forgot their girls' faces as they drank it in. What she sang was:

> 'Hither, sweet booby,
> Come hither to me,
> Your nose is a ruby
> As red as can be,
> I am your lady,
> Your pearl from the sea,
> Hither, my gaby,
> My booby, to me!'

'You've got a false rhyme there, miss,' said a voice from the shore. The voice of the Him.

Miss Winchel stopped floating, turned over, and paddled water till she stood on end. In her most dulcet tones she called across the ripple: 'I'd be sorry for myself if I was you.'

'I'd be sorrier,' said He, 'if I was you.'

Miss Winchel was charmed. 'Yah!' said she.

'I can't help that,' said He. 'You've got a bad ear.'

Miss Winchel rubbed the ache where the pen pressed heavy. 'How did you know?' she asked.

'I've a good ear myself, miss. Lady and Gaby's a false rhyme, if you don't mind me mentioning it.'

'I don't a bit,' said Miss Winchel. 'Why are they?'

'Well, because—— Well,' he began again, 'it's one of the things you *do* know if you're a poet born.'

'Is that you?'

'There was no help for it. My name's Septissimus. I'm the Seventh Son of a Seventh Son. That's why,' he explained, 'I can see you so plain, miss, where another would only see a bundle of seaweed. That's why I write poetry when I ought to be minding my business. That's why the Business doesn't pay. That's why She's leaving.'

'Hasn't She left then?' asked Miss Winchel, with one of the twiddly feelings darting through her. 'I thought She must of.'

'How's that, miss?'

'Well, she's been here every other night looking for a thing.'

'So *that's* where She sloped to after Closing-Time! What thing, if I might ask?'

'You might,' said Miss Winchel.

'I do.'

'Well,' said Miss Winchel reluctantly, 'a pearl pin.'

'Never!' said Sep.

'Ever,' Miss Winchel assured him. 'At least, half a moon.'

'Did she find it?'

'Oh no. She just said lots of sighs and Oh-dears and It's-too-bad-reellys and Ho-you-needn't-think-its and Not-if-you-arsked-on-your-bended-knees-not-muches. Tonight's the first one she didn't come to look for it.'

'It was my present to her,' said Sep. 'She must have liked it after all, you see, miss.'

'She wants it *very* much. But so,' said Miss Winchel, 'do I.' And she glimmered her beautiful treasure in the moonlight.

'What!' shouted Sep, and came into the water after it.

'Oh no, please Booby, you don't!' implored Miss Winchel, quickly making a fist to hide it in.

'I must, I must!' said Sep. 'Her fortnight's up to-night, and She's packing her box. I haven't known how to begin to bring Her round. You know how it is after a scrap-up, miss. But now you tell me She's missed her pin so badly, I'm sure if I took it back to Her she'd overlook it, and help me mind the Business.'

'What *is* the Business?' asked Miss Winchel.

'The Rye Inn, miss. Up yonder.' Septissimus pointed inland, to the golden hill with the full moon shining on it.

'Eee!' screeched Miss Winchel, 'is that rye, and is it yours?'

'Both, miss. But when my old dad pegged out, he shut one eye and said, "*You'll* never make it pay, Sep." Then he shut the other. And he was right. He used to attract the men, but I haven't his gift. She has—but I don't want Her to.'

'Does it make you feel twiddly?'

'A bit.'

'Jallasy, jallasy,' said Miss Winchel nodding.

'I suppose so. But what's the good, She says, of staying on, if She's not to be Barmaid. I'm not going to starve and you needn't think it, She says. You must get the men in somehow or other, She says. If I'd only my old dad's knack—but there, I haven't.'

'*I* have,' said Miss Winchel suddenly.

'You!'

'Let me!'

'Bit of a risk.'

'I want to swim in the golden rye on the hill.'

'It'd never work. A mermaid!'

'I want to be a barmaid.'

'It needs experience.'

'I'll give you my pearl if I can be your barmaid.'

'And what about Her?'

'She'll tell you what about,' said Miss Winchel, 'when you give her the pearl again. It'll settle your twiddles if I'm your barmaid instead of Her. Oh, take me out of the Winchel-Sea up to the Rye,' she wheedled, 'and see how I will charm the men, young and old!'

'But can you?'

'I've learned how.'

'Really?' said Sep doubtfully.

'Reelly. Didn't I you, booby?'

'Don't you flatter yourself!'

'I'd be hard put to it,' smiled Miss Winchel, 'to flatter *you*.'

'Copycat!'

'The pot called the kettle black,' mocked Miss Winchel.

'What do you mean by that?'

'Who the cap fits let them wear it,' said Miss Winchel lightly.

'Think yourself smart, don't you?'

'*You'll* have to smarten up a bit, before I'm seen walking with *you* on the Front on Sunday.' Miss Winchel tossed her head at him very archly, and to tell you the truth she was a little surprised at how natural it came to her. 'Aren't I *good* at it!' she cried.

'Fancy yourself, don't you?'

'You'd rather I fancied you, eh?'

'What *you* want,' chaffed Sep, ''s a good spanking.'

'Yah!' beamed Miss Winchel. And then she burst into tears.

'I say, I say,' said Sep, and waded right out to her, 'I was only in fun.'

Miss Winchel stopped weeping to wipe her wet face with her wetter hand, and asked: 'When what?'

'About the spanking.'

'Boo!' said Miss Winchel. 'It's not that. It's because I'm such a very *common* mermaid. I was only born in a winchel-shell, you know.'

'Winkle,' said Sep.

'Winchel,' she repeated meekly. 'I can't even speak right, you see. The mushel-men ignore me, the cochel-babies despise me, and the oyshter-mermaids don't even know things like me are.'

'*That* for the mussels and cockles and oysters,' said Sep. 'You're going to be popular with the populace, *you* are.'

'My hair's brown weed, and it ought to be green and gold. My eyes are pebbles, and they ought to be shappires.'

'But look at all the pretty rhymes to you,' said Sep. 'What can one say of an oyster but that it's moister? Or of mussels but that they tussle and hustle and bustle? And you can't say anything about cockles at all, without an effort. But a winkle! You twinkle and tinkle, the sea-spray you sprinkle, you smile like a rosebud about to uncrinkle——'

'Reelly?' said Miss Winchel, looking pleased.

'Really. Winkles are the flower of the foam.'

'Go along!' said Miss Winchel, looking pleased.

'People who call them winkles don't know. They are only winkles for short. Oysters may have their pearls, but winkles have their peris.'

'Is a peri better than a pearl?'

'You bet it is.'

'Does it charm men more?'

'You bet it does.'

Miss Winchel simpered. 'Then I may take it I have the place, though I *am* a common mermaid?'

'You'll be the uncommonest barmaid ever set eyes on,' said Sep, 'and I'll make you the famousest mermaid in Sussex. Men will come to you from far and near.'

'Will they forget their girls' faces along o' me?'

'You bet they will, whenever you say What's Yours.'

'And what will they say back?'

'Same Again, miss! Business will go up and up and up. Excuse me,' said Sep, 'but isn't that my fountain-pen you've got behind your ear?'

'It *is* a pen, but I didn't know it was a founching one,' said Miss Winchel. 'Oh, take *care*, Mr Sep, that's my bad ear, I'll thank you to know.'

But Septissimus was already scribbling an inspiration on the back of an unpaid bill, and standing upright in the water face to face with her, he read her what he had written under the moon.

Winkle a ree!
Winkle a rye!
I'll give you a kingdom if you'll never cry.
Princes and ploughmen
Shall fall into line
And come to you quick when you give them the sign.
Winkle a rye!
Winkle a ree!
Come in to the cornfield, come out of the sea.
Poets and pedlars
Whenever they're dry
Shall drink at the sign of the Mermaid of Rye.

'Oo-er!' remarked Miss Winchel. 'I can't think how you do it, Mr Sep.'

'You can drop the Mister, Miss Winchel.'

'Call me Perry,' said Miss Winchel sweetly. 'Fair's fair, I always say, don*chu*?'

'Time to be getting along,' said Septissimus.

'You'll have to carry me,' said Miss P. Winchel. 'I don't do walking.'

She paddled to the water's edge, where Septissimus picked her up and bore her away. All the winkles in Sussex gathered to see her go, chickering and chackering: 'Good luck, Miss Winchel!' while she waved her skinny hands to them and screamed: 'Good-bye, my winchels! Good-bye, my Winchel-Sea! When Old Limpet wakes mind you tell him I've bided my opening-time, and am gone to charm men young and old!'

And so she did, and so she does, to this day. No mermaid ever born equalled the name and fame of the Mermaid of Rye. The winkles were right. She is a perfect wonder.

Postlude in the Daisy-Field

I

T HE last six daisy-chains turned into white-and-gold necklets.

'Done!' cried Sylvia.

'Done!' cried Stella, Sophie, Selina, and Sue.

'Done!' said Sally.

'Done!' said Martin Pippin.

'Not you yet,' said Sue firmly.

'Are not my six tales told?'

'The rule *was*——' began Sue; but Martin interrupted her. 'Not so fast. Presently I shall remember what the rule was. But first, I must guess Sylvia.'

'Don't be too sure,' said she cheekily.

'How can I fail?'

Sylvia reminded him: 'You've failed five times.'

'There was once a blind man,' said Martin Pippin, 'and they gave him six cups and six saucers, and said: "Put the blue cup on the blue saucer; put the green cup on the green saucer; put the red cup on the red, the yellow cup on the yellow, and the pink cup on the pink saucers; and last of all, put the white cup on the white saucer." '

Sylvia. Did he?

Sue. It wasn't likely, was it? The chances were all against it, weren't they?

Martin. To begin with they were, and the blind

man made five bad shots in the dark. But they made a little mistake that sent the last shot home for keeps.

Sylvia (uneasily). What did they do?

Martin. They put the blue cup in his hands and said: 'Find the blue saucer,' and when he put it on the yellow saucer they said: 'No, silly! *this* is the blue saucer'—and they took the blue cup and saucer away and said: 'Here is the pink cup, find the pink saucer,' which the poor man missed again. Then they said: 'That's the green saucer, stupid, *this* is the pink saucer.' And they took the pink cup and saucer away.

Sylvia. Oh.

Martin. Oh indeed. For at last only the white cup and saucer were left. And even a blind man can put one and one together.

Sally. If he didn't kick the saucer out of his reach.

Martin. Nobody asked you to put your oar in.

Sue. I don't understand a bit about the cups and saucers. What *you've* got to do is to guess whose mother Sylvia's is. Don't you *see*?

Martin. I have a glimmer, after five bad shots in the dark. Am I mistaken, or did you not tell me, Sue, that your mother is Jane?

Sue. Well, she is, you know.

Martin. I knew when you told me, you know. And Stella refuses to have any mother but Joscelyn, and Sophie declares she is Joyce's, and Selina admits to Jennifer, and Sally is no one's but Joan's. When five out of six are paired, what remains? Perhaps Sylvia, that asker of questions, can answer this one.

Sylvia (desperately). Ultimathooly!

Martin. I beg your pardon?

Sylvia. You promised to tell me what Ultimathooly was.

Martin. I will tell you when you are standing on the Guessing Stump.

Sylvia. You know what this means, don't you? It means going to bed by myself, every night till I die, while the others go on playing outside. *Always*, for ever and ever.

Stella (*furiously*). It shan't, Syl. If he guesses you, I'll come to bed too.

Sophie (*comfortingly*). Me too.

Selina (*resignedly*). And me.

Sue (*reluctantly*). And me.

Sally (*confidently*). And me. But he *might* kick the saucer.

Sue. What saucer?

Sally. Jessica.

Stella. You little *idiot*.

Sue. Yes, you *are* silly, Sally. How can Sylvia's mother be a saucer?

Sophie. Now you've done it, Sue!

Selina. P'r'aps he wasn't listening, were you, Martin?

Martin. I listened with all my ears, in hopes of a clue.

Stella (*gloomily*). Then it's bed for one and all of us.

A great depression came over the daisy-field. Sylvia looked round at her five playfellows, and Stella was looking Bother-it, and Sophie was looking Can't-be-helped, and Selina was looking What-a-pity, and Sue was looking I-don't-want-to, and Sally was looking I-wonder. So Sylvia looked Who-cares, and said: 'I shan't let you. It doesn't matter. I don't mind a bit really.'

'Do you think we'd desert you?' demanded Stella fiercely.

'This,' said Martin Pippin, 'is simply blackmail.'
He put his fingers in his ears, and made his unwilling
way across the daisy-field; but Sylvia strode bravely
before him, and when he reached the Guessing Stump
she was ready for him. Her eyes were brighter than
usual, Martin thought. She faced him squarely, saying: 'Be quick about it.'

'Don't rush me,' said Martin. 'What's that smear
on your cheek?'

'Bit of dirt, I expect,' said Sylvia. 'Go on! you
heard them say Jessica.'

'One mustn't believe all one hears. Why is the back of your hand wet?'

'Spot of rain, I expect,' said Sylvia, wiping her hand hastily on her pinafore.

'Is that all you expect? Or do you really expect me to guess Jessica? Nothing is more misleading than a clue.'

Sylvia clasped her hands, and breathed hard and hopefully.

'Am I not to take the *artfulness* of children into account?'

'But,' quavered Sylvia, 'if only the white saucer is left?'

'One of these days,' Martin warned her, 'that inquiring mind of yours will land you in trouble. As for saucers, we know how crockery gets chipped in the bowl. Many a tea-cup ends up oddly matched, and blind men never know the difference. Therefore, Sylvia——' Martin interrupted himself to kick at something or other and send it flying over the Murray River. 'Therefore,' he concluded, 'I shall guess that you are *my* child, and not Jessica's.'

'Oh, Martin!' shrieked Sylvia, 'you are a *pet!*' She flung her arms round his neck. 'I wouldn't really mind if you *were* my father.'

'I'm not?'

'You know you're not. You knew you weren't. What did you kick just then?'

'An obstacle in the way of Ultimathooly. Ultimathooly, Sylvia, is the farthest bourne. It is the horizon of man's universe: farther than he can go, very nearly farther than he can see, and exactly as far as he can think. For Miss Winchel it was once the rim of a winkle-shell. When she came out of the shell,

it was the edge of rye on the hill. For you it is bedtime.' He gave her his daisy. 'There, Sylvia. Bedtime
is now so distant, that though you may dream of it
you will never reach it again.'

'Is Ultimathooly a bad or a good thing?' asked
Sylvia.

'You won't know till you get there,' said Martin
Pippin.

'Did Miss Winchel like getting to *her* Ultimathooly?'

'For all I know to the contrary,' said Martin, 'when
Miss Winchel got to Rye she looked back at Winchel-
Sea, and saw her Ultima Thule lying behind her.
There's no pinning the wretched thing down. Perhaps as your eyes go round the far horizon (skipping
black bedtime) there's some gold or rosy place where
you'd like to be.'

'Yes,' said Sylvia, 'there is.'

'May I be told?'

'It's an apple-orchard.'

'One day,' said Martin Pippin, 'when you are there,
you may look back and find it's a daisy-field.'

*

They went to tell the good news that little girls
need never go to bed again.

There was joy among the daisies.

II

Martin Pippin lolled in the grass, with his head on
the clothes-basket. The green had faded out of the
sky and the field, and the stars were as many as daisies

in the dark. The children were picking up their chains in fragments.

'The rule *was*,' Martin remembered, 'a song to go to sleep on. A song apiece. But how is it to be done? There is to be no more sleep on earth for ever and ever. I wonder,' he mused, as the children stole round the basket, 'what it feels like, never to go to bed again. What are you doing there?'

'We're giving our chains to Sib,' whispered Sophie. 'Hush!'

'What does she want with your chains?' asked Martin, in his ordinary voice.

'She's too little to make them herself, you know. Do be quiet,' whispered Sue.

'What for?' asked Martin.

'She might be asleep,' whispered Selina. 'What a pity chains break so.'

'Fixed ideas are not more breakable,' said Martin. 'If Sib is asleep, it's time to wake her up.'

'*Wake the baby!*' whispered Sally, in an astonished whisper. 'You mustn't *ever* wake the baby. There, darling.'

'But how do you know she doesn't want to be waked?'

'It's not what she *wants*,' whispered Stella, more like a hiss, 'it's what's *good* for her. Don't speak so loud.'

'Talk of dogs in mangers!' exclaimed Martin.

'*Can't* you shut up?' whispered Sylvia. 'There now, she's wide awake.'

'It is my belief,' said Martin, 'that she has been all the time. Oughtn't she to be fetched indoors, by the way? Whose child is she?'

The little girls crammed their fists over their

mouths. Suppose he had heard them giggle? They dropped in a ring round the basket, and stretched out their hands for daisies in the dark.

'What are you up to now?' asked Martin Pippin.

'We're going to begin some new chains, of course,' said Sue.

'Hadn't you better wait till the morning?' said Martin.

'We don't have to wait till morning any more,' Sophie reminded him. 'Isn't it lovely! Lo-ovely!' she yawned.

'Lo-ovely!' murmured Sylvia.

'Lo-oo-ovely!' drawled Selina.

'I wish you wouldn't yawn,' yawned Stella. 'It's catching. I can't seem to see any daisies,' she complained.

'I can,' said Sally, blinking, 'but they're shut up.'

'Daisies do at night, you know,' mumbled Sue, rubbing her eyes.

'I had an idea they did,' said Martin Pippin, 'as the sheep came to fold.'

Then he sang:

> 'The black-nosed Southdown sheep do keep
> The Southdowns cropped as any lawn.
> The grazing of the Sussex sheep
> Begins upon the Downs at dawn.
> But when the evening sky grows gold
> The Ewes come down again to fold,
>   And sleep.'

Sue (*very drowsily*). What's that, Martin?

Martin (*very softly*). A song to go to sleep on.

Sue. I'm *not* a cup, and my mother *isn't* a saucer, you know.

Martin leaned over her, and took the daisy from her right ear. 'Sweet dreams, Sue,' he whispered. 'Dream you are skipping the new moon in on Caburn.'

He sang again:

> 'The Moon, the lovely Moon,
> When the town's asleep,
> In all her silver beauty
> Wanders down the steep,
> Wanders down the steep
> Unseen by you and me
> In all her silver beauty
> To walk upon the sea.'

Selina (*drawling worse than ever*). If I walked on the sea, I'd sink.

Martin. Deep as oblivion. But sleep is deeper than the sea, and a child can walk upon it like a moonbeam.

Selina. See me go. Come too.

Martin. If you like. But even I shan't know it.

And leaning over her, he took the daisy from her ear, saying: 'Sweet dreams, Selina, as high as the moon on Wilmington, and as deep as the Birling Sea.'

A third time he sang:

> 'In Gillman's Orchard in Billingshurst
> Nightingales always sing the first;
> Under the apple-trees all night long
> You can lie in the grass and hear their song.
>
> And through the apple-bloom pink and white
> Two or three stars will be in sight,
> Like the highest, roundest, loveliest notes
> Gone up to the sky from the nightingales' throats.'

Sylvia. Is that what it's like in apple-orchards?

Martin. It was like that in one apple-orchard I knew once.

Sylvia. When?

Martin. Too far off for me to remember. It's Ultimathooly now.

But she didn't hear that, as he leaned over and took the daisy from her ear, whispering: 'Sweet dreams, Sylvia. Dream of tea-cups and apples, and winkles, and rye, and anything else you want to know about, for you've gone where the answers to all things are.'

And he sang his fourth song:

> 'The pool has caught a star
> And a moth flies through the night.
> When morning wakes, our dreaming breaks
> All in the clear day-light.'

Sophie. Good morning, Martin.

Martin. All in good time.

Sophie. Oh, isn't it? How funny. I thought it was. The moon's as bright as day.

Martin. Then go out to play with the Pharisees.

Sophie. If I knew where to find them.

Martin. Just round the corner.

She never felt him take the daisy from her ear, as he whispered into it: 'Sweet dreams, Sophie, of the fairy circus. Fly through the hoop and juggle with the world.'

Then he sang his fifth song:

> 'Moon-Come-Out
> And Sun-Go-In,
> Here's a soft blanket
> To cuddle your chin.
>
> Moon-Go-In
> And Sun-Come-Out,
> Throw off your blanket
> And bustle about.'

Stella. What's the blanket for? You only have blankets when you go to bed. I'm not going to bed. Lying down in the grass isn't going to bed. Anybody can lie down in the grass by day. I often do. Why shouldn't I?

Martin. There is every reason why you should. Would you like my coat?

Stella. Well, nobody would call a coat a blanket, would they?

Martin. They would be making a great mistake if they did.

He laid his coat over her shoulders, and as he tucked it in he stole her daisy, whispering: 'Sweet dreams, Stella. Dream of the silliest thing you ever heard in your life, for only in dreams will you wide-awake ones get your chance to agree that kings may be pawns, women be treasures, and coats be blankets.'

Then Martin Pippin sang his sixth and last song to go to sleep on.

> 'The starlings sleep under the shed,
> The swallows sleep under the eaves,
> The lark in the grass makes her bed,
> The robin tucks down in the leaves.
>
> The finch shuts his eye in the hedge,
> The elm rocks the rook to his rest,
> The moorhen dreams deep in the sedge,
> The wren has a hole to her nest—
>
> A little wee hole like a mouse,
> As secret as secret can be,
> And she slips in and out of her house
> Where nobody sees her but me.'

Sally. Doesn't the wren never go to sleep?

Martin. Now and then she pretends to.

Sally (*looking very like a wren*). Peep-peep! Was the cup-and-saucer man blind actually?

Martin. He was only a blind man by the rule of Buff. He had a handkerchief tied over his eyes.

Sally. He could have peeped if he'd liked, then.

Martin. He didn't even try. If anything, he pulled the handkerchief tighter.

Sally. Yes, well, I'm going to pretend to go to sleep now.

Martin. Don't peep.

He took the daisy from behind her ear, and whispered: 'Sweet dreams, Sally. Trot along to the place where all things are one, from the pig in the sty to the saint in the sky.'

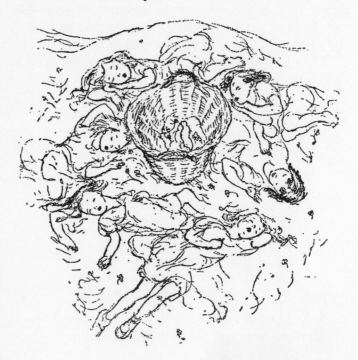

The stillness of sleep lay on the daisy-field. Its stillness could be heard in the breathing of the six children, who lay, each a little heap in the grass, with their eyes shut as tight as the six daisies on Martin Pippin's palm. Idly he made a little chain of them, and while he did so his thoughts came full circle.

'I came to send my child to its dreams,' he said, 'and none of these children is mine. I had better have gone looking for my child in the moon.'

Shaking his head at his own foolishness, he rose to drop his daisy-ring in Sib's basket. He moved very softly, so as not to wake her. But she was staring up at the moon with her eyes that knew all.

Epilogue

THE BABY IN THE CLOTHES-BASKET

I

'So,' said Martin Pippin, 'it's you, is it?'

Sib clutched the daisies without looking at him.

Martin brazened it out. 'I knew it all the time.'

Sib moved her eyes from the moon to his face and back again.

'It's a wise child, Sib, that knows its own father, and you are the wisest child I ever saw. But would your mother, whose name I have forgotten, let you eat those daisies?'

Martin saw Sophie, Sally, Selina, Stella, Sylvia, and Sue disappear down Sib's throat.

'I hope you know what's good for you,' said Martin. 'I am sure I don't, and if you want to swallow your little friends, do, my daughter. They were troublesome children, and deserve no better fate. Six into one make seven. Oughtn't you to lie over and go to sleep now?'

Sib went on staring unwinkingly at the moon.

'You insist on your tale and your song like the rest of them, do you? What can I say or sing wise enough for you, while you lie there saying nothing as hard as Little Jenkyn and I stand here saying anything as easy as Uncle Nicodemus, when he sat in his big arm-chair smoking his pipe, and Little Jenkyn sat on the foot-stool at his feet eating his bread-and-milk. They were

S i b

very happy together, not saying a word to each other
while one puffed his tobacco and the other ate his
supper. Presently a shrill voice called down the stairs:
'Nicodemus! Nicodemus!'

'Yes, my dear?' said Uncle Nicodemus from the
arm-chair.

'Nicodemus! when you went out this afternoon, did
you remember to . . .'

'No, my dear!' said Uncle Nicodemus from the
arm-chair.

The shrill voice called: 'That's you all over!' and a
door banged, and they heard no more. Little Jenkyn
took another spoonful of bread-and-milk, and Uncle
Nicodemus took another puff at his pipe.

'It's a very queer thing,' said Uncle Nicodemus, 'that when I want to remember something in particular, I can't remember anything at all. But when I'm trying to remember nothing at all, I remember all sorts of queer things that you wouldn't believe.'

Little Jenkyn stopped with his spoon in mid-air, and looked inquiringly at Uncle Nicodemus.

'Such as, for instance,' went on Uncle Nicodemus, 'I didn't remember to do what she told me to do today, and to save the life of me I can't remember now what it was I forgot to do. BUT,' said Uncle Nicodemus, 'sitting here so peaceful along o' you, Little Jenkyn, I'm remembering a dozen queer things at once.'

Little Jenkyn's mouth was so full that he couldn't make a sound; but he looked deeply interested, and Uncle Nicodemus went on.

'I remember,' said Uncle Nicodemus, 'when the Cook sold the basting-spoon by accident to the Rag-and-bone-man, and ran away for fear of a scolding, with the roast going dry on the spit, when, as good luck would have it, a passing buffalo looked in at the window and offered to baste the roast for three brass buttons and a china door-knob; and I remember he basted that joint with his own tail dipped in candle-grease, and when it came to table my Grandmother's nose turned blue at the very first mouthful; and I remember we couldn't think *what* to do till the Cuckoo-clock struck seven minutes past three, when it flashed on everybody present that she could be cured by standing on her head in the middle of a snow-storm; and I remember that, it being the month of June, when snow-storms are scarcer than they ought to be, we called a cab to take the old lady to the North Pole, to

which the Cabman said "Quack! quack!" and on looking at him we saw he was a Canvasback Duck. And
I remember that when we'd tucked my Grandmother
into the Cab, with her nose in the bluebag to keep it
warm on the way, and twopenn'orth of acid-drops to
amuse herself with, the Duck hoisted the Canvas, and
away they sailed and never came back any more. But
I remember a man I met years later at a Soap-bubble
party given by the Queen of Pennsylvania, who told
me he'd just come from the North Pole, where he'd
seen my Grandmother standing on her head on an
iceberg in the heaviest snow-storm of the season; and
her nose was bluer than ever. And I remember that
this man, who had the unusual name of Waterproof
Brown, swallowed his clay pipe in his excitement and
lay choking in the Queen's arms, with soap-bubbles
as big as gas-globes coming out of his mouth. And
I remember that just as he was at the last gasp, the
Queen's Greengrocer said . . .'

'Nicodemus! Nicodemus!' cried the shrill voice on
the stairs.

'Yes, my dear,' said Uncle Nicodemus.

'Here's the Stores man just come and delivered
everything I told you to get this afternoon: the Sunday
joint, the basting-spoon, the buttons, the china, the
candles, the Reckitt's blue, the clock, the ice, the duck,
the acid-drops, the soap, the pens, the brown water-
proofing, the clay pipe, the gas-globes and the greens
for dinner. What a memory you've got, to be sure.
I never saw such a memory in my life! Why, you remembered absolutely everything. Whatever did you
mean by saying you'd forgotten them?'

'I don't remember, my dear,' said Uncle Nicodemus
from the arm-chair.

'Isn't that you all over!' called the shrill voice on the stairs; and then they heard the door bang.

'That's what comes,' said Uncle Nicodemus, 'of stopping at the Queen's Arms on the way home.'

And Uncle Nicodemus went on with his pipe, and Little Jenkyn with his bread-and-milk.

Lie over, Sib.

No? The tale was too short for bedtime? Then let us call it a sample of the understanding which existed between Uncle Nicodemus and Little Jenkyn, who comprehended each other so perfectly, while the owner of the shrill voice comprehended neither of them. She was a native of Henfield, and had carried her voice to the World's End, where infantile wisdom and ancient simpleness meet. It shall be heard no more in the story.

Come, Sib, let us go with

UNCLE NICODEMUS AND
LITTLE JENKYN

In Search of Wisdom

UNCLE NICODEMUS and little Jenkyn lived to-
gether at the World's End, which some Africans
think is in Africa, certain Asiatics believe to be in
Asia, many Americans swear is in America, a few
Australasians suppose to be in Australasia, and all
Europeans know to be in Chelsea.

But in point of fact the thinkers, the believers, the
swearers, the supposers, and the know-alls, are wrong.

The World's End is in Sussex. And for those who have never tripped up on it, let me say that if you stand on Oldland Hill it will be to the north of you, and if you pitch on Godley's Green it will be to the west of you, and if you dwell in Folly's Farm it will be to the south of you, and from Freeks it is due east and almost next door to you.

But if you live at the World's End itself, it leads to anywhere and everywhere; to oldness, and godliness, to folly and freakishness, and to many other places and things besides. And it was from the World's End, Sib, that Uncle Nicodemus and Little Jenkyn went forth in search of the wisdom you were born with.

*

Uncle Nicodemus sat reading his Encyclopaedia. Little Jenkyn sat reading his Alphabet. Uncle Nicodemus read the last Z in his book, and closed it with a bang; which made Little Jenkyn look up from the first A in *his* book.

'Jenkyn,' said Uncle Nicodemus, 'let us go in search of wisdom, for I cannot find it at home. Get your hat.'

Little Jenkyn put his toy goose in between the pages of his book, to mark where he'd got up to, and went for his hat. Uncle Nicodemus took his stick, and they left the house together.

Now the World's End stands at the cross-roads, and in the very first minute of his search, Uncle Nicodemus found himself brought up short by a problem.

'Here, Jenkyn,' said he, 'are three wrong roads and one right one. What shall we do to discover the one that is right? Truly, truly, the road to wisdom is hard to find.'

As he spoke, a man came tapping his way along the hedge, a man whose eyes were in his ears, for he was blind. Hearing Uncle Nicodemus, he stopped and asked: 'Is it the road to Truleigh you're seeking, master?'

'Truly, that's the road we want to take,' said Uncle Nicodemus.

'Go five mile west-and-a-bit,' said the blind man, 'and five mile south-and-a-bit, and you won't be far off it.'

'Far off where, my friend?'

'The tumulus on Truleigh Hill, master, where the men of the nations gather to speak what's true. I know, for I've come from there.'

'And what did they tell you?'

'To go east to Morning's Mill by Pevensey Levels; for there,' said the blind man, 'they say I may wash my eyes bright again.'

'Truly?' asked Uncle Nicodemus.

'Truly, master. May you hear something as good as I have heard this day on Truleigh Hill.'

Uncle Nicodemus gave the blind man a pinch of shag, and Little Jenkyn gave him an acid-drop, and so they parted, one to the east and two to the west.

Presently Little Jenkyn's legs began to flag, so Uncle Nicodemus carried him pick-a-back; and the figure that climbed Truleigh Hill at noon looked from behind like one man, with very old legs and a very young head.

Just as they reached the tumulus, a thunder-cloud rolled its dark blue tide over the sun, and the earth below turned strange colours of green and yellow, that were luminous with a light of their own.

'Jenkyn,' said Uncle Nicodemus, 'it has started to spit, and truly I think it would be wisdom to go into that barn over there.'

And into the barn they went.

They were not the only people who had thought it wise to come in out of the rain. Four others were there before them. One was a young man with a dark skin, one was a middle-aged man with a fur cap, one was an old man with apple-cheeks, and one was a man with slant-eyes and a pigtail. The age of this man it was impossible to tell; sometimes he looked like a new-born babe, and sometimes older than any man that ever was. The first was an Italian, the second was a Russian, the third was an Englishman, and the fourth a Chinaman.

Uncle Nicodemus wished them 'Good Day,' and each answered in his own tongue.

'Eh? eh? eh?' said Uncle Nicodemus. He said it three times, because he did not speak Russian, or Italian, or Chinese. The only answer he understood was the apple-cheeked Englishman's, who said: 'Welcome.' Little Jenkyn looked in their faces and smiled. The four faces reflected his smile, and there was no need of words between them. All five smiles said 'Welcome' as plain as anything.

'Sit you down, man and child,' said the Englishman, 'and tell us what's brought you here.'

'The hunt for wisdom brought us up the hill,' said Uncle Nicodemus, 'and the rain brought us into this barn.'

'Then the rain did you a good service,' said the Englishman, 'for in this barn sit four wise men. We were just arguing which of our countries had wrapped up the greatest wisdom in a few words.'

'What tongue were you arguing in?' asked Uncle Nicodemus.

'I forget,' said the Englishman. 'All four of us speak all the tongues on earth.'

'Then go on arguing in plain English,' said Uncle Nicodemus.

'Very well,' said the apple-cheeked old man, 'and you and the child shall be the judge of it.'

Uncle Nicodemus sat down on a heap of hay, took Little Jenkyn on his knee, and said: 'Bring out your parcels of wisdom.'

The apple-cheeked old Englishman said: 'In my country we have a saying: Three may keep Counsel if Two be Away.'

'In mine,' said the dark-skinned young Italian, 'we say: A Burden which one Chooses is not Felt.'

'We say in mine,' said the fur-capped Russian, 'A Word is not a Bird, once Flown you can never Catch it.'

'If you have Two Loaves,' observed the Chinaman, 'sell One and buy a Lily.'

Having spoken, they fixed their eyes on Uncle Nicodemus, and waited for him to pronounce which of these bits of wisdom was the wisest. Uncle Nicodemus scratched his head.

'To tell you the truth,' said he, 'I'm not quite sure what any of your sayings means. All four seem empty to me.'

'Then each of us will fill his saying with a tale,' said the Englishman, 'to throw a light on it and prove its wisdom.'

'Tell your tale first,' agreed Uncle Nicodemus, 'and let me and Little Jenkyn hear how three may keep counsel if two be away.'

The apple-cheeked Englishman opened his lips, and began.

MANY years ago there was a Sussex man called John Hammond, who had a wife, a child, and a secret. He lived, with Jane his wife and Dick his son, in a cottage in a field, both of which belonged to Farmer Moggridge, for whom he worked. It was Hammond's ambition to own the cottage and the field himself. The farmer had named his price, and for ten years Hammond had been saving it up in his tobacco-jar. Into this he put sixpence a week from his wages, any little extras made from odd jobs after hours, Jane's earnings from lace-making, and Dick's from mushroom-gathering. He was just sixpence short of the mark, when he came back to supper one night, full of his secret.

'What do you think, Jane,' he said, sitting down to his cheese and onion, 'there's bricks in our field!'

'Bricks?' said she.

'Bricks!' said he. 'You know that overgrown dip by the hollow oak at the far end of the hazel copse? Well, as I was coming along through the nettles, I stumbled on something hard. I stooped, thinking to find a stone and I found this.' And Hammond placed on the table a beautiful red hand-made brick.

'Well I never did!' said Jane.

'But you soon shall do,' said Hammond jovially, 'for I examined farther, and that queer dip in the field is one of the old brick-kilns of long ago, overgrown and forgotten. From what I can see, there's enough bricks there to build a fine house, and over and above that bricks to sell. Those hand-made bricks fetch a good price now, when they can be got. It isn't a brick-kiln, it's a gold-mine, is this field of ours.'

'It's not ours yet, dad,' said Dick.

'Come Saturday it will be though,' said Hammond, 'when I put the last sixpence to Moggridge's price. Keep counsel, you two, not a word of this to a soul.'

'Not a word!' cried Jane and Dick in one breath. And all three went to bed hugging their secret.

The next day Jane went to buy some soda at the village shop, kept by Miss Pounce. Miss Pounce was one for a gossip, and while Jane was counting her change, she heard all the news.

'Mrs Moggridge has a new black satin mantle,' said Miss Pounce, 'and my nephew, the one that works for Farmer Batty you know, is getting a new thatch to his cottage, and a pig-sty as well. But then,' said Miss Pounce, 'he has a good master, not like that skinflint your husband works for. 'Tis a sin Moggridge doesn't thatch that roof of yours instead of buying satin mantles for his missus, for after all,' said Miss Pounce, 'she had a new black alpaca dress only last March.'

'Pooh!' laughed Jane, 'I'll soon be having a new silk dress myself, and we'll not need to be beholden to Mr Moggridge for a new roof, a new sty, or a new house.'

'How's that?' asked Miss Pounce.

'Well, if you won't tell a soul——' said Jane; and she leaned over the counter and did a bit of whispering.

That same morning, Dick Hammond lost six good marbles to Bob Moggridge at school.

'That clears *you* out,' said Bob tauntingly.

'Pooh!' said Dick, 'what's a few old marbles? I'll soon have enough marbles to fill both my pockets.'

'How's that?' asked Bob.

'Ah, wouldn't you like to know!'

'I know this much,' jeered Bob, 'you're saying more than your prayers. How's a poor man like your dad going to buy you pocketfuls of marbles?'

'Why, you musn't let on to anybody,' said Dick, 'but——' And he too did a bit of whispering.

The consequence was, that when at the end of the week John Hammond added the last sixpence to the tobacco-jar and carried the price of the property to the farmer, Mr. Moggridge said: 'You're too late, Hammond, I sold that field yesterday for five times the price to Barton the Builder. There's bricks in that field.'

'How came you to know?' asked Hammond, very downcast.

'My missus had it from Miss Pounce, who had it from *your* missus,' said Farmer Moggridge, 'and my boy Bob had it from your own son's mouth.'

'Ah,' muttered John Hammond, 'three may keep counsel if two be away.'

And when, in the new field he was moved to, he dug and found oil, he kept his own counsel, and told neither wife nor child till the field was bought and paid for.

'Now,' said the apple-cheeked Englishman to Uncle Nicodemus, 'is not that the best of wisdom?'

'Before I call it best,' said Uncle Nicodemus, 'I must hear what the rest have to say. Let the Italian here tell us why a burden that one chooses is not felt.'

'With pleasure,' said the dark-skinned young man.

The Light Burden

ELISA, her husband Marco, and her little boy Beppo, lived in the village of San Domenico on the hill. With them lived Neddo, their donkey, who one evening, after he had carried a double load of charcoal to the house, fell lame. This was a nuisance, for the next day was market-day, when Neddo's panniers were piled with olives and lemons and figs and persimmons to be sold in Florence, at the foot of the long hill.

'Tomorrow we must carry the baskets ourselves, that's all!' said Marco.

'I'll come too, and help!' cried Beppo.

'Little darling!' said Elisa, who thought the child the very best child in the world.

Next morning they set off gaily down the hill, Marco with a basket of lemons on his back, Elisa with another of persimmons, and Beppo with his own small basket full of figs. Beppo was very proud of himself, and strutted along, boasting: 'I am as strong as Neddo! We don't need Neddo at all!' Then he spied a toy milk-cart, quite a big one, lying by the roadside; it was broken, and evidently the rich man's son who had left it there had no more use for it. But Beppo thought it the finest treasure he had ever seen.

'Oh, let's take it with us!' he cried.

'No, Bambino,' said his father, 'we have too much already; we'll hide it under this old wall, and take it on our way back.'

In Florence they sold half the lemons, half the persimmons, and all the figs. With the money, Elisa
bought some things she needed at home, pots and
pans, a tall rolling-pin to make macaroni with, a pair
of boots, a hammer, and three pounds of rice. On
her own back she carried the basket with persimmons and lemons in it, on Marco's she strapped the
other basket full of the hard heavy things, and the rice
she gave Beppo to carry. Then they started to walk
the miles up the hill.

Soon Beppo began to cry. It was the end of the day,
not the beginning, the hill went up instead of down,
and his basket tired his wrist.

'I don't want to carry it any more, it's such a
burden!' he sobbed.

'Give it to me then,' said Marco, and took it from
him. After a bit they came to the hiding-place of the
milk-cart, and Beppo rushed to the wall and dragged
it out.

'Look, Papa, look!'

'Let it alone,' said Marco, 'we've enough as it
is.'

'But Papa, I want it!'

'My strong little donkey,' said Marco, 'if you want
it, you can carry it yourself.' Beppo picked up the
cart, and trudged on gaily.

Half a mile farther on Elisa stopped with a sigh.
'For goodness sake let's rest a bit,' she grumbled;
'my back will break if we don't. What a burden this
basket is!'

'Give it to me then,' said Marco. The second
basket was transferred to his own shoulders, and on
they went again. Half a mile farther Beppo sat down
in the road.

'Now what is it?' asked father.

'My legs are tired, Papa.'

'Put down that cart then.'

But Beppo hugged his toy. 'I'm not carrying it with my legs; my legs are tired because the road is steep. I want to be carried.'

'Little darling!' cried Elisa, and picked him up in her arms, milk-cart and all.

On they went, and Elisa sang to Beppo, and Beppo span the wheels of his cart and laughed. When they reached their home Elisa started getting supper, while Beppo played with his toy; but Marco went into the stable, scratching his head.

'Neddo,' he said, 'just you explain this. Beppo wept at carrying a basket weighing three pounds, and laughed at carrying a toy that weighed six. Elisa grumbled at a burden of fruit that may have weighed a stone, and sang while she was burdened with Beppo, who weighs three stone at least, not counting his milk-cart. What do you make of it, eh?'

'Master,' said Neddo, 'a burden which one chooses is not felt.'

'I see,' said Marco. 'Now tell me one thing more. Do *you* feel the burdens we put upon your back?'

'Do I not!'

'What, a strong beast of burden like you!'

'The burdens are your choice, not mine, master!'

'I see,' said Marco. 'And how is your lame leg doing?'

'Badly, thank you,' said Neddo, and blinked at his master. Or was it a wink?

'Now,' said the dark-skinned young Italian to Uncle Nicodemus, 'is not this excellent wisdom?'

'It seems so,' said Uncle Nicodemus, 'but the Russian's wisdom may be more excellent still. Let him tell us why a word is not a bird, and once flown can never be caught.'

'Then listen,' said the Russian.

A Word is not a Bird

MISCHA and Ivan were friends, and loved each other like brothers. This vexed the jealous Vassili, who was friends with no boy. He was a mischief-maker, this Vassili. He would go to Mischa and say: 'Do you know what Ivan said to me today? He said he was only your friend because you are stronger than he is, and can protect him when he is bullied.' 'That's what he said to you, is it?' laughed Mischa; 'when he says it to me, I'll believe it.' Then Vassili went to Ivan and said: 'What do you think I heard Mischa saying of you yesterday? That he only valued your friendship because you are cleverer than he is, and can help him with his lessons.' 'You heard him say that, did you?' scoffed Ivan; 'when *I* hear him say it, I'll know it to be true.'

Old Petroff the stone-breaker, who sat in the road outside the school, nodded to himself. 'Wise boys! wise boys! they know better than to trust the word of a mischief-maker—*that* word won't fly far!'

One day when Mischa was going through the wood, he heard the cry of a partridge attacked by a hawk. He ran to the spot, and caught the bird as it fluttered towards the earth. Its wing was slightly hurt, and he decided to take it home and nurse it in a cage. At that moment Ivan came running through the trees crying: 'Where is it? where is it?'

'Where is what?'

'The pretty partridge I saw pursued by a hawk—I mean to save it and take it home with me.'

'Aha!' laughed Mischa, 'but I was ahead of you, you see.'

Ivan's face fell a little—'But I saw it first, Mischa!'

'We can't claim all our eyes see,' said Mischa, good-humouredly, and carried the bird to his home, where his little sister Vera was sad because it was hurt, but Mischa told her it would fly again when the wing healed.

Now Vassili had been lurking in the wood when the thing happened, and he began telling the other boys how Ivan longed for the partridge, and how Mischa boasted of being first in the field. He sowed the idea of envy in the air, where an idea, my friends, sows itself as fast as dandelion seed. The boys chattered of it till Mischa and Ivan too picked up what was in the air, and a constraint fell between them.

One day Vassili, passing Mischa's house, saw the bird-cage hanging open outside the window, with not so much as a feather in it. He ran to the school crying: 'Mischa's bird has been stolen!' and the boys ran to Mischa laughing: 'Go and look at your bird-cage, Mischa! Ivan's got the better of you after all!'

When Mischa saw the empty cage his blood went to his head, and he rushed to Ivan's house crying: 'Give me back my bird!'

'I have not got your bird,' Ivan declared.

'Who else coveted it?' said Mischa angrily. 'Give it back, you thief!'

At the word 'Thief' Ivan turned as pale as Mischa was red; Mischa, still angry, went away, but felt as though he could have bitten his tongue out, all the same. Near his home, his little sister Vera ran and tugged his coat.

'Come quick,' she cried, 'and save the partridge again!'

'What do you mean?'

'You said it would fly when the wing was healed, so I tried today, to see, and it has only fluttered to a fork of the cherry tree, where I can't get it, and the hawk can.'

'Then it was *you* who opened the cage!' cried Mischa. His heart was heavy in him as he recaptured the partridge, and caged it safely; all the time the word 'Thief!' rang in his ears.

As he passed, Petroff the stone-breaker looked up. 'So you've caught your bird, eh, Mischa? But a word is not a bird, once flown it cannot be caught.'

Is not that good wisdom? If the tale does not satisfy you, let me add that Mischa, instead of going home, carried his bird straight to Ivan, saying: 'Take this, and call me anything you like.' Then Ivan looked at him and called him 'Friend!' and there was a second word flown after the first. And tell me now, have you ever heard better wisdom than *that*?

'Before I agree,' said Uncle Nicodemus, 'let the Chinaman tell us why, if you have two loaves, you should sell one and buy a lily.'

The Chinaman smiled blandly, and began his story.

Two Loaves and a Lily

Lo WING and Li Wong were poor men. They
had a hut to sleep in, and that was all. Each day
they had to consider how to get the loaf that keeps
life in the body. Sometimes the one and sometimes
the other got it. It was in one of the hard times when
food was scarce, and even those who had been rich
men did not prosper. So how could Lo Wing and
Li Wong hope to? In those times the rich were poor
and the poor were beggars. The loaf that was the life
of their bodies was their first thought on waking in
the morning, and they spent their day in getting it, to
divide between them in the evening. Then they slept
till morning. Then the thought of the loaf began
again.

One day Li Wong had luck. As usual, he and Lo
Wing had parted at the door of the hut and gone
different ways, for what cannot be found on one road
may be found on another. Li Wong had gone into the
city by the East Gate, and he had barely entered the
street when his toe struck something and sent it
spinning. Quickly he pounced on what his toe had
struck, for the sound of it told him it was a coin. And
so it was—exactly the price of his loaf. Full of delight
he ran to the loaf-seller's, but when he reached it he
stopped and stared. Just outside sat an old woman in
a blue dress, and on her knees was a pot with a lily in
it. It seemed to Li Wong, such was its beauty, that
he was looking at a lily for the first time in his life.

Perhaps he was. Who knows? Day after day we look on things we do not see. Then one day, all in a moment, we see them.

When the old woman perceived Li Wong gazing on her lily, she held it towards him persuasively. 'Buy?' said she. The lily on its green stem stood upright in the air; the shape of its petals, their colour and their texture, made the man's heart tremble within him. He forgot the hunger in his belly because of the new hunger in his soul. The old woman said 'Buy?' once more. 'How much?' whispered Li Wong. She named the price of a loaf of bread. Li Wong fingered the coin in his pocket, and then shook himself roughly. Could one starve? He hastened into the shop, and bought the loaf, and came out quickly, without looking at the lily-seller.

He found, or made, no more money that day, and at evening, when he returned to the hut, discovered that Lo Wing had been less lucky than he. 'If you had not got this loaf,' said Lo Wing, dividing it in two, 'we should have gone hungry to bed.' Li Wong nodded; he ate his bread, bit by bit; yet he went hungry to bed. He dreamed of the lily. He woke and saw the moon float over a hole in the roof, and he thought of the lily. He slept, and dreamed of the lily. In the morning, a small white shining cloud hung over the rice-fields. He thought of the lily. He avoided the city, and sought the day's loaf outside it. Again he was lucky. A farmer had some work to be done, and had sprained his foot. Li Wong stayed and helped him, and for what he did the farmer's wife gave him a loaf of her own baking. He put it in his shirt, and went back; but when the moon rose, he kept his eyes on the ground. From the hut door Lo Wing called: 'If you are dejected because you have made nothing, it does not matter. I have our loaf.' 'I too have our loaf,' said Li Wong slowly. 'You too! what luck! we have two loaves, one for today and one for tomorrow. We shall sleep with easy hearts tonight. Come in and eat.'

But Li Wong stammered: 'Wait! wait!' and turned and ran to the city as hard as he could. Would she be there? She was, and the pot was on her knees. She lifted her wrinkled face with a smile, and in her wrinkled hand the lily. 'Buy?' said she. 'How much?' whispered Li Wong. The lily was so beautiful that it seemed to him without price. But it was still the price of a loaf. 'I have no money,' said Li Wong hoarsely, 'but take this.' He gave her his loaf, and she gave him the lily. He carried it back to the hut, up-right, between his hands. When he came in, Lo Wing did not ask where he had been, he only looked at the lily and breathed: 'Oh!' The two beggars put the lily in its pot in the middle of the hut, where the moonlight fell upon it through the hole in the roof. They broke their loaf, and ate it, keeping their eyes on the lily, and they lay down satisfied in body and soul.

What do you think of Li Wong's wisdom, old man and child? Could one starve?

'Well, Little Jenkyn,' said Uncle Nicodemus, 'there are the four tales, and the four bits of wisdom they carry. What do *you* think?'

*

All the time the tales were being told, Little Jenkyn had been scribbling on a bit of slate he had found in the barn, with a piece of chalk he had found on Truleigh Hill. Now, when Uncle Nicodemus asked his opinion, Little Jenkyn looked up, then he looked down, and then he went on scribbling.

'In case your memory is short,' said Uncle Nicodemus, 'and very likely it is in such a short little person as you are, let me remind you of the four sayings.

The Englishman says: Three may keep Counsel if Two be Away.

The Italian says: A Burden which one Chooses is not Felt.

The Russian says: A Word is not a Bird, once Flown, you cannot Catch it.

And the Chinaman says: If you have Two Loaves, sell One and buy a Lily.

All these four sayings seem to me to be just as wise and just as foolish as one another. Perhaps if we put our heads together we shall come to a conclusion.'

Uncle Nicodemus put his head down to Little Jenkyn's head, and in so doing brought his eyes level with the slate.

'Bless my soul!' cried he to the four men, 'while you have been talking the child has been writing. He has not been listening to your tales at all!'

'Let us hear the child's writing,' said the Chinaman.

'It is in four pieces,' said Uncle Nicodemus, 'all in rhyme. The first piece says:

> 'Three who keep counsel,
> So people say,
> Only keep counsel
> When two are away.
> Take two from three,
> That will leave one,
> One can keep counsel
> If he tells none.'

'Bravo,' chuckled the Englishman. 'The child listened well to my story, and it is as plain as a pikestaff he thought it a wise one. The prize for wisdom is mine!'

'The second piece,' said Uncle Nicodemus, 'goes like this:

> 'My basket is heavy,
> My burden is dour,
> I don't choose to carry it
> More than an hour.

My baby is lovely,
My baby is light,
I choose to carry him
Morning and night.'

'Charming!' cried the Italian. 'The child took my story in perfectly, and it is clear as daylight he understood its wisdom. The palm goes to me.'

'The third is as follows,' said Uncle Nicodemus:

'A word may be a white bird, a word may be a black.
If you let a bird fly, perhaps you'll get it back;
If you let a word fly, you cannot stop its flight—
Keep your black word in the cage, and let fly the white.'

'Good!' exclaimed the Russian. 'The child knew what I was talking about, and let it sink in. The crown of wisdom is certainly mine.'

'Let us hear the fourth piece,' said the Chinaman; and Uncle Nicodemus read:

'A Loaf for a Lily. The mouth must be fed,
But the eyes and the spirit ask also for bread.
If you have two Loaves, give one then and there
In change for a Lily that someone can spare.
A Loaf for a Lily. 'Tis little to give.
By bread and by beauty we all of us live.'

'The child not only listened to my tale,' said the Chinaman, 'he understood it; and at least he found it as wise as the rest.'

'Then unless somebody can produce new wisdom,' said Uncle Nicodemus, 'we are just where we were.'

'Good day!' said four voices at once in the doorway of the barn; and in came a Burly Belgian, a Dumpy Dutchman, a Frivolous Frenchman, and a Smiling Serb.

★

'And a very good day!' said Uncle Nicodemus. 'You arrive in the nick of time. I and this child have come from the end of the world in search of wisdom, and each of our friends here has offered us his best. Sit down, if you please, and give us your opinion as to the wisest rule a man can live by.'

'I cannot do better,' said the Burly Belgian, 'than offer you a wise saying we have in my country, and it is this: A Good Neighbour is better than a Bag of Money.' And pulling a sausage out of his pocket, he bit off the end.

'In my country,' said the Dutchman, 'we say that More Belongs to Dancing than a Pair of Dancing Shoes,' and taking a round red cheese from his bag, he cut off a slice.

'In mine,' said the Frenchman, breaking a *brioche* in three parts, 'If the Triangles made a God they would give Him Three Sides.'

'And we say,' said the Serb, 'that Every Man Knows the Lining of his own Cloak.' And he took something out of his wallet and began to eat it, but what it was I can't tell you, because I don't know.

'There!' said Uncle Nicodemus, 'do you hear, Little Jenkyn? Instead of discovering wisdom in what we've already heard, we are given twice as much to think about. That is, if these last four sayings *are* wisdom, and not foolishness.'

'Let the others speak for themselves,' said the Frenchman. 'As for me, I'm prepared to defend my saying with a tale.'

'One more or less can't hurt,' said Uncle Nicodemus.

The Frenchman looked at the three parts of his *brioche*, and told the following tale.

If the Triangles made a God

ONCE upon a time, the world was in a state of confusion, because it couldn't find God. Where He had got to, nobody seemed to know, and the Things all came together and said: 'Since He is not there, we had better make Him.' And the Wind, blowing by, murmured: 'What does He look like?'

'That's an easy one,' said the Man, 'He has two legs, two arms, two eyes, a nose and a mouth.'

'You are very nearly right,' said the Lion, 'except that He has four legs, no arms at all, and a mane.'

'Of course He has no arms,' agreed the Wren, 'but He has only two legs, and you've left out the wings.'

'You've counted His legs wrong, Jenny,' buzzed the Bee, 'and you've forgotten His sting and His honeybag.'

'He hasn't got a honeybag,' hummed the Hornet.

'Yet He is full of honey,' said the Rose, 'and oh! His scent!'

'Just so!' said the Skunk. 'But I don't see where the honey comes in.'

'He is bright,' said the Sun.

'He moves,' said the Sea.

'Things grow in Him,' said the Earth.

'You are all of you wrong,' said the Monkey, 'except the Man. I agree with the Man. He is exactly like the Man said. Only, of course, He has a tail.'

The Man didn't look too pleased with the Monkey's

pat on the back. But he said: 'Well, we've all got our ideas, suppose we go away and make them.'

Which they did; and when they met again, and produced their ideas of God, it was found that the Man's had the shape of a man, and the Lion's of a beast, and the Wren's of a bird, and so on down to the Mite's in the cheese. And the Wind blowing by murmured: 'If the Triangles made a God they would give Him Three Sides.'

'How's that for wisdom?' said the Frenchman, swallowing the three parts of his roll all in one.

'I'll leave it till I've heard the Belgian here say why a good neighbour is better than a bag of money,' said Uncle Nicodemus.

'By all means,' said the burly Belgian, and finished his sausage and began his tale.

A Good Neighbour

THREE families lived in a lane. Their houses were separated by their fields and gardens to be sure, but they were the only families that did live in the lane, and you'd have to walk three miles in either direction to find other habitations. It was a lonely place, and if you settled down there you had to work to live, unless you were well-off before you came.

At the top of the lane lived Nicholas Moke and his old wife; at the bottom of the lane lived Joseph Baron and his nine children; and in the middle lived Felix Wappers, with Jeanne his wife, and Marie his daughter, and Paul his son. The Wappers had lived there always, in a comfortable home which Jeanne kept in as good order as Felix kept the land outside it. The Mokes had a superior sort of house which had been standing empty for some years; it was known that whoever bought it must have a bit of money behind him. The day they moved in old Madame Moke poked her head in its fine lace cap out of the window, and saw a woman standing at the door below with a basket on her arm.

'What's your business?' asked the old woman. 'I don't buy of tramps.'

Jeanne Wappers, for it was she, laughed heartily. 'Save us!' she cried, 'I've nothing to sell; but as you're new-comers and maybe have nothing in the house, I just ran across to ask you to accept these few lettuces and half a dozen eggs.'

'Well, you can leave 'em on the doorstep,' said Thérèse Moke suspiciously; Jeanne Wappers looked surprised and a trifle hurt, and she slowly laid her neighbourly offering on the step and went away. Then old Madame Moke said to her husband: 'That's what I call a busybody; no doubt she was making an excuse to get inside and nose round, and see what we have. Lock up your money-bags, Nicholas, for this is a lonely sort of place we've come to.'

And the Mokes neither visited nor invited their neighbours, the Wappers, but kept themselves to themselves, being looked after by a man and his wife, who acted as cook and coachman and everything else into the bargain.

As for the Wappers, they could take a hint as well as another; and being independent folk shrugged their shoulders at their fine neighbours and lived contented as before.

Then one day Marie Wappers came running in saying: 'There's such a big family moved into the old tumble-down cottage below us! The father has nine children, the oldest is thirteen, and the youngest is nine months.'

'And what of the mother?' asked Jeanne.

'There isn't a mother,' said Marie.

'Save us!' ejaculated Jeanne; and she filled her big basket and ran down the lane. She knew that old tumble-down cottage was no place for a baby without a woman to look after things. And she was in the right of it; for Joseph Baron wasn't a strong man, his children were pale and sickly, and they had brought poverty with them into their hovel. There was little food in the cupboard, and few coverings on the beds. The big family looked up as Jeanne bounded in, and plumped her heavy basket on the table saying: 'Welcome, neighbour! I've come to see if there's anything I can do for you, while you're settling in.'

Anything indeed! there was everything. The townbred Barons hardly knew how to begin to light the fire in the broken stove, and bake when the fire was lit, or to hoe the weeds in the garden, and dig when the weeds were hoed. To make a long story short, the Wappers took them on; and Jeanne carried off the baby and the two youngest children bodily till the hovel could be made cosy; Felix Wappers stepped round to patch the roof, and brought a load of firewood and potatoes while he was about it; Marie trotted in and out, showing the little girls how to make fires and cook, while Paul got the little boys into the garden and set them weeding and planting. In another twelvemonth the Barons were a rosy, happy, handy family, their home was weather-proof and their garden productive. If anything went wrong, it was 'Run round to the Wappers' about it; and the Wappers never failed them. And when on the road Felix Wappers and Joseph Baron saw old Nicholas and Thérèse Moke driving in their carriage, in their broadcloth and lace, looking sour and suspicious, and scarcely deigning to glance at their shabbier neighbours, Felix would laugh and say: 'There go the money-bags.' And Joseph would clap him on the shoulder and say: 'A good neighbour is better than a bag of money.'

Then one day it got round that the old Mokes had been robbed overnight, by their own cook and coachman. They had gone off, taking all the valuables and cash along with them, leaving their masters destitute and helpless.

'And serve 'em right!' said Joseph Baron.

But Felix Wappers looked at his wife, and Jeanne Wappers ejaculated: 'Save us! I wonder if the poor souls have anything to eat?'—and she fetched down her basket, and began to put things in it.

'How's *that* for wisdom?' asked the burly Belgian.

'I'd rather not say,' said Uncle Nicodemus, 'before the Dutchman here tells why more belongs to dancing than a pair of dancing shoes.'

'It's a plain story,' said the dumpy Dutchman, 'with a plain meaning.'

Dancing Shoes

MRS GROSCHEN was an admirable housewife; she excelled in cooking and sewing and all the domestic arts, and she wished to make her daughter Trude as house-wise as herself. She began by training her in such simple things as bed-making, potato-peeling, and marketing; but Trude's feather-beds were never properly plumped up, she always left the eyes in her potatoes, and she always came home from market with the wrong change. When Mrs Groschen pointed these things out to her, she pouted and said: 'Well, Mother! if only the beds had more goose-feathers in them!' or 'Well, Mother! if only Father grew the right sort of potatoes!' or 'Well, Mother! if only I had a pretty purse with three compartments, like Meenie Gulden's!' Then, Trude was quite sure she would be a perfect bed-maker and potato-peeler, and would always bring back the right change. 'You see, Mother,' she explained very earnestly, '*nobody* can work properly without the very best things to work with.'

'*I* see,' said Mrs Groschen, plumping up a first-rate bed with her capable arms, peeling potatoes just so with her capable hands, and counting the change just right with her capable wits.

As Trude grew up, she became a very pretty girl; her hair was fairer and thicker than Meenie Gulden's, her eyes were bluer, and her mouth was redder. But she was lazy and discontented, and her neglected plaits did not shine like Meenie's well-brushed ones,

her blue eyes did not sparkle like Meenie's merry
ones, and her red lips, that turned down, were not so
pleasant to see as Meenie's paler lips that turned up.
At summer picnics and winter skating-parties plain
Meenie, not pretty Trude, was the popular one; the
pies she brought, and the figures she cut on the ice,
were so deftly made, that the boys struggled to sit
beside her at the feast, or cross hands with her on the
frozen Zuyder Zee. Trude went home glumly, saying: 'Well, Mother! if only I had a new Delft dish to
bake my pie in!' or 'Well, Mother! if only you'd buy
me a new pair of skates!'—she was quite sure her pie
would be as good as Meenie's, and her figures of eight
even better. And then Hans Winkle would eat out of
her dish, and take *her* hands on the ice.

When Hans Winkle became twenty-one, his
parents gave a big dance in his honour. Everybody
was invited, young and old, and all the girls began to
think about their frocks, and to practise their dancing-
steps. Mrs Groschen bought some pretty red and
yellow silk, so that Trude might make a new dress to
go in; but Trude cut it badly, and sewed it with such
big stitches, that Mrs Groschen ripped it out overnight, and put it together again; and though it looked
better, Trude had cut it so narrow that there was not
room to jump about in.

'You'd do well to practise your dance-steps, all the
same,' said Mrs Groschen.

'Well, Mother! if only I had that pair of gold
dancing-shoes in Dietrich Hoogh's shop window, I
wouldn't need to practise. They're the best dancing-
shoes he ever made. Do buy them for me, Mother!'

'I've spent enough already on your new silk,' said
Mrs Groschen.

So Trude teased her Father to buy her the shoes—
'And then, Father, Hans Winkle will ask me to dance
with him first of all.'

Mr Groschen thought that wouldn't be so bad, for
the first dance may lead to a wedding, and he went to
Dietrich Hoogh's shop, and bought Trude the shoes.
When they came home, Trude put them on, and stuck
out her feet, twisting her ankles this way and that.
'How pretty they look; Meenie Gulden will have to
dance in those old worn leather shoes of hers.'

But Meenie was practising steps in her old shoes,
and had made a perfect fit of her new frock in blue and
purple cotton, with a full skirt and close-fitting body.
And on the night of the dance Trude came in in her
twice-made dress, looking like an ill-set bed of tulips.
And her feet slipped clumsily on the floor, for all her
gold shoes; while Meenie in her shabby leather ones
stepped upright and trim as a hyacinth in a pot. And
it wasn't Trude that Hans Winkle asked to dance the
first dance with him.

So Mr Groschen said to Mrs Groschen: 'What was
the use, then, of buying gold shoes for Trüdchen?'

And Mrs Groschen said to Mr Groschen: 'More
belongs to dancing than a pair of dancing shoes.'

'There's wisdom for you!' said the dumpy Dutchman to Uncle Nicodemus.

'I dare say there is,' said Uncle Nicodemus: 'but I
should like this smiling Serb here to tell us why every
man knows the lining of his own cloak.'

'Very good!' said the Serb, and beamed, and told
his tale.

The Two Cloaks

THERE were once two brothers, Alexander Karovich the elder, and Boris Karovich the younger.
Their father had a castle in the mountains, the walls
were covered with tapestries, the furniture was splendid, the chests were full of costly stuffs, the cellars of
gold and jewels. On another part of the mountain was
a monastery, the home of mendicant Friars. And in the
valley below, exactly midway between the castle and
the monastery, lay the village, of which old Duke
Karovich was the lord. When he lay dying, he sent
for his sons, and said: 'My sons, I shall shortly leave
you. You, Alexander, will become Duke in my stead;
but divide with Boris the treasures in the castle. Be
good to the peasants and generous to the poor.'
Then he died.

During the time of mourning, Boris's eyes were red
with weeping, but Alexander's eyes were dry. The
servants regarded with admiration his air of noble
melancholy, while the swollen eyes of Boris only commanded their pity. After seven days, Alexander came
to Boris and said: 'It is time to make the division.'
Boris rose, and the two brothers together examined
the contents of the castle. As they passed from room
to room, Alexander pointed out this and that to his
brother, saying: 'Look at these two great chairs of
silver and turquoise. Do they not seem made for the
lord and lady of the castle? I am not yet married,
but one day I shall be. However, one of these chairs
is yours.'

Boris said gently: 'Keep mine and welcome, brother, against your wedding-day.'

In another room Alexander said: 'Here is the service of gold plate my father used at his banquets. Will you have half of it? What a pity you are not the duke! I would not deprive you of half the service necessary for the entertainment of your guests.'

And Boris said simply: 'You are the duke, not I, keep the whole service.'

In the bedrooms, the proud and noble Alexander sighed: 'If I have a big family, how suitable are these rich couches and coverings for a duke's children!'— and Boris asked for none of these things.

It was the same in the cellars, where the treasure was stored; as Alexander began to divide the gold and jewels, he paused to remark on the heavy cost of a duke's estate.

'Do keep it all,' urged Boris.

'It would perhaps be better,' agreed Alexander.

At last they came to the division of their father's wardrobe; the rich clothes seemed fit only for a duke, and one by one Boris ceded them all. In the last drawer lay two carefully folded mantles. One of these was more sumptuous than any other garment in the wardrobe; its cloth of gold was so encrusted with jewels, that Alexander needed all his strength to lift it. His sparkling eyes scarcely noted the plain brown cloak which lay beneath it in the bottom of the drawer.

'Why did we never see our father wear this cloak, I wonder!' exclaimed Alexander; 'it is more fit than any other for a Duke Karovich—but perhaps you, Boris, feel you have a claim on it?'

'Oh, no,' smiled Boris; 'you, not I, are the Duke

Karovich. Of all our father's cloaks, let me have this one.' And he laid his hand on the poor brown stuff.

'Gladly!' said Alexander generously; 'I grudge you nothing.' And so the division of the goods came to an end.

'And now,' said Alexander, 'where do you think of living? I imagine that when I marry, my servants and my lady's, and our children and their servants, will occupy all the bedrooms in the castle.'

'Perhaps,' said Boris, 'there may be a room at the monastery for me.'

'A good idea,' said Alexander. 'How sorry I am to part from you! Well, you must come often to visit me. I will let you know when it is convenient.'

So saying, he put on the grand cloak, and Boris put on the poor one; and together they went out of the palace where the peasants were waiting to greet them.

At sight of Alexander, who was seven feet tall, the peasants shouted as though they had seen the sun rise; he stood there in his magnificent cloak, smiling proudly upon them, scattering gold and silver from a bag at his girdle. 'How great a Duke is ours! how splendid! how beneficent!' cried the peasants. They hardly noticed Boris, in his old brown cloak; and while they shouted, he slipped away to the poor monastery on the other side of the mountain. The friars welcomed Boris gladly, and in time he became one of them; but begged as a special favour that he might always wear his father's old brown cloak, which was permitted.

So the two brothers lived out their lives on the mountain above the village. At first, Boris saw something of Alexander—though the new Duke did not send too often for the poor friar. He ceased to do so entirely, after he had married a proud and noble lady, who gave alms to the friars at her gates, but preferred not to receive them as brothers. So the humble Brother Boris passed among men unnoticed, while wherever Duke Alexander went he was praised and cheered. 'There goes a great man!' said the world. There was only one opinion about it. The strange thing was, that though his proud lips smiled, and his hands scattered money, Alexander's eyes grew more and more unhappy with the years; while the eyes of Brother Boris, who had no money to give away, grew more and more shining as time passed.

At last the brothers died on the same day. Then people remembered suddenly that they *were* brothers, and it was arranged that they should lie in state, side by side, in the courtyard of the castle. When all the country-side flocked to pay their last respects to the Duke, they found him stretched in his magnificent cloak beside his brother in his shabby one.

Suddenly, among all those who had come to pay homage to greatness, a wondering woman cried: 'Why, look who lies here by our Duke! It is the poor Friar who sucked the poison from my baby's throat!'

A child said: 'Oh, it's the man who saved me from a wolf in the forest. The wolf tore his hands while I ran away.'

A man said: 'I remember him too. He climbed down a precipice where I had fallen, and bore me up on his back, though it was almost certain death for both of us.'

An old woman said: 'When the storm killed my husband and my three sons by lightning, he showed me God's face, and saved me from despair. He was a Saint.'

One and another had some such tale to tell of Brother Boris, and one and another ended his tale with: 'He was a Saint!' in tones of wonder, and as though they knew this for the first time.

'Mother,' cried a little boy, 'why does Duke Alexander look so sad in his grand mantle, and why does Brother Boris look so happy in his old one?'

As though in answer to the question, a gust of wind blew through the courtyard, out of nowhere as it seemed; and in passing it lifted one corner of the jewelled mantle, and revealed to all the world a stained and dirty lining, of such cheap stuff, and so moth-eaten, that it was unfit for a Duke or any man to wear next to his skin. The next moment, passing over Brother Boris, the wind whirled his brown cloak almost inside out, and the lining was of the purest silver silk, so that for a few seconds the thin old face seemed to smile out of a shining cloud. Then the gust died away, the two cloaks fell back upon their wearers, the one so splendid, the other so poor; and the Mother whispered in a tone of awe: 'Every man knows the lining of his own cloak—but who else, except God?'

'That is my story,' said the Serb. 'And now compare its wisdom with the rest.'

'When it comes to comparisons,' said Uncle Nicodemus, 'I must first ask Little Jenkyn.' He leaned down to the child. 'Have you been listening, and what do you think? Is the Frenchman wisest when he says: If the Triangles made a God they would give Him Three Sides? Or the Belgian, when he says: A Good Neighbour is better than a Bag of Money? Or the Dutchman, who says: More belongs to Dancing than a Pair of Dancing Shoes? Or the Serb, with his: Every Man knows the Lining of his own Cloak? Well?'

All through the last four tales, Little Jenkyn had
been scribbling on his slate, as busily as he had
scribbled during the first four, with the bit of chalk he
had picked up on Truleigh Hill; and now he held it
up for Uncle Nicodemus to see. As before, four poems
were written on it, and Uncle Nicodemus read them
aloud to the company. The first poem ran:

> 'He sits aloft, He sits alone,
> Scarcely seen and barely known,
> And Man and Snake and Owl and Ass
> Look for Him in a Looking-glass.'

'What does *that* mean?' muttered Uncle Nicodemus.

'That,' said the Frenchman triumphantly, 'means
that the child has seen the wisdom of my saying about
God, though an old man couldn't.'

The second poem ran:

> 'Neighbour, good Neighbour,
> Your purse may be thin,
> But your acts are worth more
> Than a Bushel of Tin.
> When living is heavy
> With burdens untold,
> Good Neighbours are better
> Than Silver and Gold.'

'Well said!' cried the Belgian; 'the wisdom of *my*
saying could not be better put!'

'Let's hear the third poem,' said Uncle Nicodemus,
and read:

> 'Dance with your feet, and dance with your heart,
> And your Slippers, though shabby, will play a good part;
> Dance without pleasure and dance without skill,
> Though your Shoes be of gold you had better stand still.'

'Good! good!' puffed the Dutchman. 'The child knows a wise word when he hears it.'

The fourth poem on Little Jenkyn's slate ran:

'I saw a Rich Man swagger
In a costly Cloak of Vair,
And all the world said praisingly:
"What a Great Man goes there!"
But only he who bore the cloak
About him closely coiled
Knew what mean stuff the lining was,
How torn and worn and soiled.

'I saw a Poor Man wander
In a common Duffle Coat,
And all the world said carelessly:
"There's one of little note."
But only he who wore the coat
Knew that which kept him warm,
The lining of the purest silk
That clothed unseen his form.'

'No more need be said,' said the Serb. 'The child decides for *my* saying.'

'So far as I can see,' said Uncle Nicodemus, scratching his head, 'he decides for you all. Unless we can find one wiser still, we shall never get the question settled at all.'

Just as he finished speaking, the door opened, and a brown-skinned Haytien slipped into the barn.

★

The Haytien stood there without saying a word, looking round the company from Uncle Nicodemus to the Apple-cheeked Englishman, the Dark-eyed Italian, the Fur-capped Russian, the Pig-tailed Chinaman, the Frivolous Frenchman, the Burly Belgian, the Dumpy Dutchman, and the Smiling Serb. Last of all he looked at Little Jenkyn, and Little Jenkyn looked back at him.

'Good day to you,' said Uncle Nicodemus. 'This morning I and this child left home in search of wisdom. In this barn we sheltered from the rain, where these eight men were all of our mind. One after another they have quoted a wise saying from their own countries, and told us a tale to prove its wisdom. Thus we have found out that wisdom is of all sorts and kinds, and is to be found in every land on earth. But the wisest wisdom of all seems to be wanting, in spite of much talk. Now you come from strange and distant parts, where perhaps you also have wise sayings. Is there one you can tell us?'

The Haytien listened very attentively, and when Uncle Nicodemus finished speaking he opened his lips. Uncle Nicodemus leaned forward, cupping his ear to catch the wisdom which would come forth; but before a single word could escape, the brown man shut his mouth again.

'Don't be ungenerous,' said Uncle Nicodemus. 'If you know a wise word, say it.'

The Haytien opened his lips a second time—and shut them again.

'Out with it!' said Uncle Nicodemus.

The Haytien opened and shut his lips for the third time.

'Come, come!' said Uncle Nicodemus.

The Haytien opened and shut his lips for the fourth time.

'Well, well!' said Uncle Nicodemus.

After the fifth time he said: 'Fie! fie!' and after the

sixth, 'Dear, dear! how shall any man judge of your wisdom if you *won't* talk?'

For the seventh time the Haytien opened and shut his lips.

Uncle Nicodemus took up his stick, and beckoned to Little Jenkyn, who was scribbling on his slate again. 'Come along,' said Uncle Nicodemus; 'the rain has stopped, the sun is shining, our search is done for the day, and now we'll go home to tea.' He bade 'Good day' to the barnful of wise men, who bade it him again in their own tongues; then Uncle Nicodemus and Little Jenkyn went out of the barn, and walked down Truleigh Hill till they came through Freeks, and reached their own door at the World's End. Just as he laid his hand on the latch, Uncle Nicodemus felt a touch on his shoulder. It was the brown-skinned Haytien, who had followed them silently like a dog; and now, to the great surprise of Uncle Nicodemus, he opened his lips and spoke.

'Sir,' he said, 'we have one very wise saying in my country.'

'At last!' cried Uncle Nicodemus. 'What is it?'

'This,' said the Haytien. '*Before you speak, turn your Tongue over Seven Times.*'

'And what does *that* mean?' asked Uncle Nicodemus, prepared to hear another story.

The Haytien opened and shut his mouth seven times, thought better of it, and went away; and Uncle Nicodemus and Little Jenkyn went into the house, where they found on the floor the A.B.C. and the Encyclopaedia just where they had left them when they set out on their search for wisdom. The toy goose was still at letter A.

Little Jenkyn dropped his slate and picked up his

goose, and Uncle Nicodemus picked up Little Jenkyn's slate. On it was written:

'As I did drive my flock of geese
I found a lock with seven keys.
I turned them all from first to last,
And still the rusty lock held fast.
I threw the keys behind my back,
And heard my geese say *Quack-quack-quack*.'

'Little Jenkyn,' said Uncle Nicodemus, 'I'm afraid you've taken to writing nonsense.' Then, settling his spectacles upside-down on his nose, he began to read his Encyclopaedia backwards.

★

'Lie over,' said Martin. 'It's time you went into your forest of dreams. Which for any Sussex-born child is St Leonard's Forest, where a man may look and find and never know it.'

Then Martin sang Sib this, for a song to sleep on.

'O have you seen St Leonard a-planting out his Forest?
Come, look up from your water-can and put your spade
    away!
I've searched through the trees from the Holmbush to
    the Goldings
For an old holy Forester with hair going grey—
O have you seen St Leonard, Child at play?

Is he swimming in the Hammer Pond, or piping in the
    Shepherd's Field
Or sleeping sound in Barnsnap in the heat of the day?
Is he supping in the Carter's Lodge, or sowing in the
    Lilybeds,
Or falling down upon his knees on Doomsday Green to
    pray?
O have you seen St Leonard, Child at play?

But the gold-headed Child at play in Little Goldings
Looked up from his digging, laughed and answered,
    Nay!
And went on planting acorns and watering his beech-
    nuts,
And the Pilgrim with his scrip and his staff went away—
Went looking for St Leonard, and left the Child at play.'

*

'Asleep, Sib?'
Martin peeped into the basket. It was empty.
There was no baby in the clothes-basket. Martin
looked down at the grass. There were no children in
the daisy-field. The grass grew uncrushed at his feet.
Not even the print of a little girl's cheek, or her
shoe. Nothing but daisies.

GILLIAN HAS THE LAST WORD

'BEDTIME, Martin!'
Somebody was calling across the Murray River.
Martin picked up the clothes-basket and crossed the
bridge to the flower-garden at the end of Shelley's
Lane. There was no light in the cottage because

Martin didn't possess a candle-stick. But the moon fell on Gillian standing in the doorway, and the moment he saw her Martin remembered that he had married her that afternoon.

'You've been gone a long time,' she said.

'How long?'

'Seven minutes.'

'What did I go for?'

'To find the source of the Murray River. Did you find it?'

'I found it seven times,' said Martin, 'and lost it. Here's a clothes-basket instead. It might come in useful one day when we've something to put in it.'

'There's a daisy in it already,' said Gillian.

'Now I wonder,' mused Martin Pippin, 'how that got there?'

'Stop wondering,' said Gillian. 'It's time.'

'It is never time to stop wondering,' said Martin, 'and above all, to stop wondering about time. For when we say bedtime, before we can know what we mean, we must turn the world upside down. And when we say seven minutes we might as well say eternity. The Prophet Mahomet——'

'You're nearly asleep,' whispered Gillian.

'You're too wide awake. The Prophet Mahomet,' said Martin, 'knew all about *that*. When Uncle Nicodemus pulled out the plug——'

'Sit down then,' said Gillian. 'The sleepier you get, the more you talk.'

'And the more I talk,' said Martin, 'the sleepier I get. Which is the real and only reason for stories at bedtime. Sit down beside me with your back to the clothes-basket, look at the moon over Rackham, and listen while I tell you what happens when

Uncle Nicodemus pulls out the Plug

UNCLE NICODEMUS was giving Little Jenkyn his bath.

As he washed the dirt off Little Jenkyn's knees into the water, he said: 'There's a Joy-Wheel at Blackpool.'

As the soap slipped away and he fumbled for it under Little Jenkyn's legs, he said: 'King John never found those jewels he lost in the Wash.'

As he squeezed the sponge down Little Jenkyn's back, he said: 'Mr Blondin went over the Falls of Niagara on a tightrope, wheeling his wife in a wheelbarrow.'

As he pulled up the plug, he said: 'One day the Prophet Mahomet upset his water-jug, and as he stretched out his hand for a basin to catch the falling water, he was carried by an angel up to heaven, where he stayed two years.'

Just then the plug, sucking down the bath-water, sucked Little Jenkyn down with it. Little Jenkyn had always known it would.

Bath-water is soapy. Little Jenkyn shut his eyes tight, and did not open them again till the roaring sound stopped. When it did, and he unstuck his eyelashes, he found himself sitting on the edge of a big black pool. There were high rocks all round, and no way in or out but the one Little Jenkyn had come by, which was a round hole in the rock above the path that went along the water. The rocks had numbers of such holes in them, on every side; Little Jenkyn gazed thoughtfully at one on the opposite side, and King John in his gold crown came out of it. He stood for a moment staring into the black water, then he tucked up his velvet gown, put up his ringed hands, and dived in. When his head appeared again, it was on Little Jenkyn's side of the pool. It no longer had his crown on it.

King John swam until he reached the edge on which Little Jenkyn was sitting exactly as he had arrived; and puffing and panting, the King pulled himself up, and sat on the edge by Little Jenkyn.

'There, you see!' he said. 'I've lost my crown again, and my rings have gone where all the others are. Hundreds of crowns and thousands of rings must be lying there after all this time. Which comes,' he explained softly, 'of their never taking them off before my bath-time. Don't you let them bath *you* in your jewels, will you?' Little Jenkyn shook his head. 'That's right,' said King John. 'It's better to send your jewels to the Dry-Cleaners than to the Wash, remember that. I'm afraid I must leave you now, Little Jenkyn, and go and get another crown out of the Treasury.'

So saying, he picked his way along the path until he found a good-sized hole, into which he wormed himself.

Little Jenkyn continued to look at the water. In it he saw the reflection of a big gold Wheel, lit up with coloured lights; but when he looked up he could not see the Wheel overhead, for the rocks were too tall. Their sides were smooth and slippery, and couldn't be climbed. He fixed his eyes on a spot high up that seemed to be swelling; soon it swelled right forward, like a blown-out balloon, and burst. Out of the immense hole that was left poured the Niagara Falls.

The Falls rushed down into the black pool with so much force that it bubbled like a boiling saucepan, and among the fierce black bubbles rising and falling spun rubies and sapphires and emeralds. Golden crowns were flung up out of the boiling and fell back again, golden chains writhed in and out like snakes, and golden rings tossed here and there in showers.

'Stop, Mr Blondin, stop!' cried a wee little voice far up in the heavens.

Little Jenkyn lifted his eyes to the top of the rocks, and there was Mr Blondin wheeling a golden wheelbarrow along a golden rope. In the wheelbarrow sat Mrs Blondin, kicking her tiny heels in a frenzy. 'Stop, stop, stop!' she cried.

'If I stop, Mrs Blondin, we'll fall into the Falls,' said Mr Blondin, in a deep far-away voice.

'We won't, Mr Blondin, we won't! Stop just one second and let me catch a gold ring.'

'You wouldn't catch a gold ring, Mrs Blondin, Niagara would catch you.'

'I want rubies and emeralds!' shrieked the little voice.

'Stop kicking, Mrs Blondin,' said the deep one.

'I want garnets and pearls!'

'Stop wriggling, Mrs Blondin.'

'I want diamonds and sapphires!'

'Sit still, Mrs Blondin, or I'll tip you out.'

After that the far-away voices, little and deep, said no more, and the golden wheelbarrow passed out of sight. Niagara stopped pouring through the hole, the black pool stopped boiling, and Little Jenkyn knew for a certainty that it was the source of the Murray River. In its polished ebony waters he saw again the gold illuminated Wheel, going round and round under the water.

'Then why don't you,' said the Prophet Mahomet, 'if you want to so much?'

Little Jenkyn considered.

'It will cost you nothing,' said the Prophet Mahomet, 'or it will cost you everything. And everything and nothing are exactly the same as each other, just as inside and outside are, for the inside is the outside of the outside of the inside, and the outside is the inside of the inside of the outside.'

Little Jenkyn nodded.

'And Up is Down,' went on the Prophet Mahomet, 'and Down is Up, and Here and There are neither there nor here.'

Little Jenkyn began to rock backwards and forwards.

The Prophet Mahomet said: 'Now is Then, now and then, and Then is Now.'

Little Jenkyn leaned over the edge of the water.

'Topsy is as good as Turvy any day,' said the Prophet Mahomet.

Little Jenkyn dropped into the water, and perched on the topmost seat of the big gold Wheel.

The Wheel went on turning, bearing him down deeper and deeper into the depths of the pool. By the jewelled lights round his seat Little Jenkyn saw wonders. Dolphins and comets and herons, flower-girls, dukes, and the Great Khan of Tartary; mountains and fountains, aeroplanes and dragon-flies, mermaids and meringues, and the Pyramids of Egypt; mice and horses and giraffes and mammoths and ideas. Once he caught sight of King John, swimming under the

water, and King John snatched at his green and crimson
lights as he rolled away; once he saw Uncle Nicodemus's pipe, with smoke rising out of the bowl.
The deeper he sank in the pool, the higher he rose in
the sky. From his seat in the Wheel Little Jenkyn
saw all the things that ever had been, and everything
that never was; and whatever he saw was long ago
over and still to come. It took him two years to get
round to where he had started. When the big Wheel
reached the edge of the pool where Little Jenkyn had
dropped off, he had seen all. So he took the hand held
out by the Prophet Mahomet, who put him back into
the hole, and gave him a push. Little Jenkyn shut his
eyes tight, because bath-water's soapy; and when the
roaring in his ears had stopped, and he unstuck his eyelashes, Uncle Nicodemus was lifting him out of the bath.

'At the end of which time,' said Uncle Nicodemus,
'the Prophet Mahomet came back to earth, and found
himself catching in his basin the first drop spilled out
of his water-jug.'

'That, Gillian,' said Martin, 'is your bedtime story.'

'I see,' said Gillian, stroking his head which was
now upon her lap. 'Lie over.'

'What for?'

'It's as much as you can do to keep your eyes open.'

'It's more,' said Martin Pippin with his eyes shut.
'And as I said before, and if I didn't say it then I say it
now, which is all the same thing, for in the future the
present will be the past——'

'Lie over,' whispered Gillian.

'——one child's going-to-bedtime is another child's
getting-up-time.'

But Gillian was singing him a song to go to sleep on:

'Moon for your cradle,
Dark for your cover,
Star for your night-light,
Me for your lover,
Hushaby, hushaby
Martin, lie over.'

'Because, when you come to think of it——' said
Martin Pippin.

Gillian put her finger on his lips. 'No more talking.'